AFTER

THE

LIES

BY
MANDESSA SELBY

Zora is an imprint of Parker Publishing LLC.

Copyright © 2008 by Mandessa Selby
Published by Parker Publishing LLC
12523 Limonite Avenue, Suite #440-438
Mira Loma, California 91752
www.parker-publishing.com

This book is a work of fiction. Characters, names, locations, events and incidents (in either a contemporary and/or historical setting) are products of the author's imagination and are being used in an imaginative manner as a part of this work of fiction. Any resemblance to actual events, locations, settings, or persons, living or dead, is entirely coincidental.

ISBN:
First Edition

Manufactured in the United States of America
Printed by Bang Printing, Brainard MN
Distributed by BookMasters, Inc. 1-800-537-6727
Cover Design by Jaxadora Designs

Parker Publishing, llc
www.Parker-Publishing.com

PROLOGUE
Paris, France 1861

Lucien Delacroix sat at the baccarat table fingering his cards. The man across from him stared at the dealer, a droplet of perspiration rolling down his pale pudgy cheek. Never wager what you cannot lose. Luc's opponent was a fool but then gambling often attracted the gullible who thought wealth and prestige awaited them on the next turn of the card, or flick of a dice.

Luc smiled at the beautiful blonde woman seated next to his opponent. Her hair was piled high on her head with sparkling crystals sprinkled through her sausage curls. She had brought Luc luck with her lush, exotic beauty and her flirtatious air. Only a few minutes earlier she had slipped her room key into Luc's pocket with a whispered invitation. The key he wouldn't use despite her hunger and his need. He wondered if she would be so eager to engage his company if she knew the truth. The bastard son of a Louisiana plantation owner and his quadroon mistress, white enough to pass, yet still dusky enough to be interesting. On impulse, he flipped her a gold coin. The coin somersaulted through the air and she snatched it deftly, catching the coin in both her hands. She slid the gold inside the bodice of her gown with a bold, suggestive wink that told Luc exactly what he could expect should he decide to accept her tempting offer.

Luc had everything any man could want: wealth, education, and privilege. But a jarring dissonance of discontent crawled inside him. What more could a man of his success expect? What more did he want?

A tiny voice nagged at him. Acceptance, the tiny whisper said. Acceptance to be who he was openly, without subterfuge, at home in New Orleans as he was able to do in Paris. A gallant dream. An impossible one. Luc had no illusions about who he was and what he was.

Luc glanced around the opulent casino, richly decorated with red and black velvet draperies, dark blue Persian carpet, and ornately carved furniture. The gaming tables, surrounded by the well-heeled patrons of the establishment, tantalized with the promise of easy money. Elegantly dressed gamblers surged back and forth between the bar and the stairs leading to the second floor bedrooms where the casino's women plied their thankless trade.

Swirling smoke cast a blue haze over the assembly. The polished crystal of the candelabra caught the light and reflected it back on the walls in a delicate prism of dancing colors, flittering about the room. The finest of Parisian society laughed, played, and flirted with each other, then discreetly withdrew for a moment of pleasure in one of the upstairs bedrooms.

Luc knew he could have the blonde. But he also knew her body would not satisfy him. What would? His sister, Esme, would laugh at him, telling him to forget what he could not acquire. To be happy with what he had. Her wise financial ability had made them both wealthy, so they had little to worry about. They owned a discreet mansion on the Boulevard Du Maison, a small country house in Burgundy and a fashionable townhouse in Monte Carlo. They traveled in style in their own lavish carriages accompanied by servants. Their wine cellar was the envy of Paris. Luc wished he could have Esme's devil-may-care attitude toward life.

He tried to lose himself in the game, but a disturbance distracted him. Immaculately dressed in black satin evening clothes, Henri Pierpont clutched the arm of a woman of color who wore a yellow evening gown laced with seed pearls. She struggled against Henri, her delicate face frantic with fear. Henri never took rejection lightly. Luc despised the man, his sexual appetites as well as his depravities were legend in Paris.

The woman cried out, her brown eyes showing spiraling apprehension. No one aided her. Several men laughed in amusement and turned away unwilling to interfere. Luc dropped his cards on the table and pushed his chair back. He wasn't a hero, but he hated brutality of any kind, especially toward women. He had seen the results of Henri's careless cruelties one too many times.

Luc pushed through the crowded room thick with bodies drenched in cloying perfumes. He grabbed Henri's arm. "You are hurting the lady."

Henri snorted. "She's hardly a lady." His glance was filled with contempt as he gazed at the young woman who desperately tried to twist out of his grasp.

Luc yanked Henri's hand away. A purplish bruise was already forming on the white skin of the woman's arm. "Must I repeat myself?" He squeezed Henri's hand. Years of privilege had made Henri soft.

A hush slowly spread over the salon. Even the dealers stopped calling out the winners as heads swivelled about to watch the drama unfold.

Henri pulled back, a snarl on his face. "She's a black whore! Who cares?"

Luc's teeth clenched, his rage escalating. "I care. Every woman deserves respect. Apologize, or we meet in the morning."

Henri blanched. "You would duel over a whore?" His voice seemed more curious than alarmed.

Stupid man, Luc thought. History was littered with the bodies of men who had fought over whores. "A woman is a thing to be treasured no matter her station, no matter the circumstances." Luc touched the dark skin of her cheek.

Henri roughly shoved the woman away. "I will not fight over a whore."

The woman staggered into Luc, who steadied her. "Merci, monsieur." She smiled, then turned and disappeared into the crowd.

Luc released Henri's hand.

Henri straightened his jacket lapels. "Now what shall I do to amuse myself for the evening?"

Luc smiled. "My offer is still on the table."

Henri flicked his hand in the air. "I do not waste my time with impetuous American puppies." His eyes held contempt.

"Pity." Luc turned away, the evening spoiled.

From across the room the owner of the casino, Marie Severin rushed after Luc. Marie tapped him on the forearm with her fan. "You are so gallant, cherie. How can I repay you for ridding me of that boorish oaf?"

Luc took her hand, bowed and kissed the tips of her fingers as though she were a queen rather than a woman of the night. "No payment is needed, Madame. Thank you for the offer, but perhaps, another time."

She giggled. "Whenever you are ready, I will be waiting." She flicked her fan at the entrance to the room, "I have been informed that your hired man is waiting in the foyer. He says it is urgent." A delicate brow rose in a coquettish manner. "Tell me you are not meeting that red-haired countess I saw you with the other night at the opera. She is not really a countess, nor is her hair truly red." She folded her fan with a snap, a knowing smirk on her lips. "I know all your weaknesses, Monsieur."

He bowed again. "You are my only weakness, Madame. If you will excuse me. I must see what is so urgent that I am sought out in the middle of the night." He turned and stepped toward the foyer.

———⌒⌒⌒———

As Luc opened the door to his apartment on the Rue du Sienne, he found his twin sister, Esme, waiting for him at the door in the parlor, sitting on the edge of a chair, twisting her hands.

At sight of him, she jumped to her feet. "At last, you are back."

Any person, upon seeing them, would know immediately they were twins. They had the same oval-shaped face, same color greenish eyes and curly dark hair, but in Esme the features of her face were softened. Luc's features were more angled and harsh.

Esme's face was marred by a worried, frantic frown. Her dark hair fell about her shoulders, framing a pale, ashen face. She turned green eyes on him.

She threw herself into his arms, almost sobbing. "Papa wants you home immediately. The South has declared war on the North."

CHAPTER ONE
Mexico, 1873

Callisto Payne wanted a bath. No, she craved a bath more than her next breath. Her clothes itched and her curly black hair was coated with a thick layer of gray dust. Her mouth was so dry, she could barely spit.

Damn rustlers! Two days of hard riding after a pair of stupid bastards and all she got for her trouble was dirty and smelly. You had to be a special kind of dumb to steal cattle from the most powerful rancher in Mexico and think you could get away with it. Wealthy ranchers had money, money they used to hire Callisto to get their cattle back.

She was hot, tired and impatient for the job to be ended. Callie shifted her position on the flat boulder, scorching hot in the late afternoon, as she watched the rustlers in the desolate valley below. The stolen herd of dun-colored cattle, flanked by the bandits, moved through a cloud of thick, billowing dust.

A scorpion, unsettled by her movements, scuttled off the boulder and into a crevice—its dangerous tail held high and pincers on the defensive. The white hot sun blasted the bleak desert below.

Her partner, John Wildcat, hunkered down behind a rock ten feet to her left. She motioned her head toward the valley. He grinned, his bronzed skin crinkling around his mouth showing the whiteness of his straight teeth. Like her, he must be thinking about the fat bounty they'd collect for the return of the cattle and the thieves. A few more dollars in the cookie jar that brought her closer to her dream.

Though all the men in her tiny village respected her abilities, only John Wildcat worked with her as an equal. He didn't seem to notice she was a woman, caring only that she was the best tracker he'd ever taught. Each one of their successes increased their stature as well as their price. Callie was proud that she had made more money in a couple months than most men in the village made in a year.

Callie scanned the sweltering desert floor below. Cactus stuck thorny arms into the sky. Birds twittered at each other from the nests they'd made inside the juicy interior of the cactus. A jackrabbit nibbled at a few stray grasses then bounced away as the shadow of a hunting hawk circled it overhead.

In another day, the rustlers would be in the flats and there would be no place to ambush them. She and John had to strike tonight. Once darkness fell, they would give those rustlers the surprise of their mangy lives.

Hot summer sun beat down on their heads. Callie retied the edges of her bandana protecting her mouth and nose from the heavy dust, then resettled her wide-brimmed hat, pushing strands of escaping black hair behind her ears. The baggy denim trousers and old plaid shirt she wore irritated her skin.

She could afford better, but preferred her older brother's cast-offs. Rafe had left several years ago to make his fortune and never returned. She still missed him. Wearing his clothes gave her a sense that he was with her somehow.

She slid backward off the rock and met John at the bottom of the ridge. The hot air dried the perspiration on her skin before moisture had much of a chance to form.

"What do you think?" John rested his tall, lean body against a rock. He chewed a piece of tough jerky. They took their meals whenever they could. Lines of exhaustion scored his dark face.

Like Callie, he was dark-skinned with tightly, curled black hair and deep brown eyes, the product of their Negro-Seminole heritage.

Callie gazed thoughtfully at the sun. "We take them after nightfall."

"Why?"

After two years of working together, he still quizzed her, making her work hard for his praise. Although his patronage had cemented her reputation as the best tracker in Sonora, he pushed her to improve her skills. She made sure she could meet his challenges. "I think they'll water the cattle at Diablo D'Oro springs before heading into the flats."

The springs, hidden deep in the foothills, were shaded by massive cottonwoods and protected by huge boulders, rattlers, and jackrabbits. Most people knew the springs were the last water until the Rio Grande which appeared to be the rustlers destination. Callie didn't know why they wanted Mexican cattle when there were plenty of wild cattle roaming through Texas.

He nodded his approval. "We wait."

Callie grabbed the reins of her horse and pulled herself into the saddle. They still had a heap of riding left to do before the rustlers bedded the cattle down for the night.

She set off across the desert, keeping a low mound of hills between her and the rustlers. John followed.

Darkness fell. The sun dipped behind the mountains to cast long purple shadows on the desert floor. Callie and John found a bank of rocks near the springs which hid them from view. They settled down to wait for dark as the rustlers watered the cattle and made camp near the springs, just as Callie had predicted.

They left more sign than a herd of buffalo, Callie thought as she watched them. White men had no idea how to travel through the desert. If they had been smarter rustlers, they would have made for the heavy sands to the north where the cattle tracks and the dust would blow away in the desert winds in a few minutes. It was a drier, thirstier area, but it would have been a lot harder for Callie and John to find them. But then again, they probably weren't expecting to be followed.

The night grew cold. Callie napped beneath the stunted branches of a cottonwood, while John watched the sky darken until twinkling stars dotted the black sky and a sliver of moon rode low on the horizon.

When Callie felt the time was right, she went south and John went north through clumps of mesquite bush to approach the camp. The restless movements of the cattle covered the small sounds she made as she crept forward to survey the camp.

The two rustlers lay on the ground, blankets tucked around them fending off the night chill and facing the still roaring fire, an empty whiskey bottle on the ground between them. They obviously felt safe enough to let down their guard. Stupid, Callie thought. Once they realized Callie and John were there, they would open their eyes, first seeing the bright blaze. By the time they looked away, their eyesight would take too many precious seconds to adjust to the night. Then they would have to struggle out of their blankets to find their guns. Stupid.

She searched for John and saw him tucked up against a rock waiting for her. She waved and he waved back. They had played this game many times. One rustler began to sing. A smile spread across Callie's face. Boy, were these two going to be surprised. They'd never know what hit them.

She waited until the rustlers' snoring filled the air over the crackling fire. Then she and John struck. Callie jumped to her feet and with an ancient Seminole war cry landed between the sleeping figures.

Their eyes popped open, and they both scrambled awkwardly for their pistols. She smacked the nearest one on the side of the head with her rifle butt. He fell back like a sack of flour still tangled in his blankets. John jumped the other man and clubbed him into semi-consciousness. The two rustlers sprawled, mouths hanging open. Callie smiled at the sight, delighted at the ease of the capture.

Pulling out his hunting knife, John grabbed the nearest rustler by his stringy hair and yanked his head up. He put his knife against the man's white throat and looked at Callie. "Dead or alive?"

Callie shrugged. "More money if we bring them back alive." Brought back alive, Callie could turn them over to the rancher who would probably hang the two rustlers. That was enough entertainment to keep the village humming for months. "Ain't had a good hanging in months." She had no sympathy for thieves who preyed on the hard work of others.

John sheathed his Bowie knife, a look of disappointment on his shadowed face. "Damn, Callie. You take all the fun out of the hunting."

Callie understood his dissatisfaction, but the money was too important to throw away so thoughtlessly. "Let's get 'em tied before they wake up. If they escape, we'll lose the bounty." She took off their boots, while John tied their feet and hands. By the time they woke up, they were secure and even if they could get away, they wouldn't get far in bare feet.

Callie made herself a cup of coffee and sat down across from the rustlers, ignoring their struggles. In her mind, she added up the money hidden in her old boot. Her share of the bounty would buy another two acres for her mother. She could almost see the fertile farm they would have. Colorado, Wyoming, Montana. Even Texas. Any place they wanted.

Since the end of the Civil War, her people had been saving every cent they earned in order to return to the United States and purchase land. Owning their own land, free and clear, without the fear of being part of the next Indian relocation was a dream the whole tribe had. They had learned that the white man did not honor the treaties they negotiated. Especially when the white man wanted something on Indian land.

When would her people find peace? First, they had left Florida to escape slavery. Now they were persecuted for being Seminole. Her people needed land, enough property to provide for everyone. Owning land meant roots. Roots equaled a future. Callie and her people were

desperate for a future, and would do anything to create their destiny.

Shaded by a towering cottonwood tree, Luc Delacroix stood in the dusty village square surrounded by sandy-colored adobe buildings shaded by the trees. His horse drank heavily at the stream which meandered down the center of the village. Two black and white spotted dogs lapped at the water, then scampered away nipping each other's heels.

Children played tag in the dirt, their laughter light and merry. They seemed to have no cares, no worries. Luc had never had a childhood where he'd been able to romp with such a sense of freedom. He envied them.

A young woman in a colorful, flounced skirt and a high-necked blouse pranced by, catching his eye. Her gold hoop earrings sparkled in the sun complimenting her golden chestnut skin. She grinned at him with a toss of her head. Curly black hair flew about her shoulders in wild abandon. She was pretty and Luc felt a moment of tension. He hadn't been with a woman since he'd left Washington D.C. and given up his mistress.

Pretty Jennifer. Luc would miss her pliant body and seductive wiles, but duty had ordered him to Fort Duncan in Texas, and Jennifer was not the type to enjoy being in the middle of nowhere. They'd parted and Luc knew within hours she had a new protector.

"Dear God," Lieutenant Reginald Cooper muttered, taking off his hat and wiping his forehead with the back of his gloved hand, leaving a smear of dirt across his skin. "There isn't a decent place anywhere in this forsaken town for a drink and a bath." Reggie's usual charm and wit seemed to have abandoned him since they'd left Washington. His charm was his trademark, and dependent on a social setting in which he could shine.

Luc laughed. "Reggie, you're too far from home to expect the comforts of home to just be there for you. As though on command."

Reggie lifted a blond eyebrow. "I like my comfort. Unlike you, I didn't volunteer. I was assigned this little enterprise."

"Snob. Where's your sense of adventure?" Luc slapped his canvas gauntlets against his blue-clad thigh to rid them of the dust embedded in the seams. If anything, it was the dust that bothered him the most. The finely grained dust seeped into every pore, the seams of his uniform, and no matter how clean Luc kept his clothes and his quarters, there was always a feathering of powder on everything.

Reggie snorted and said, "At Bull Run."

Luc didn't reply. Bull Run had been the first battle for both of them during the Civil War and Luc knew that the idealism he had carried with him had also been sacrificed during the fighting. How could they have been so silly to think that war was romantic? War was dirty and bloody, and the screams of the dying fueled Luc's nightmares.

Luc had known Reggie since that battle. In the beginning, he had been less cynical. But in the aftermath of the war, Luc had watched Reggie grow a bitter shell about him. Coupled with his brother's death was the loss of the ancestral fortune and home that had devastated his family, and Reggie couldn't seem to recover. He sent home as much of his pay check as he could afford to help his widowed mother and two sisters, but the amount was a pittance of what they were used to. And now one sister was engaged to be married and expected Reggie to foot the bill for a lavish society wedding. Luc understood Reggie's discontent. "Then consider this a new beginning."

Reggie shaded his eyes with his hand. "I wish I had your confidence."

Despite his brave words, Luc still searched for a new beginning, too. His father, who had fought for the South, had disowned him because of his determination to fight on the side of the Union. Once the war was over, Luc had stayed in the Army. He enjoyed military life, much to his amazement, a decision that further alienated him from his father.

Luc had no regrets, even though he had to keep his race a secret, otherwise he would be hounded out of the service. One drop of black blood made him black forever. The North, for all its bombastic rhetoric about saving the Africans from the savagery of slavery, was just as blind to the humanity of the black man as the South had been.

Though his decision to remain in the Army, determined to find his place on the frontier, had been more rewarding than he'd ever suspected, he paid for it with a hidden guilt that surfaced periodically and left him feeling ashamed. He betrayed his own race by hiding his origins.

Reggie turned and loosened the saddle girth on his tired horse. The animal stood, head down, blowing small puffs of dust with each breath through distended nostrils. The unrelenting heat brutalized both animal and man.

Reggie placed his hat back on his head, hiding the blond curls that had drawn the attention of two little girls who gazed at his hair in awe. "We should have stayed in Washington," Reggie said. "General Lewis took quite a shine to you, Luc. He'd have taken us with him to London where we could be dancing the night away with titled English beauties desperate for rich American husbands."

Luc grinned. The idea had appeal. He loved London, but he'd chosen a different path and Reggie had followed him. "I've already done that."

"Now who's being the snob?" Reggie laughed and slapped Luc's shoulder.

Another billowing of dust rose in a cloud about his hands as Luc slid his gauntlets through his belt. He slapped at the shoulders of his uniform and rubbed at the gold insignia on his collar.

Reggie nudged his arm. "Look there. Those must be your darkies."

Three young men exited the front of a shabby mercantile store. They wore shapeless pants and brightly colored shirts with their long hair loose under their hats. They stared intently at Luc and Reggie, curiosity deep in their black eyes.

Luc tensed at Reggie's prejudice. Though he felt a kinship to those young men, he could never reveal it. The position he'd carved out for himself in the army had become too important for him to give up, despite the guilt. He liked the privileges of the white man. As the years went on, he found the lie easier to say. His conscience bothered him less and less.

When he was alone, he counted his successes. He fought bravely, led wisely, garnered the respect of his peers, superiors, and his men. Wasn't that what he had always wanted? What more did he want?

Commanding the Black soldiers, now called Buffalo Soldiers by the Indians, most of his career, he'd been able to prove their worth to the Army. But in his gut he knew if the world didn't consider him white, he would have never been given the chance in the first place.

He studied the group of men. Although young, they had hard, ruthless eyes and tough bodies. He liked that. He had no time to be a nursemaid. The type of man he'd been sent to recruit as a scout was an integral part of the Army's plan to stop the Comanche Indians from preying on the settlers moving west. He could make excellent soldiers out of these men.

Even before he'd left Fort Duncan, the rumors of 'Delacroix's Darkies' had begun to make the rounds. Luc smiled at the thought. The Negro-Seminoles he had already recruited and trained had proved themselves more than capable of doing the job from the moment they'd been enlisted. He had hated to see them posted to other forts where they face faced hostility from the white officers they served under, and betrayal from the white government who employed them.

Though considered some of the best trackers in the country, the skills of the Negro-Seminole scouts were treated with contempt by too many of the officers. Yet the army needed the Negro-Seminoles if they were going to win the war against the Comanche, no matter how much the officers and bureaucrats scorned them.

A tall, imposing man with skin the color of burnished mahogany, stepped onto the street. Clad in the clothing of a Seminole chief, his bright-colored patchwork shirt stood out against the duller red of the turban twisted about his head and the elaborate beaded belt about his waist. Feathers had been tucked into the folds of the turban and bobbed as he walked toward Luc. The three men who'd been standing in front of the general store fell into step behind their chief as he approached.

"I'm Lieutenant Delacroix." Luc held his hand out to the chief.

The chief examined Luc from head to foot in a slow, deliberate manner that left Luc feeling as though the other man could see beneath his skin to the secrets he had buried so deeply. Only when the chief had finished his scrutiny did he hold out his hand to Luc in a gesture of friendship.

"Welcome to our village." The chief's voice rumbled with a timbre that insured respect. "I am William Nightowl, chief of Panther Clan. What is your business?"

A crowd began to gather around them. Women, wearing knee-length skirts with elegant embroidery and ruffles, hugged little children to their sides. Luc wanted privacy and he had an assembly instead. "Chief Nightowl, we wish to speak to you about recruiting some of your men for the Army Scouts to fight the Comanche." Luc had been to two other villages on his recruiting quest and this was the last one. The other villages had not been cooperative and he'd come away with nothing to show for his efforts.

The chief gave an expansive gestures. "You are welcome in my home. Come. Do not worry about your animals. My sons will care for them." He led the way toward a one story adobe structure set back from the square with a large garden on one side and an oak tree shading it.

Inside, Chief Nightowl motioned for Luc and Reggie to sit on two sturdy stick chairs. The chief sat across from them. A handsome woman with sparkling eyes brought cups and poured water into them. Then she served oranges before fading into the shadows.

"I have heard from our sister villages to the south that you are here to take away all my young men." Nightowl eyed Luc.

"I'm offering jobs at a fair wage and forty acres of land to any man willing to join the Buffalo Soldiers and fight against the Comanche."

Stroking his chin, Nightowl seemed to ponder Luc's words. While Luc waited patiently, Reggie moved restlessly. For all his bravado, Reggie had no talent for diplomacy. He hungered for action. Tapping his finger on the table, Reggie radiated discomfort. Given the choice, Luc would have left Reggie in Washington and brought someone more sympathetic to the Seminole. But Reggie had been assigned to him and now Luc was stuck with him.

"This is true? Forty acres of land." A light shone in the chief's dark eyes. "Where is this land?"

Luc stirred. Nothing had been written down, only discussed in vague promises. "I don't know where. My chief did not discuss all the terms with me." Luc took a sip of water, hoping he was making some sort of headway.

Chief Nightowl's eyes narrowed. "How do I know you will keep your word when the time is right?"

Luc could only repeat what he had been told. "My chief has guaranteed you will be rewarded in land."

While Nightowl thought, Luc felt his heart sink. He could see that the chief had heard similar promises before. Why should he believe Luc now? Hell, Luc had seen the government renege on written treaties with all the signers in agreement. Promises and handshakes had little value outside the bureaucratic enclave who felt no obligation to the native peoples who had inhabited the land long before the white man had arrived. Luc had no way to reassure the chief, only the hope that his superiors would honor their word ... this time.

Luc's first priority was to get recruits. With the stream of settlers coming west over the Overland Trail, protection against the Indians was paramount. The Comanches, the fiercest of them all, escalated their violence daily. Something had to be done. The more scouts he had, the better the chances of eradicating the threat. "I realize the Seminole are brother to the Comanche."

Nightowl shook his head. "The Comanche are brother to no one."

"Then it would serve your interests to help us."

"If I allow my young men to leave, who will protect my village? Who will help with the harvest?"

"The Mexican government has given permission to my chief to patrol the entire Rio Grande Valley to ensure your safety."

The chief laughed, a skeptical look in his dark, intelligent eyes. "Your white armies will now protect the Negro-Seminoles?"

Luc didn't miss the man's sarcasm. "You have my word." What was he saying? He doubted the government even knew these people were here.

"What about the word of your chief?"

Reggie slapped the table. "We speak for them."

Chief Nightowl glanced at Reggie, but said nothing. Then he turned his eyes back to Luc. "I will talk to my young men." Chief Nightowl stood.

Outside, a commotion started. Luc heard the bawling of cattle. He stepped out, Reggie behind him, into the hot afternoon sun and saw a small herd of twenty cattle being driven through the village square by a man on a horse and a boy on a mule. Two other men, tethered to a horse by long ropes, staggered after them.

Luc heard whispers of rustlers, and a little boy pointed at the men being pulled along behind the horses of the others. One of the rustlers stepped into a pile of cow dung and screamed a rough curse word. The boy who held his rope jerked it and the man fell to his knees. He scrambled to get to his feet again, looking more afraid than before. The boy didn't slow his mule one step.

The rustlers ought to be scared. Luc knew cattle rustlers in Mexico were hung without benefit of trial. His momentary sympathy evaporated when one spat at him.

The man and the boy halted their animals near Chief Nightowl. The boy grinned. "Caught them, sir, just like I said. Wasn't hard, they left enough sign for a blind man to follow."

Luc examined the two trackers. The older man was grizzled and hardened, his face a network of wrinkles and leathery skin, but the boy's face was still delicate, unformed. He must be around fourteen, yet Luc could see that the boy was capable of a man's job despite his lack of age. Damn, the man was too old for recruitment, the boy too young.

Luc turned his attention back to the other men who clustered around the two, congratulating them. Cocky, the boy preened. The other young men grinned while asking about the bounty. Desert life was stamped deeply on their youthful faces. They had lived a hard existence, and though the Army would be just as difficult, Luc had faith that they would be great soldiers.

The boy faced him. Their eyes connected. Luc felt a jolt race through him. His mouth went dry. The kid smiled. Luc turned away. What the hell had just happened?

CHAPTER TWO

Luc saddled his horse, ready to return to Fort Duncan with the five new recruits. He'd hoped for more men, but Chief Nightowl had been adamant. No more than five able-bodied young men could be spared. The others were needed in the village.

"Lieutenant Delacroix!" A clear, high voice called from outside the ramshackle lean-to that served as the stable.

Luc turned to find the boy, who'd paraded his captured rustlers through the town, standing in a shaft of sunlight that cast his face into dark shadows yet illuminated his dark curly hair. A strange, disturbing sensation crept through Luc's body. He pushed it away. He didn't have the time for the odd feelings swirling inside him. "What can I do for you, young man?"

"I've come to join the Scouts, sir." An excited glint lit the boy's cinnamon-brown eyes.

Luc bit back a laugh. This boy was too young and Luc regretted that he couldn't accept the offer. "The army is no place for children."

"I ain't no--" He stopped, pressing dainty lips tightly together.

"How old are you, boy?"

He lifted a softly rounded chin. "I'm ... fourteen. I work hard, and I'm the best tracker in the village."

Luc laughed. Short and scrawny, with a too-pretty face to be male, the boy had a voice that hadn't broken yet. Luc had already seen too many boys die in the war and knew he couldn't stomach the loss of one more. "Go back to your mama. You can sign up when you're older." He cinched the saddle and guided his gelding out of the stable into the morning sun.

The boy put a small hand on Luc's arm. "But sir ..."

The hairs on the nape of Luc's neck rose. He studied the brown hand on the dark blue sleeve of his uniform. The boy's nails were clean and groomed, the hand delicately formed. Stunned, Luc stared at the boy's upturned childish face. Luc waited a second for the curious sensation to pass. "Sorry, son, but you're just too young." Luc nodded at Reggie, who tightened the saddle cinch, jerking at the strap. His horse tended to hold its breath while being saddled and once Reggie had mounted, it would let it out and then the saddle cinch would be loose. Reggie, finally satisfied, swung into the saddle.

Luc gazed regretfully at the young boy. "I know you can do a man's job, son, but the Army is no place for a child." Luc swung into the saddle and turned his horse toward the lane that lead out of the village. He glanced back once to see the boy standing in the center of the lane, hands on his hips, scowling.

Luc glanced quickly away. He didn't understand the strange reaction he had just experienced. Nor did he understand the sense of regret as he rode away.

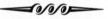

Callie stared after the soldiers as they cantered out of the village, the chosen five following. She choked on the desert dust, her temper rising. That man had no reason to turn her down. She was a good as any man they'd chosen. She didn't like the way he'd looked down his nose at her, like she was nothing but dirt. He was probably laughing at her now.

She'd show him, she was a better tracker then all of them put together. When the chief had told her about the promise of land, Callie had known then what she had to do. She would volunteer and help the Army in its war with the Comanche.

She yearned, no lusted for that forty acres more than most of the people in the village did. Her mama could have a beautiful garden. And Callie would build a good, sturdy house to keep them warm and dry. With Rafael gone, the future of her family rested on her shoulders even if she was just a woman.

Land ownership meant safety and stability. No government agent could force her to ever again live in the worst of situations. Callie's parents had refused to be herded onto reservations like the rest of the tribes in the East. They had journeyed to Mexico in the hope of freedom. But Chief Nightowl didn't know if the Mexican government would always allow them live here. Her Seminole family had lost most of their tribal lands to the white man, because they could prove no legal claim. Owning the land, with a deed that said so, meant no government could ever force them to leave again.

Callie stamped across the dusty square to her mother's house. The more she thought about Lieutenant Delacroix and his condescending attitude, the angrier she became. He had flashed his white teeth at her like she was just a kid and told her to run home to her mama. With hands clenched and mouth set in a grim line, her blood boiled. No man ever told her what to do. Not even a handsome white man.

She forgot to wipe her feet on the woven mat by the front door, and dragged desert sand across her mother's spotless wood plank floor. Callie tossed her hat on the small table between the two chairs in front of the fireplace, and walked through the tiny house searching for her mother.

The kitchen was also empty and the rear door hung open. Outside, she found her mother on her knees in her garden, pulling weeds from around the shoots of her young tomato plants and singing to her beans.

Callie plopped down to sit cross-legged next to her mother. Her mother was tall and graceful with black hair quickly turning silver. She wore her long hair braided and then looped into a figure eight at the nape of her neck. She had an oval face with serene brown eyes and a gentle mouth. In Callie's mind, she was the most beautiful woman in the village despite the network of wrinkles radiating outward from her mouth and the corners of her eyes.

"I told you he wouldn't take you." Bessie Payne's dark eyes filled with maternal understanding. She smiled and patted Callie on the knee with a long, slender hand.

Callie couldn't help the pout that pulled her lips downward. "He told me I was too young."

"And how old did you tell him you were?" Bessie picked a green worm off a plant.

"Fourteen."

Her mama sat back on her heels and chuckled. "Callie, you have courage, but knocking five years off your age ain't going to make that man change his mind. There are some things in this world even you can't change."

Callie brushed at the tears gathering in the corner of her eyes and bit her lips to control her temper. When she was back in control, she said, "We need that land. They said forty acres. Think of the garden you could have."

"Ha! Where is this land?" Bessie eyed her dubiously. "I've heard that promise before."

Callie hadn't thought to ask. "He didn't say."

Bessie eased a worm off the branch of one of the tomatoes. "For all you know, this land could be right, smack dab in the middle of a desert and good for nothing but coyotes and rattlesnakes."

The American government couldn't be that cruel. Someplace along the chain of command, someone had to remember that people needed to live, had to remember their responsibilities. Callie knew she was being naive, but she had so dreamed of taking her mother away from this god-forsaken place. "Does it matter? The land would be ours. Mexico is not our home." She knew her mama longed for the tranquil beauty of the swamps where she had been born. She told Callie stories of her home, but Callie was desert-born and had no idea what her mama had been talking about.

Bessie shook her head. "Maybe not, but it's a place to stay. I've lost my husband and my son. I'm not going to lose you, too."

Callie hugged her mother. "You won't lose me. All I have to do is serve two years, Mama. And we can have everything we ever dreamed of. The Army is paying thirteen dollars a month. That's a fortune! At the end of the year, we'd have land and money. Enough to make a good start."

Bessie kissed Callie's cheek. "I've made my home here. I'm content."

"You only stay because you hope Rafe will return."

Bessie eased a weed out of the ground. "He's coming back. I know it. I can feel him."

Callie bit her lips. "He's dead, Ma. He's never coming back. He died the same way Daddy did." She jumped to her feet, angry at her mother's blindness.

"Callie, you can track rustlers and dress like a man, but everyone knows you're a grown woman. How can you hide what you are among strangers?"

Callie lifted her chin. "I can do it. Half the time, no one here even remembers I'm a woman."

Her mama looked her up and down. "Only because you insist on wearing trousers and acting like a man." Her voice turned wistful. "If you put on a skirt and blouse like the other young women, you would find a good man to marry you and care for you. Mr. Hernandez in Calimesa would marry you in a minute."

"I don't want to spend the rest of my life serving a man all his meals. And Mr. Hernandez just wants a maid to help him in the store, and take care of all his kids. I want to be free." Her lips trembled. "Please understand, Mama."

Bessie sighed. "If you want to go, I can't stop you." Tears slid down

21

her round cheek. "I'll never forgive you if you die. I couldn't bear it, Callisto Payne."

That was her mother's way of saying "go." Callie smiled. She would get her land and show Mama she could do it. "I won't die, Mama. I promise." Callie ran into the house to pack. Elated that her dream had finally had come within reach.

Rafael Payne, watching the herd of Army horses moving sluggishly along the trail, fingered the alligator tooth threaded onto a leather thong and tied about his neck. His mother had long ago given it to him, a reminder not only of their home in the damp swamps of Florida, but a reminder that the Seminole were unbowed and still fierce. Rafe used the tooth as his totem, as his reminder of what he wanted.

The herd of horses raised a huge cloud of dust. A hundred horses and only four men to guard them. Rafe watched them in disgust. In all their arrogance, the army thought the horses safe because the distance between Fort Clark and Fort Duncan was so short, but a Comanche scout had seen the herd leaving and raced to inform Rafe and the other warriors.

Rafe glanced at his brother-in-law, Three Wolves. Three Wolves gestured to the others in the war party and they began to spread out, lust for the horses and the wealth they would bring plain on their faces. Wealth that Rafe lusted for as well. The wealth that he had once promised his mother.

Beyond Three Wolves, Night Feather, the tribe's war chief, watched the horses, a measuring look on his face. Though their band was small, only seven warriors with their families, they were brave.

"Black Fox." Wild Willow Woman's voice broke into his thoughts. When he had become a member of the small band of Comanche, he had taken the name Black Fox.

He smiled at his wife. "Willow, are you ready?" His wife was a beautiful woman with sharply chiseled features, dark eyes, and a generous mouth. In all his life, he would never have thought such a proud woman would take him, a half-breed, as a husband. She was the reason he had become a warrior with her clan. He had fallen in love with her the first time he'd seen her with her shy expression and beautiful face.

"I'm ready, husband." Willow's voice was soft and husky. "Are you thinking of your family again?"

"I think of you and our son, and the money Juan Valenzuela will pay for the horses that we can use to buy more ammunition." And information, Rafe thought. Information was what was truly important.

He wasn't quite certain how he'd made the transition from soldier to honorary Comanche war chief, but here he was preying on the white people who had once called him a dog and whipped him. He would never forget the whipping, nor the anger that still beat inside him at the humiliation. He had deserted that night, never to return.

Wild Willow Woman touched his arm. "We will have many fine horses by nightfall. Our son will be proud. But only if you come back to the present." Her smile was indulgent, though her feral eyes gleamed with a ferocious light. Willow, like most Comanche, relished warring with the white men.

"Are you ready?" He watched the army horses clomping along the trail, their heads drooping in the heat, their tails thick with dust. Their handlers were even less alert. This was almost too easy.

Willow nodded. She leaped onto her paint pony and grinned savagely, gripping her brand-new Winchester rifle with strong brown hands. Rafe had stolen it for her as a wedding gift. If not for her, Rafe would be dead. She had found him half-dead in the desert.

Night Feather gave the signal. Everyone jumped on their own ponies, and with blood-curdling whoops, they descended on the unsuspecting soldiers.

The herd of horses broke into a sudden run, charging forward with a surge of energy. A huge cloud of dust rose billowed to the blue sky. The soldiers fired their pistols, the popping sounds of the discharges speeding past Rafe's head.

Three Wolves raised his rifle and fired. With a scream, one of the soldiers fell off his horse. Willow let out a war cry and charged from Rafe's side, aiming her rifle. Coal black hair flew behind her as she bent low over the thick neck of her horse. Pride flashed through Rafe as she raced toward the soldiers. The sensation kept him from stopping her. She would be safe on her own. She'd already made many kills before he'd married her. Comanche women were as fierce as their men.

He concentrated on the leader, lifting his rifle and squeezing the trigger. His target slumped over his horse, then tumbled to the ground, the horse racing away reins flapping.

The raiding party spread out, two raiders taking control of the horses, leaving the two remaining soldiers exposed.

Willow chased one of the soldiers. The man wheeled his horse in an attempt to evade her. Her horse veered, mirroring his maneuver. With one quick pass, she shot him. Even from the back of a horse, Willow could be unerringly accurate. The soldier shrieked and plunged to the ground.

Willow's horse spun, sliding to a stop. She jumped down, taunting the soldier, sheathing her rifle and reaching for her lance. Her arm rose to spear the man. He pushed himself to his feet and tried to run. Willow caught him, plunging her lance into his back. He fell with a cry, his legs twitching before he lay still. She raised her bloody lance and screamed in victory. Rafe's admiration soared. Today she'd counted coup twice. Yes, their son have more than one reason to be proud even though he was barely two years old.

Rafe turned his attention to the last fleeing soldier. He signaled Kicking Moon, a boy barely sixteen, who heaved forward, chasing the last soldier. The soldier dragged his animal to a stop and dismounted. He knelt on the ground and raised his rifle. As Kicking Moon drew closer, the soldier fired. Kicking Moon jerked backward, but retained his seat. He bore down on the soldier. The soldier's rifle fired again, but he missed. Kicking Moon's horse slid to a stop. Then the young brave leaped on the soldier. A knife flashed. Kicking Moon stood, blood dripping from a wound in his leg. He raised his blade and cried out in triumph. "Black Fox, today I am a man."

Rafe laughed. He knew the feeling, the exhilaration of victory. The battle had ended leaving Rafe to gaze at the dead bodies of his enemies. He said a short prayer for their souls. Even though they had fought as best they could, they had been out-matched by the seven warriors of the Comanche war party.

Willow thundered up. Blood dripped along the edge of her lance, spattering her face. She reminded him of an avenging angel. "We have horses." She raised her lance to the sky and whooped.

Rafe could only gaze at her, admiring her beauty, her wildness and her strength. He loved her to the depths of his soul. Of all the young men who had vied for her hand in marriage, she'd accepted Rafe.

The raiding party herded the horses south toward the river to meet the men who would trade them for money, guns and more cartridges.

Thoughts of home consumed Rafe. He would pass near his village. Though he never regretted his choice, nostalgia for his mother and sister filled him with an aching pain. He worried that if he tried to see them, the Army would find out. He couldn't endanger his family.

The last time he'd seen Callie, she'd been a long-legged, gangly twelve-year-old, just coming into the first bloom of womanhood. What had she become in his absence? Was she married? Did she have children? Was she well? Was she happy? She must be sad at his absence, but he had no way of letting her or his mother know he was alive.

Shaking off his morbid thoughts, he turned back to Willow. Battle always left him with excess energy.

She leaned over to caress his cheek. "I am proud of you, Black Fox. When we return to the village, we will have a feast that will be remembered for many a season." The look on her face promised him more once the fires had dimmed and everyone had returned to their dwellings.

Rafe touched her black hair, braided with colorful beads and leather strings, wondering how he could have been so lucky as to win the heart of this fierce, proud woman.

—⟨⟨o/o/o⟩⟩—

Luc stood in the shade of an overhang, wiping his forehead. Fort Duncan, a combination of stone and adobe buildings, sprawled in the fertile valley below flanked by the Rio Grande and the town of Eagle Pass. Texas was a desolate land good only for the wild cattle that lived there. Yet Luc liked Texas despite a barrenness that was so different from the excesses of Paris and London.

A ribbon of sweat trickled down his cheek into the trimmed edge of his beard. After a week in the saddle chasing Comanche, he couldn't wait to get out of his heavy wool uniform and into a cool bath. At moments like this, he missed Paris, but not enough to abandon the military life he'd come to enjoy so much.

Dog-tired, he turned and led his horse, Liberty, into the stable. The stable smelled of manure, wet hay, and horses. As he passed down the long row, a chicken fluttered in front of him and raced away.

The Comanches had stolen a hundred army horses and killed four soldiers. He sorrowed for their loss. Good soldiers, all of them. When he had come to Texas he had thought war with the Comanches would be like war with the south. But he had learned quickly that the Comanche followed no rules and their guerilla style of war made the army look like idiots.

The deaths weighed him down. No matter what he did, the endless war continued. He traded war in the East for war in the West. Only the bloodstained landscape changed.

He led Liberty into a stall, then loosened the cinch.

"Lieutenant Delacroix!" A voice called, hesitant and almost shy.

He turned around and saw a boy dressed in baggy trousers and a loose plaid shirt. A wide-brimmed hat protected his thin, youthful face from the harsh sun. For a moment, his heart raced.

The boy straightened his narrow shoulders and stared straight in Luc's eyes. "You told me I could sign up when I was older. I'm older, sir."

Luc almost laughed. "That was two weeks ago."

"You didn't say how much older." The boy grinned, showing a small dimple in one cheek and even white teeth.

Luc narrowed his eyes, ignoring about the strange feeling whirling in his gut. He had to admire the lad. "You are persistent."

The kid smiled. He had a sweet smile. "I followed you all the way here and you didn't know."

"That wouldn't be hard. You knew which direction I was going. We didn't try to hide our tracks."

The boy studied him. "I know something you don't."

"Boy, I don't have time to play games." Too tired and too irritated to make sport, Luc's amusement turned to annoyance.

The boy's brown eyes danced. "Know why Army horses are prized by the Comanches?"

"Why?" Luc patted Liberty's rump.

"Because you have the best horses in the world. The Comanches can trade them for weapons, ammunition, and food."

Intrigued, Luc leaned forward. "Explain yourself."

"I know where your horses are." The brat sounded smug, even cocky.

The little scamp. "Where?"

The boy grinned. "I'm not tellin'."

Luc raised an eyebrow. "You're going to tell me now."

The boy grinned. "You want your horses back?"

"Of course."

"Let me join the Scouts and I'll take you."

Luc shook his head. "You're too young. The army isn't a nursemaid." Though he doubted this boy would ever need a nursemaid, his eyes told of experiences even Luc wouldn't understand.

"I saw them. Passed right by me while I was following you." He put his small hands on his narrow hips. "In fact, the whole herd passed right by you, too, and you didn't see a thing."

Luc stared hard at the boy, his anger growing. "Tell me where they went." He could get a fresh patrol on the trail first thing in the morning.

The boy shook his head. "Not until you sign me up."

Luc wanted to shake him. "You don't even shave yet."

The boy touched his smooth chin. "Indians don't shave. No facial hair. I inherited that from my mama."

"What's your name, boy?"

"Cal. Cal Payne, sir."

Luc pulled the saddle off his horse and tossed it at the boy. The kid caught it and tumbled on his butt.

"Take care of my horse." Luc grinned. "Then come by my office when you're done and sign your papers. We leave in the morning."

Luc walked away. He had to admire Cal. That boy had refused to give up. The army needed men like that. Halfway down the feed aisle, he turned around to look at Cal struggling to his feet with the saddle. His smile broadened. The army wasn't the place for a kid, but he'd grow up knowing how to be a soldier. Luc would make a man out of him.

Callie pushed the saddle off her stomach and battled her way to her feet. She glared at Lieutenant Delacroix's back. She didn't like him. He was too prideful for his own good. Typical white man. Although he was pretty to look at, he was stupid.

He probably didn't know anything about surviving on this side of the Mississippi. Maybe she should reconsider her decision to join the scouts. Naw! Not a chance. She figured she'd probably have to spend all her time keeping his white ass out of trouble. What did he know about tracking? Nothing. What did he know about living off the land. Nothing. What did he know about the Comanche? Nothing. Callie knew everything.

She hefted the saddle to one shoulder and staggered down the feed aisle to the tack room. She flung it over a storage rack. She'd love to punch that man in the mouth. He made her feel crazy inside, like she couldn't think anymore.

Joining the scouts was supposed to be simple. She'd earn her land and muster out of the Army. She didn't need to be thinking wicked thoughts about a man ... any man.

"You be careful with Mr. Luc's saddle, boy," a man said.

"Who you callin' a boy?" Callie spotted an old colored man sitting on a three-legged stool mending a harness. He wore a stained leather apron over baggy denim pants. Tightly curled, iron gray hair crowned his head. Brown eyes were deep-set in a coffee-colored face.

The old man shifted the harness. "Mr. Luc had the saddle made special in London."

Callie studied him. "Maybe he ought to go back to London. Texas is no place for a tenderfoot."

The old man grinned, revealing red gums and a couple of teeth in the bottom jaw. "You a feisty one, little man."

Callie bit her lip. "Don't you call me a 'little man.'"

The old man burst into a hearty laughter. "You and me are gonna get along just fine. But you watch your mouth around the officers. Most of them white boys don't think nothing about strippin' down a Black man and whippin' us like we was back on the plantation."

Her mouth fell open. "Including Lieutenant Delacroix?" She waited for the answer hoping that the handsome Lieutenant Delacroix wouldn't be so cruel, that he was different.

The old man shook his head. "The Lieutenant's a good man. He volunteered to lead the Black soldiers. Not like most of the officers who think we don't know nothin' about soldierin'. All we're good for is pickin' cotton and shinin' shoes."

"You mean the Buffalo Soldiers?"

"Yes sir, little man. That Lieutenant Delacroix and his black boys followed that Apache, Screamin' Coyote, all the way into Sonora and drug him back." He bent over the harness for a moment. Then he smiled. "An' fore that he fought the war betwixt the States."

"I'm surprised he didn't get killed."

The old man laughed. "You a evil one, little man. What's your name?"

"Cal."

"Well, Cal, you big enough for that name."

Callie stuck her hands in her pockets and poked out her chest. She liked him. "I can take care of myself, old man."

"You call me Silas. I take care of the horses and the saddle mendin' round here. Nobody knows more about horses than me."

In spite of her herself, Callie sat down on a stool, drawn to the old man. He was like her father. That is, what she remembered of her father. He'd always been spinning yarns, telling tales, and sharing his life stories with her. "How come you know so much about horses, Silas?"

"Back in Virginia, I was a slave. Took care of the Master's horses. Master Charles had himself the best stable in the state. When the war come, I stole me seventeen horses and made my way up north and joined the Union Army. Been with Mr. Luc ever since."

The war in the east had been like another yarn spun around the camp fire. News had been scanty, and Callie doubted much was true. What the men in the village didn't know, they made up. "Did you do any fighting?"

He buffed the metal rivets that held the harness together. "I did some, but I don't want to do no more killin'. It's hard on the soul."

"Then why are you here?"

Silas smiled. "I owe Mr. Luc my life. Now I take care of him."

Callie stood and turned back toward the stable. "Looks like I'm doing the same thing. I have to rub down his horse."

"There's worse jobs," Silas said with a knowing glint in his dark eyes.

Callie walked back to Luc's horse. She grabbed a ratty blanket and started rubbing the animal down, then she groomed the animal until the gelding's hide shone like silk. For some reason, she wanted Luc to be proud of her, and if that meant showing him she could take good care of his horse, then she would.

—⊙⊙⊙—

Luc opened the door to his office. A wave of heat hit him like a slap as he entered. The office was small and cramped with four desks. One of which was occupied by Reggie who sat with his dust-caked boots propped up on an open drawer, reading a report. He glanced up over the edge of the report. "How did patrol go?"

Luc tossed his hat on his desk. "Badly. Not a sign of the Comanches, but I may have located the stolen horses." He pulled out his chair and sat down stifling a yawn. He rubbed his face and eased his legs out. He desperately wanted a decent night's sleep. He'd spent the Civil War aching for the exact same thing, and here he was wanting it again. And he'd thought life in Texas would be boring.

Reggie's feet hit the floor. "Where?"

"We'll find out tomorrow." If a snot-nosed boy who didn't even shave proved to be wrong, Luc would look like a fool. But then again, Cal was desperate to join the scouts, Luc didn't think he'd lie about something so important. In fact, he didn't think Cal would lie about anything. There was a directness in the boy's eyes. Not the type of sliding-off gaze that indicated a lack of truth.

Luc had a momentary flash of finding the bodies of the soldiers who had been herding the horses to the fort. The soldiers badly needed the replacement horses. Once Luc spoke to Major Adams about what Cal had related to him, the Major would send them out again to track the Comanches down and get those horses back.

Luc examined the mail that had been neatly stacked on his desk. Most of the envelopes contained bills for grain and for supplies for the troops. But one letter leaped out at him. The postmark said Paris, and his name was written in the loopy feminine script that belonged to his sister. Esme! He reached for it, anticipating the latest gossip. The letter was open. He glared at Reggie.

"I am your adjutant," Reggie pointed out. "You did give me permission to open your mail."

"I believe I did mention to abstain from opening those marked 'personal'.

And this one is definitely marked personal." He was thankful Esme was willing to help him keep his secret. He didn't want Reggie--or anyone else--to learn about his deception. He'd be cashiered out of the army, or worse. He didn't know what the worse could be, but he knew he would suffer the effects of the humiliation for the rest of his life.

"Just trying to help," Reggie replied with an impish grin. "Are you going to introduce me to your sister? She's coming, you know." A salacious gleam brightened Reggie's blue eyes as he picked up a small portrait Esme had painted of herself that decorated the corner of Luc's desk.

"No." Luc snatched the painting from his aide's hands. He studied his twin's face. She wore a stylish, evening gown of virginal white--an ironic choice. Her shining blue-black hair, swept up in the newest Parisian style, exposed ruby and diamond earrings hanging from her delicate shell-shaped ears. Her green eyes, glowed with mischief. She was outrageous and Luc loved her. Her antics had kept him amused since their childhood.

Reggie tapped his fingers on the desk. "Why not?"

Luc raised an eyebrow. What would Reggie think if he wooed Esme, married her, and discovered she was a woman of color? Reggie's well-bred ancestors, a line he could trace all the way back to the Mayflower and probably England, would disown him.

Luc almost laughed out loud at the thought. Though he doubted he had anything to worry about. Reggie wasn't Esme's type, he was too tame, too average. Esme liked men with culture and class, yet with a hint of mischief that complimented her own.

But then again, Luc hadn't seen Esme in five years. She could have changed.

Reggie frowned. "I assume by your silence that you feel I'm not good enough for your sister." A touch of hostility tinged his voice. Reggie didn't take rejection lightly.

Luc chuckled. "Correct on the first try."

Reggie's eyebrows rose in surprise. "I'm most respectable. Any woman would be delighted to have me."

"Any woman, but Esme." Luc removed the letter from the envelope.

"If she gave me a chance, I could change her mind."

Luc studied him over the edge of the letter. "You may try all you want. But I warn you, my sister has a trail of broken hearts behind her a mile long."

Luc scanned the letter quickly. Her lover had died, and Luc felt a moment's sorry even though he had never met the man. Esme had loved him very much. With him dead and Luc gone, she no longer had a reason to remain in Paris. The idea of visiting him had occurred to her. She'd decided to visit him and eventually make her way to San Francisco. She had heard the city was an interesting place and she felt it was the place to start anew.

Luc had a hard time picturing his sophisticated, Paris-educated sister, whose favorite pastime was strolling the Champs d'Elysses, in the wild and untamed West. Where would he put her? The three rooms assigned him on officers' row were abysmally small and filled with insects. Weeds grew through the wooden slats of his floor and water leaked through the roof during the summer storms. Fort Duncan was a long, long way from cosmopolitan Paris.

Esme considered anything less than the finest European accommodations, with the best linen sheets, nothing more than a hovel. The picture of his sister on a bumpy, dusty stagecoach, with the great unwashed hordes, amused him. Haute French society would pay millions of francs to see Esme Delacroix out of her element and uncomfortable. As a matter of fact, he would enjoy seeing that way also.

He read her letter again. From the time-table she'd given him, she should be arriving in New Orleans soon, where she intended to visit their father.

A stab of guilt pierced him. Luc hadn't spoken to his father in twelve years. His father had been furious when Luc ad joined the Northern army instead of the south's colored brigades. But Luc's politics and his father's politics didn't exactly match, and the old man, whose support Luc had depended on through his years in Paris, had been withdrawn.

Luc regretted his father's anger, the rift between them, but if Luc were honest with himself he was as much at fault as his father. Like his father, Luc's pride had been hurt. He understood his father's position, but his father had refused to understand Luc's. The only time Luc had written to attempt an explanation, the letter had been returned unopened.

He wondered what Esme thought she could to help make peace between them. Though she had kept in touch with her father, their correspondence had been sporadic. In the last two years, Esme had written several times, but their father had not answered. Luc hoped that her trip to New Orleans was fruitful.

Esme, as outrageous as she was, wasn't impulsive. She planned her scandals and stunts with precision. What did she have in store for him? He grimaced at the prospect of her arrival. Esme was always up to something, and he wondered what she was up to this time.

CHAPTER THREE

Callie sat, tall and proud, in the saddle of her brand new horse. She loved her new mount, but hated giving up her mule, Ocala. Since childhood, the feisty mule had served her well. But Ocala wasn't fast enough for the grain-fed army horses. So she had turned Ocala loose in a corral. Mules were smarter than horses and Callie had been sorry to give the old mule up.

She would have been issued a uniform, but none had been small enough to fit, so she continued to wear her baggy pants and loose plaid shirt. Good thing, too. How would she change in front of all the men who comprised the patrol? None had been from her village. Her friends would have shielded her but they had been sent to other forts. These men would be less understanding if they discovered she was a woman.

She'd been given a private room in the barracks. Lt. Delacroix had secured it for her, telling her that her age had allowed him to manage the special privilege. Callie had been grateful. She wouldn't have to wash and dress in front of the whole barracks. Though the soldiers had a pleasant, almost kindly, attitude to her, treating her like a little brother. She knew if they found out what she was, she would be treated harshly.

She shot a glance back at Lieutenant Delacroix. Her commanding officer radiated authority. He rode at the head of the patrol, his eyes constantly scanning the horizon. Sometimes he watched her.

Delacroix interested her in a way she'd never before experienced. With his black hair and piercing green eyes, he was unlike any other man she'd ever seen. His sculpted cheekbones and full mouth fascinated her. Just being near him made her go hot and giddy on the inside. She'd never felt so odd with any of the men in her village. They were like brothers to her. But something about the Lieutenant was very un-brother-like.

She shifted in the saddle. The horse glided in an easy way that Ocala had never had. Filled with confidence and hope, Callie envisioned her future stretching out brightly in front of her. She'd prove to the Lieutenant she could to do the job. And in the end, the Army would be grateful for what she'd done and they'd pay her with land.

The long, hard ride to Mexico took them across the Rio Grande, away from the fertile areas alongside the river, and into a desert, scorched by the hot sun, inhabited only by bugs and rattlesnakes.

Callie ranged far ahead of the patrol. She stopped, dismounted and crouched on the ground. Clutching the reins of her horse, she studied the tracks in the sand. Even though the horses had been herded this way over a week ago and the sand had almost returned to its natural, rippled state, the sign was still there. Faint and almost gone, but she knew how to read the desert. She smiled, surprised at the cunning of the Comanche raiding party.

The evidence of the large herd of horses passing through was clear to someone who knew what to search for. A broken twig, horse hair, a bush knocked aside with rocks turned over--all showed that a large herd of animals had passed. On the edges, were deeper tracks of horses with riders. She believed the band of Indians was small, from what she could see maybe four or five warriors, but the Comanche were masters at concealing their numbers.

She heard a horse cantering toward her. She didn't look up, knowing it was Lieutenant Delacroix. She always sensed when he was near. The skin on her body heated and the hairs on the back of her neck rose. Callie tried to shake off the feeling. She remounted and turned her horse to face him, glad the white man, Reggie Cooper, hadn't come to check on her.

Lieutenant Cooper treated the soldiers worse then dirt. Silas had warned her to stay out of his way. If he treated his men so badly, how would he treat a woman?

"Sir." She settled her wide-brimmed hat low on her head to shade her eyes. The glare off the sand burned her skin. In the distance, a storm formed, but Callie doubted it would come this way. She hoped not. It would erase what was left of the horse sign, and then she'd be out of the Army because she couldn't do her job.

Lieutenant Delacroix leaned forward on his saddle. "Well, Payne?"

"Five, maybe six, riders heading south on unshod horses pushing the herd hard" She peered at the ground. "They came through here about a week ago. The sand is already settling back."

Every time he looked at her with his piercing green eyes, she thought he would see right through her disguise and realize who and what she was. That thought sat in the back of her mind, never to be forgotten, making her remember she had to be careful. He was a man who saw beyond the obvious. Once slip on her part and he would guess her secret.

"Any idea where they're heading?" Lieutenant Delacrois asked.

"Tres Cruces." She pointed at a ragged ridge of mountains, so distant she could barely make out the peaks.

Delacroix shaded his eyes as he stared in the direction she pointed. "Why would they go there?"

Callie knew. Tres Cruces was the hangout for every outlaw in Mexico. "Tres Cruces is a very bad place. Juan Valenzuela is there. He's a bandit. Comanche trade with him. He pays them in rifles and ammunition." Her horse fell into step next to his. "Valenzuela is not a good man. Everyone avoids the area. Only outlaws go to Tres Cruces."

They rode silently for a few minutes and then Callie stopped and frowned.

"What's wrong?" Lieutenant Delacroix asked.

She studied the trail. "A smaller herd with two riders split off and headed back north toward the river."

"Splitting the herd to throw us off the trail?"

She shook her head. "Maybe, but I think they probably intend to keep some of the horses for themselves. Which trail do you want me to follow?"

"The main herd."

She paused and looked into his green eyes, pushing down an attack of nerves. He made her so jittery she couldn't concentrate on what she was going to say. "The Comanches are long gone. This trail's a week old. They didn't head straight for Juan Valenzuela's hideout, but zig-zagged to make tracking more difficult. If we follow on their heels, we'll stay a week behind. I can show you another way and head straight for the hideout. We'll probably miss the Comanche, but we might get there before Valenzuela has moved the horses to one of his other bases."

He glanced at her. "How do you know?"

She took a deep breath, worried about the consequences of giving him advice. "The zig-zag pattern is an old Seminole trick."

"But you have no proof they are heading there."

Her knees started shaking. She bit the inside of her lip. "There's no place else for them to go. According to a couple of rustlers my partner and I caught about six months ago, Valenzuela has been stock-piling weapons. The Comanches need those weapons and ammunition. They are going to trade the horses for guns. If you want those horses back, I think we should head straight there."

He pushed back his hat and studied the horizon. "How much further?"

She let out a breath, glad he wasn't staring at her anymore. "Four days, three if we ride hard. But you'll need more men. Valenzuela has a hundred banditos. I figure that's why he wants the horses. He thinks he can be El Presidente." Contempt infused her voice. Valenzuela had boasted he would rule all Mexico. Callie doubted his claim. If a superior force like the French couldn't hold Mexico, how did Valenzuela think he could?

He frowned. "Valenzuela can be whatever he wants, but he does it without my horses. We'll use the men we have." He whirled his horse and headed back toward the patrol.

Callie followed at a slower pace, scanning the landscape. A jackrabbit jumped out startling her horse. He was going to get her killed attacking Valenzuela. Was he loco? Valenzuela's hideout was well guarded, set in a deep valley with a dozen places perfect for ambushing unwanted visitors. Forget buying the land. She'd be lucky to escape with her life. And she promised to her mama not to get herself killed?

＝ー✺✺✺ー＝

Callie ran a hand over her horse's flank, settling the rangy gelding. The animal shifted its weight from side to side as she finished rubbing it down and feeding it the grain the army brought along for food. Callie felt grimy with the day's dust and had tried to clean herself as best she could.

Once the decision had been made to attack Valenzuela, the Lieutenant had marched the patrol long into the dark. All the men were exhausted. Callie was in better shape because she often only slept a few hours in a night.

Lieutenant Delacroix had ordered them to make camp in a deep canyon which offered protection from the night. A shallow pool beneath a tiny waterfall fed by the runoff from the mountains beyond provided water. The chilly pond was hidden by a thick grove of trees and heavy underbrush. The Lieutenant had commanded her to water their horses, and then help set up camp closer to the mouth of the canyon.

The strong aroma of coffee and cooking food emanated from the direction of the camp. Callie's mouth watered. Though hungry, she wanted privacy to wash and maybe even change her clothes first for the clean ones she carried in her saddle bags.

Callie waited for the men to settle down with their food, then slipped back to the pond. The moon had risen over the peak of the rocks.

The night sky twinkled with the distant stars. As a child, her mother had taught her she could make a wish on a star and it would come true. She'd grown up enough since then to know that wishes didn't come from stars, but still as she searched for a place that would shield her from prying eyes, she couldn't resist a glance upward and utter a short, hopeful wish for the army to honor its promises.

The pond was a contrast of shadows, dark against silver light. Water cascaded over the cliff above, creating a soothing, invitation that made Callie want to lay down next to the edge of the pond and take a nap. Callie knelt and ran a hand through the cold water. She splashed her face and washed the back of her neck.

She tossed her saddlebags down and opened one flap to draw out a clean shirt and trousers. She hunkered down in the concealing darkness of a bush, carefully listening for anyone else around. She heard the rustling of desert mice in the rocks and the twitter of night birds in the scrub oaks, but no other sounds. Satisfied she was alone, she began to unbutton her shirt. Her skin itched beneath the bindings around her chest. She gazed longingly at the pond, wanting a bath, but knowing she probably shouldn't risk it.

She heard a twig snap. Callie whirled around to see Lieutenant Delacroix, his shirt hanging open, his muscular chest shiny in the starlight.

He watched her with a strange expression on his face. "You're out here to take a bath, too?"

"Yes, sir." Callie closed her shirt, irritated at the loss of her privacy, panicked by his presence. She'd almost betrayed her secret.

"Come on." He reached for her, but she jumped back. "Let's get this over with. We have to be up and in the saddle before down."

"I don't think bathing with you would be proper, sir."

"What isn't proper about a bath?" His eyes narrowed as he studied her

She flushed under his scrutiny. "Us in the same pond, at the same time."

He tilted his head at her, his green eyes curious. "Why?"

"You're white and I'm black." Callie couldn't catch her breath. Her village had many handsome men, but this man looked magnificent.

Something in his eyes shifted and the amusement that had been there a moment ago was gone replaced by something she couldn't interpret.

Her eyes shifted back and forth, trying to avoid her gaze landing on him. She wanted to examine every aspect of his body, but she didn't dare. The pulse in her neck beat so hard she was surprised he couldn't see it.

Fortunately, the Lieutenant didn't seem to notice her panic. He leaned his tall, lean body against a rock. "Then, help me with my boots." He sat on the ground and held up one foot.

Callie's fingers trembled as she re-buttoned her shirt. She grasped the heel of his boot in both hands and pulled hard. Inch by inch, the black leather boot slid off. He wriggled his toes and sighed in relief. Then he held out the other foot. Callie tugged off the second boot and he repeated his toe wriggling. She sat down and watched him, amazed that he could take such pleasure in being barefoot.

"If there is one thing I hate, it's breaking in a new pair of boots." He stood and began unbuttoning his trousers.

Callie covered her eyes with her hands. She wouldn't peep she told herself, though she peeked anyway.

"Son," he laughed. "we both have the same materiel. You don't have to be ashamed."

Heat rose across her skin. She wondered if she touched herself would she burn. "But, sir, I've never seen a white man's ... or any man's ... you know. My people do not expose themselves."

"You're in the Army now, son. Finding privacy is almost impossible. I respect your people's teachings, but the Army is your family now."

Callie stared at him. He'd taken off his shirt, his back and shoulders silver against the moonlight. He tossed the shirt at her and she clutched it to her chest, inhaling his scent.

Callie's thought her heart would stop. She gasped for breath. She'd never before understood how the other women could get all lathered up about the men of the village--until this moment.

Lucian Delacroix was beautiful. His chest gleamed, each muscle clearly defined. He had a line of black hair trailing down his stomach disappearing into his trousers.

"Son, modesty and privacy are two luxuries we soldiers can't afford."

Her grip on the shirt tightened as he stripped off his pants. White long johns clung to his powerful thighs and rear-end. His muscles rippled with every step.

Callie was lost. Sheer strength of will kept her from pulling her own shirt off and joining him in the pond. She wanted to feel his hands on her skin. She wanted ... she shook her head not knowing what she wanted, but she scuttled backward away from him, embarrassed.

He pushed through the underbrush, calling back over his shoulder, "You can have the pond when I'm done, Payne. Until then, stay here and protect my virtue." He shimmied out of his long johns and flung them over a bush.

Callie saw a white flash as he splashed into the pond. She lifted his shirt to her nose to breathe deeply of his aroma, heavy in the folds. A tingle traveled through her, that radiated outward like the ripples on the surface of the pond.

His voice raised in song in another language. Callie listened. She recognized French. A French priest had come to her town a long time ago to set up a school.

How had Lieutenant Delacroix learned French? He had a French name and spoke English plainly enough without an accent. Who was this man? Where had he come from?

Callie peeked through the underbrush, transfixed and terrified. He stood in water to his waist as he ran a bar of soap over his shoulders. His face and hands, dark against the stark whiteness of the rest of his body.

He soaped his chest. The ditty he sang changed, taking on a mocking tone. He washed his hair and then sank beneath the surface. Callie held her breath, waiting for him to surface.

When he didn't rise, Callie jumped to her feet and raced to the edge of the pond. She stepped into the water to her ankles, staring at the spot where he'd disappeared. Terror grew inside her.

She heard splashing and suddenly, he surfaced right in front of her, bouncing out of the water like a fish.

Startled, she stepped back and sat down hard on the sandy edge. The Lieutenant jumped out of the water and she saw him from neck to knee in all his glory. Oh God!

He grabbed his shirt from her hands and then hauled her to her feet, his fingers warm on her arms. Fire blazed from the very core of her body and spiraled outward. All she could do was gaze at his man thing. She was fascinated.

"Here." He handed her his soap, then reached for his underwear and trousers and stepped into them. "Nothing like a bath to put a new slant on a man's perspective." He shook his head and crystal droplets flew in all directions.

One of the drops landed on her lip. She swiped her tongue across her mouth. She could almost taste him. The heat inside her grew more intense until she thought she would erupt into flames. The sight of him climbing into his clothes, one leg raised, and the other solid on the ground, showed corded muscles in his thighs. He moved with such raw power and grace, he reminded her of an Apache warrior she'd once seen in Hermosa. He'd had the same power. She remembered being fascinated by him, but her mother had jerked her into a store and she'd lost sight of him.

What was wrong with her? She'd never reacted to any man in her village like this. Not one had roused such strong emotions in her.

Dear God! She lusted after a white man.

One of the girls in her village had run off with one of the French soldiers who had been in the patrol conscripting the men. The scandal had rocked the village to its foundation. How could a good girl like that run away with a white man?

The town still gossiped about the old scandal. No one heard another word from her. Everyone assumed she was dead.   Callie   didn't need this problem. Lusting after a white officer would not only get her dismissed from the Army, but her mother would be so disappointed in her. The shame! She shuddered at the thought of being the object of gossip. She'd caused enough scandal already by donning pants and tracking rustlers.

She stared at the Lieutenant. He'd pulled on his pants and had slipped on a clean shirt. His strong fingers fastened each button with care. How would his long elegant fingers feel on her bare skin?

She sniffed the soap. "What is this smell?"

"Bayberry. Good isn't it?" He grabbed his boots and stamped into them, then turned to Callie. "Enjoy your bath, Payne." He slapped her on the back. "You did a good job today."

He disappeared through the underbrush back to the camp. Callie listened to him crash through the bushes. He made too much noise. Typical white man.

When the sound of his passage ended, she undressed quickly, slid into the water and washed herself.

The idea that he had given her his soap sent a chill down her spine. He had used this same soap. Odd that he would give her his soap. Soap was precious. She sniffed it. Bayberry, he'd said. She'd seen bayberry soap at the store in Sonora. She'd wanted it, but the price had been beyond her means. She'd only had money for essentials. For fancy people, the shopkeeper had told her when he'd slapped her hands as she'd reached for it. Now she had some and she inhaled the scent. It was so different from the sharply scented soap her mother made from lye and animal fat.

She ran the soap over her body. The sensual scent covered her skin and left her tingling. The soap, soft and gentle, lathered up in a luxurious manner. She spread the lather over her aching breasts and down to the hidden core of her body. His soap. His smell.

She found she couldn't end her bath. She wanted to go on forever lathering her body with his soap, smelling like him. She didn't want to return his soap. She wanted to use it down to the last sliver.

She heard movement in the brush. Swiftly, she slid into the water until it covered her to her chin.

A figure moved through the grove. She narrowed her eyes to filter out the side images. The other white lieutenant, the mean one with the blond hair and icy blue eyes, seemed to be slinking through the grove of trees.

Callie eased back until she stood behind the little waterfall and watched him. He leaned against a tree and she could make out his fingers tugging open a tobacco pouch and pouring a line of tobacco into a piece of paper. He rolled a cigarette. A match flared. After a few moments, the scent of tobacco drifted toward Callie.

She waited until Lieutenant Cooper had finished smoking and left. She pulled herself out of the water and hastily dressed in clean clothes. She cut a square from the end of her soiled breast binding, then sliced a small chunk of the soap from the bar, and wrapped it in the square. Carefully she hid the treasure in her saddle bag.

She crept into the camp. The fire had burned down to dim embers. Most of the men slept. Delacroix sat in front his open tent, reading by the light of a small lantern. He cradled the book in his hands as though it were more precious than gold.

All her life Callie had wanted book learning. A spurt of envy rose in her as she approached. "Here's your soap, sir." She handed him the block. "Thank you."

"You're welcome."

She sat down next to him to peer over his shoulder. "What are you reading, sir?"

"The Count of Monte Cristo by Alexander Dumas."

His gentle voice held the cadence of Southern gentility. Silas said the Lieutenant fought for the Union. Why had he done that, when his voice reflected the deep South? When she'd been a child, just after the war ended, a wagon train of southern officers rolled through town, staring at Callie and her people with hatred. How could the Lieutenant be so different? He treated the black soldiers like equals.

Callie touched the outer edge of the book. "I've always wanted to read."

"Didn't you have a school in the village?"

"I didn't have time for school. I had to support my mama." Though her brother had been sent for a couple years. He'd learned to read and write, and Callie had always felt a little touch of envy for him.

An odd look crossed the Lieutenant's face. "Would you like to learn to read? I can teach you."

She couldn't accept. She'd be too close to him. That would be too unsettling. He did things to her heart she didn't understand. "No, thank you, sir." She slipped away into the darkness, trying to put distance between them.

———⟨ɷɷɷ⟩———

Luc watched Cal disappear into the darkness. Something about that boy bothered him, but he couldn't put a finger on it. He was as skittish as a newborn foal and as sensitive as a girl. Luc closed his book and put the bar of soap back in its waterproof oilskin bag.

His patrol was spread out about him, feet pointed toward the dead fire. Reggie slept apart, his tent pitched behind Luc's as though not wanting to be associated with the Buffalo Soldiers. He'd chided Luc for being too lax with his men, but Luc know these were men who could fight and whose loyalty had been hard-won.

Then he doused the fire with the last of the coffee, entered his tent, lay down on his cot and rolled into his blankets to sleep. He tossed about for awhile, thinking of Cal. He'd seen the eagerness on the boy's face when he'd offered to teach him to read, but Cal had withdrawn. If Cal wanted to learn to read, why not allow Luc to teach him?

He fell asleep and dreamed about Cal Payne. In his dream, Cal came to him and offered his body, a body heavy with breasts and long hair that spilled about his shoulders framing his elfin face.

Luc sat straight up in the bedroll, wide-awake, cold sweat pouring down his face, his heart racing and hands shaking. No, he couldn't be that way, craving the company of men. It was a sin. It was not natural. He could lose everything he'd sacrificed for. These thoughts had to stop. He must control himself. He wasn't sure how, he just knew that he must.

The dream slipped away from him and he lay back down, but sleep was a long time coming.

CHAPTER FOUR

In the morning, as the first light brightened the sky, Luc and his soldiers stole through the foothills of the mountains. The peaks were brown and desolate, yet Cal had insisted a fruitful canyon was hidden just behind the rocks.

At mid-morning, Cal rode back from his scouting expedition with new information. Cal refused to meet Luc's eyes. He continued to act skittish and distant. Luc remembered the part of his dream when he'd was kissed Cal. His lips were soft and sweet, like a woman's. Luc shook his head to clear himself of the erotic vision.

"I found the bandit camp," Cal said as his horse fell into step with Luc's.

"How far?"

"About two miles back in the foothills." Cal wiped his face with a worn kerchief. "I counted twenty-two banditos."

Reggie spurred his horse forward. "I don't like this."

Luc twisted in the saddle to look at Reggie. "Don't like what?"

"Attacking them," Reggie said. "We're outnumbered. Twenty-two to thirteen is not good odds."

Luc laughed. He glanced back at the men following him. With the exception of Cal Payne, and his newest private, all of the men with him had been in his command for almost two years. Men he trusted. His sergeant-major, Abraham Parker, had fought with him in the Civil War. His men were the best, hand-picked for their courage, ferocity, and fighting skill. Luc would rather have these Buffalo Soldiers at his back than any other men.

"Thirteen to twenty-two." Luc smiled. "I think our bandits are outnumbered by us." He glanced back at Abraham and the Sergeant-major nodded in agreement, his black face a contrast to the sandy desert.

Cal cleared his throat. "Begging your pardon, sir. I've dealt with outlaws before. They put up a good fight, but they have very little at stake. The only thing they have in common is greed. They'll turn tail and run if they don't see a clear victory. Valenzuela pays for loyalty. His people won't stick around to defend him if they think the odds are too great."

Luc nodded in agreement.

Reggie scowled. "What does this darkie know?" His gaze swept over the whole patrol implying that none of them knew anything. Reggie annoyed him at times, but he was good officer despite his feelings

Luc ignored Reggie, but saw Cal's face tighten for a brief second, then the boy's expression went completely blank, hidden behind a careful mask.

"What I know," Cal said in a tightly controlled voice, "is that Valenzuela attacked my village twice. When he saw we weren't giving up, he went after less determined folks."

"I think our Cal has more experience under his belt than I thought." He noticed Cal's lips twitch like he was fighting a smile.

Cal suddenly sat straighter in the saddle, his puny shoulders thrust back. Luc suppressed a smile. Little Cal's attempt at acting like a man amused him. Unbidden, his dream came back and Luc's amusement faded. Was he attracted to a boy? Mon Dieu! Luc shied away from the appalling thought.

"Let's get going," Luc spurred his horse. Liberty jumped ahead. The Sergeant-Major called for double time and the whole patrol set off toward the foothills and Valenzuela.

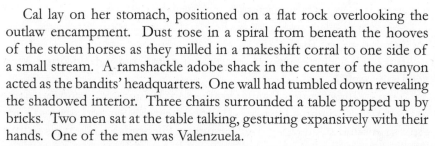

Cal lay on her stomach, positioned on a flat rock overlooking the outlaw encampment. Dust rose in a spiral from beneath the hooves of the stolen horses as they milled in a makeshift corral to one side of a small stream. A ramshackle adobe shack in the center of the canyon acted as the bandits' headquarters. One wall had tumbled down revealing the shadowed interior. Three chairs surrounded a table propped up by bricks. Two men sat at the table talking, gesturing expansively with their hands. One of the men was Valenzuela.

Cal watched the outlaw, a feeling of anger rising inside her. She hated Valenzuela. He had destroyed her village two times and kidnaped two young women. Even though the men of the village had followed in an attempt to rescue them, the women had never been found. Cal scanned the encampment counting the outlaws again. Five more had joined the band during the night. The odds had changed.

Next to her, Lieutenant Delacroix watched, his fancy binoculars pressed to his eyes, as he scanned the surrounding peaks looking for guards. The heat of his thigh against her's made her uncomfortable. She scooted over slightly to put some distance between them. She wondered what he saw through his binoculars and envied him his ownership of them.

The bandits were preparing to move out. Pack animals stood patiently against hitching posts while the bandits fixed and ate their lunch. A dozen men hunched over bowls of food. They'd eaten in shifts. One set guarded the canyon, while the other ate.

"Let's get back," Lieutenant Delacroix said, "I want to surprise them while they're still eating."

"Luc," Reggie said, "don't you think it would be easier to surprise them in the canyon? You could station the men on the rim and fire down on them."

"I don't want to injure any of the horses and ... I want prisoners." His voice was grim. "We'll attack them now while they are off guard. In the canyons they'll be alert and be ready for trouble."

Callie slid across the hot rock and down the back side of it. Her feet hit dirt and a cascade of pebbles rained down on her. "I can slip into the camp, sir, and take out a few of them. Just to even up the odds." She would start with Valenzuela. He was arrogant and cocky. He'd be easy to kill.

He flashed an amused smile at her. "Have you killed before?"

She'd never had to before, but couldn't let him know. "Rustlers don't take kindly to bein' captured."

Respect flared briefly in his eyes. She looked away ashamed, aware she had earned it under false pretenses.

Lieutenant Delacroix shook his head. "I'd just as soon you stayed here and kept an eye on things."

"But, sir," Callie objected, "you're out-numbered two to one. You need everyone."

"That's a direct order, Payne. You're here because you can read sign, not because you fight." He reached for his horse's reins and stepped into the stirrups and swung a leg over the horse. He headed back to his patrol hidden in a small pocket canyon a hundred feet away.

Callie resisted the urge to stamp her feet in frustration. She wanted to be in the thick of the battle. Her horse moved impatiently. Callie soothed the animal as she reached for her brand new, army issue Springfield carbine, and shimmied back up the rock. Even if the Lieutenant said stay put, she could still shoot from where she was. She owed Valenzuela for a lot of deaths in her village. Not even Lieutenant Delacroix was going to take that away from her. She found a comfortable spot on the rock to watch the bandits' camp, ready to help the minute the Lieutenant and his men shot into view.

Luc and Reggie had set up their plans after their first study of the canyon. Luc nodded and Reggie set off, taking six men in one direction to flank the outlaws, skirting the canyon walls, staying out of sight until he was on the far side. They had agreed on fifteen minutes to get in position before engaging the enemy. Once the shooting started, Luc and his men would stop the outlaws from escaping down the canyon trail to the desert.

Luc's men picketed their horses in the small pocket canyon. Luc then motioned his men to hide in the rocks. He didn't anticipate a lot of resistance. He'd read a report on Valenzuela. The man was dangerous, but only when the odds were in his favor. Luc and Reggie had decided on a big show of force to trick Valenzuela into believing they had more soldiers than they did.

Gunfire erupted from the other end of the canyon. Startled, Luc glanced back. His men were only half way to their positions. "Damn it, Reggie." He half shouted. Reggie hadn't given Luc enough time. Luc waved at the Sergeant-Major. "Get the men into their positions."

A bullet whined past his ear. He fell to the ground reaching for his Colt. He spied an outlaw on an outcropping. Luc sighted down the barrel and pulled the trigger. Behind him he heard his men scrambling to get into the rocks and then return the outlaws' fire.

A thunder of horses hooves sounded. The ground vibrated beneath him. The outlaws had stampeded the horses and were heading them straight for Luc.

He dashed for a cluster of boulders. Seconds later, the lead mare of the stolen horses dashed past him. His own people began firing. He pressed himself against the canyon wall. He had no place to go. The horses streamed past him. He glanced up. He could scale the wall if needed. Over the edge of the wall, Cal stared down at him, his eyes dark with alarm.

With his Colt in his hand, Luc fired at a mounted outlaw heading straight for him. The outlaw jerked out of the saddle, blood blossoming on his chest.

More gunfire erupted. One of the stolen horses stumbled against him,

45

knocking his Colt out his hand. Weaponless, he groped for the Colt, but another horse knocked him over. A second later, another one crashed into him, crushing him against the canyon wall. The horse screamed, blood spurted from it's neck and with head flopping, slid down to roll against him, pinning him tight to the rock. Pain exploded in him. His legs went numb beneath the massive bulk of the dead horse.

Luc shoved, but the limp animal would not roll away. An outlaw thundered up to him, sighting down his rifle at Luc. Luc waited. For a moment the outlaw seemed suspended in slow motion. Then a shot rang out and he was lifted out of the saddle, blood ripping from a gaping wound in the side of the head. The outlaw rolled over his horse's flanks to be trampled by the stampeding animals.

A second later, Cal dropped down next to Luc and handed over his side arm. Luc took the pistol and with Cal to cover him began shooting at the departing outlaws.

When the battle had ended and the dust settled, five outlaws, including Valenzuela, had escaped, ten were dead, and the rest prisoners. The only casualty to Luc's patrol was one of Reggie's men, Private Thomas Hawkins, who'd been caught in the crossfire. Hawkins, who had been with Luc since 1866, had been a good man. Luc didn't look forward to telling Hawkins' wife about her husband.

The Sergeant-Major formed a squad to roll the dead horse away from Luc and free him. When he was free, Luc found he could barely stand. The weight of the horse had stopped the circulation in his legs and they were numb. With the Sergeant-Major's help, he walked about stamping his feet until feeling returned.

While he worked the feeling back into his legs, Luc set about restoring order to the chaos. He sent a detail to round up the stampeded horses and sent their only medic to check the wounded. He also sent two men to check out the wagons the bandits had been loading to see what else they had stashed away.

Luc saw Cal calming the new private who was bleeding badly from a wound on his leg. The private was barely older than Cal. Yet Cal seemed to be much older.

Blood stained Cal's arm and Luc didn't know if he'd been wounded, or if the blood belonged to someone else. Cal had saved Luc's life with his quick thinking, and Luc was grateful. Cal helped the wounded boy to his feet and eased him over to a rock. While the boy shook, his face contorted with pain, Cal cleaned a gaping wound and bound it with bandages.

Luc had been worried the boy wouldn't know what to do, would freeze when the firing began, and then Luc would have another death on his conscience. But he hadn't.

As though sensing Luc's gaze, Cal looked up, then turned away again. Though Cal seemed calm and tranquil, Luc could see his hands shaking as he tore a bandage into two edges and tied it tight about the other boy's leg. For some reason, Cal's reaction made Luc feel better. The boy had feelings, deep feelings that he tried to hide beneath a veneer of bravado.

The captured outlaws had been tied hand and foot to each other. They sat in a circle talking quietly amongst themselves. They were an odd mix of Mexicans and Texans. Two soldiers guarded them.

Reggie dusted himself off as he approached Luc. "Shall we interrogate the prisoners now?"

Luc glared at Reggie. He pulled the other man aside. "I told you to give me fifteen minutes to get in position."

Reggie shrugged. "Private Hawkins signaled me you were ready."

Luc shook his head. Reggie had to be mistaken. Luc knew Hawkins had been a careful soldier. "Hawkins knew better than to act on his own."

Reggie shrugged again. "I heard gunfire and thought you'd started without me. I wasn't going to wait until the party got heated up. I thought you had left yourself exposed to enemy fire."

Luc glanced at the Sergeant-Major who talked to the medic while the medic checked out a scrape on his neck. "Sergeant-Major told me Hawkins was the first one down."

Reggie's mouth twitched. "I don't know where the first shot came from. Maybe the bandits ..." Reggie waved his hat at the prisoners. "They were shooting off their guns for the sheer joy of it. You're going to take some darkie's word over mine. Damn it, Luc. We've known each other for years. I'm a seasoned combat officer. I knew what I was doing."

Maybe that was the problem, Luc thought. He and Reggie had known each other for too long. Reggie over-stepped his bounds too many times and one day he'd go too far and Luc would have to put him back in his place. Reggie wouldn't like that at all. All the blue-Boston blood would roil up and explode at the insult.

"We'll talk about this later, Lieutenant," Luc said, his voice full of promise. "Let's interrogate the prisoners."

The outlaws were a scruffy lot--dirty, tough-looking and angry. Obviously they hadn't been expecting anything like a raid on their encampment.

Luc stood in front of them for a moment, watching them watching him. "What did you trade the horses for?" Luc finally asked.

No one answered. They kept their mouths shut and their eyes answered him with a cold and unblinking stare filled with indifference.

Reggie hit one of them across the mouth. The man's head snapped back. Blood trickled from the corner of his mouth. He spit out a tooth. The yellow object bounced off Reggie's boot and than onto the sand. Reggie face twisted to an ugly grimace.

Luc fought the urge to laugh at the insult. "I think you have your answer."

"I can make this scum talk." He raised his hand to hit the man again.

Luc grabbed Reggie's wrist. "Enough." Luc gestured to the Sergeant-Major. "Let's get our guests on their horses and move out." He wanted to be as far from the canyon as possible before Valenzuela thought to regroup and maybe attempt to take back when he considered to be his.

Luc turned around and saw that Cal was gone. He moved through the milling horses and finally heard the sound of someone puking in the bushes.

He found Cal bent over a depression in the canyon floor. The boy's eyes were glazed over and his whole body shook. His shirt was torn along the seam of the arm from shoulder to wrist and wet blood stained the fabric. He'd lied about having killed before. Luc recognized the signs of the boy's fear.

"You better have the medic examine your arm."

Cal glanced at the blood. "I'm fine, sir. Just a little scratch." He probed at the wound with a grimy finger.

"I don't think so. I'll walk you over to him." Luc reached for Cal, but Cal jerked back.

Cal wiped his mouth. "I'm really all right. I'm just not feeling good. Must have been something I ate."

"You don't have to lie to me, son. It's hard staring someone in the face and then taking his life. I know. I've done my share of killing."

Cal uncapped his canteen and washed his face, rinsing out his mouth and spitting into the sandy dirt. Then he dribbled the water down his arm. The trickle of water turned bright red. "I thought ... I could do it. But now I don't know."

"Killing is a part of war. You can't avoid it." Luc had been sick for a week the first time after his first battle and the lives he'd ended. He'd curled up in his tent and shook with more than his fears. He'd worried that killing would become too easy. That he would like it. But as the war had progressed, he'd found a neutral area in his mind where he could distance himself from his feelings yet still manage to obey orders.

Cal wiped his mouth with the cuff of his shirt. "I didn't like it at all.

My Mama told me to revere life. But I kept seeing all the people dead in my village because of these banditos and I thought I could kill them all without thinking. I didn't know it would bother me so much."

"You'd best learn to handle your feelings now, son. Otherwise, you won't be any use to me." Luc knew he couldn't afford to coddle Cal, but he couldn't let the boy suffer. "Thank you for saving my life, Payne. I'm in your debt."

Luc left Cal to care for his wound. The two men he'd sent to check on the wagons, had also searched the outbuildings of the camp and come running back for him to take a look. What he found shocked him. Freight boxes filled with rifles and a couple thousand rounds of ammunition. U.S. Army issues rifles. Brand new. The stolen rifles the Army had been looking for several months.

Luc stared at the boxes.

"What did you find?" Reggie asked as he entered a building.

"Take a look." Luc pointed at the boxes.

Reggie bent over the boxes, eyebrows raised. "Someone is getting ready for a war."

Luc didn't know what Valenzuela was preparing for, but Cal had mentioned he wanted to be the President of Mexico and was stashing weapons. Cal had called that right. "I saw some wagons behind the barn and a bunch of mules. Get the mules hitched up to the wagons and organize a detail to load these boxes."

"We can't take them," Reggie objected. "They'll slow us down."

"I'm not leaving anything. If we do, Valenzuela will be back to claim them. Then this day will have been worthless. I don't waste my time."

"We don't have the manpower to assign drivers to the wagons."

Luc rounded on Reggie. "We're officers in the United States Army, we will do whatever it takes to get these rifles back to Fort Duncan. We'll take them all."

Reggie continued to argue. "A smart man would cut his losses. I don't think Valenzuela is going to come back here."

"I'm not willing to take that risk." Luc turned and stepped back out into the sunlight. He shaded his eyes and scanned the canyon. He had the sense he was being watched.

He glanced around and saw Cal standing in the shade of towering tree watching him with an inscrutable look. Cal had saved the day and Luc put aside any reservations he had about letting the young boy join the Scouts. Cal had proved his worth. And Luc smiled at him, but Cal didn't smile back. Instead he turned and walked toward his horse.

Pain radiated down Callie's arm every time her horse slipped on a rock, or rolled in the shifting sand. Callie could hardly wait for Lieutenant Delacroix to order the men to made camp for the night. She wanted privacy to tend her wound.

The horses the Lieutenant had recaptured trotted ahead of the unit. The prisoners sat on their horses, a dispirited lot, with their guards alert to their every move. Private Hawkins' body had been wrapped in his bedroll and slung over the saddle of his horse.

Night fell and finally Delacroix called a halt. Callie slipped gratefully from her horse to the ground. She rubbed down her horse and fed it and then slipped away into the brush to clean her arm. She tried not to think about the man she'd killed.

All her life, she'd been taught that human life was sacred. Even on the hunts with John Wildcat, she'd managed to avoid killing. And now she felt strange. Even though the outlaw she'd killed would have thought nothing about murdering her, she still wallowed in guilt.

In the darkness, she sat on a rock and slipped her shirt off. She dribbled water on her arm and then carefully removed the herbs her mother had made up for her for just such an eventuality. She ground the herb into a powder and then mixed the powder with a little water to make a paste. She spread the paste over her wound. She would live, but probably would have a scar for life. Though the wound wasn't overly deep, it was painful.

When she was done, she pulled a clean shirt out of her pack and put it on after making certain the bindings about her breasts were secure. And then she turned toward at the camp. A small fire lit the center of the camp. To one side, Lieutenant Delacroix's face was illuminated by the flame as he issued orders. Callie could just hear the sound of his voice over the sighing of the desert wind, over the activity of the men as they picketed and tended to their horses, and prepared food. The enticing aroma of coffee reached her. The outlaws were off to one side, a guard standing over them, rifle cradled in the crook of his arm.

Callie could see the outlaws talking amongst themselves and from the way they leaned toward each other, their bodies tense, she could seet they were planning something. Why the hell hadn't the Lieutenant posted a guard where she was? The way she was situated, she could see everything going on at the camp and no one could see her.

Should she tell the Lieutenant about his vulnerability? Just because he'd captured a couple outlaws didn't mean he was in charge of them. If Callie were Valenzuela, she'd try to get her people back. Not because of any loyalty, but because people liked to brag and without even realizing what they'd said, they'd give everything away. Valenzuela's survival depended on keeping secrets.

She decided not to say anything. She doubted Lieutenant Delacroix would listen to her anyway. Even though she'd proven her worth to the unit, he still treated her as if she were a child. She'd just stay alert and be ready to handle this by herself.

She reached into her pack and drew out some dried meat. As she chewed on it, she drew her legs up and rested her chin on her knees. Her eyelids grew heavy and slowly she drifted off to sleep.

Callie woke with a start. Commanding her eyes to adjust to the darkness, she rolled to her feet. The heat of the rock had cooled and she shivered in the cold night air.

How long had she been asleep? A quick glance at the camp showed her the men spread out in their sleeping bags and the fire reduced to dim embers. The herd of horses moved restlessly as they grazed the meager desert grasses. A guard stood out against the moonlight as he circled the horses keeping them bunched.

Callie stretched her senses to the limit, feeling that something wasn't right. But what? She searched the darkness and slowly stood trying to shake the feeling of uneasiness.

She circled the camp, keeping her eyes on the desert landscape, searching for anything out of the ordinary. Though the desert looked peaceful, her feeling of uneasiness deepened.

A form rose from the camp, slowly and stealthily. Callie dropped to her knees to keep the moon from outlining her against the horizon. Another form rose and moved away from the camp. The outlaws were getting away.

Callie jumped to her feet and yelled, "Lieutenant, the banditos are getting away."

The sleeping soldiers erupted into a frenzy of activity, jumping to their feet as the two banditos dashed for the brush and a rocky outcrop. Callie raced after them. After all they'd done to capture the varmints, she wasn't about to let them get away.

She headed toward them and was rewarded as they turned in her direction. The soldiers organized themselves into search parties. Callie yelled at them.

The banditos swerved away from the sound of her voice. She heard Lieutenant Delacroix issuing orders. In the next second, she felt a blow and was thrust back. She reached out and grabbed the outlaw's shirt, hanging on as best she could. The man tried to dislodge her, grabbing her wrists and yanking. She slid down his body and grabbed onto his leg. After all the hard work of capturing him, she wasn't about to let him escape.

Shots rang out and she heard the sound of horse's hooves. The outlaw tried to run dragging her with him. She clutched tight to his leg. She felt a blow to the side of her head. She almost lost her grip, but managed to hang on. She felt his hands pounding on her shoulders and back. The harder he hit, the harder she clung to him. He grabbed a fistful of her hair and yanked.

Pain started at the side of her head and traveled down her spine. Bright lights exploded behind her eyes. The outlaw fell down and rolled, landing on top of her. She felt a sharp elbow in her ribs and she couldn't breathe. Two soldiers grabbed the outlaw and jerked him to his feet.

Lieutenant Delacroix bent over Callie. "Are you all right?" he asked in an anxious voice.

Callie couldn't answer. She fought for air, but her chest felt paralyzed.

"Cal! Talk to me." He touched her ribs and she shoved his hand away.

Callie pushed herself to her feet. Her whole body ached. She had the feeling she'd broken something, but she couldn't speak. She shook her head at the Lieutenant. She clutched her side and tried to walk away, but her feet wouldn't obey. She stumbled. As she rolled back to the ground, she smelled the faint spicy scent of Lieutenant Delacroix's soap. He ran his hands down her ribs and then gently unbuttoned her shirt and touched the binding around her chest.

"What's this?" he asked.

She tried to push his hands away, but each move increased the pain. "Don't. Please, don't."

"Hold still, son. Let me help you."

She stared at him, willing him to just go away. Then darkness seeped into the edges of her vision and the world went black.

CHAPTER FIVE

Esme leaned against the wood railing of the steam ship and watched as the tugboats angled it into it's berth. New Orleans spread out in front of her. Paris had always been fun, but New Orleans was the home of her childhood, the place of her most cherished memories.

Men, women and children gathered on the levee to watch the ship being fitted into its slot.

Esme smiled. Until this moment, she had not realized how homesick she had been for the sights, smells and sounds of her home. How good it felt to be back?

A man stood apart from the others. He was handsomely dressed, though his face was lined with age. Gray hair curled back over his ears beneath the narrow brim of his dove gray hat. His eyes met hers and she studied him with an appraising eye. He bowed slightly and she nodded at him. Then he turned to speak to a more shabbily dressed man who turned on his heel and headed toward the gangway.

"That's Jonas Ramsay," a voice said.

Esme turned to find Captain Henderson standing behind her. She had enjoyed a slight flirtation with him during the trip, but he turned out to be a man most devoted to his wife and family. When Esme found out, she backed away.

"And who is Jonas Ramsay?" Esme inquired.

"One of the wealthiest men in New Orleans. Though rumor says he invested heavily in a China venture, and is nervous because his ship was due before Christmas, long before I set course for London." Esme glanced back at the man on the levee. He walked back and forth and then suddenly turned and left the levee. "Is he looking for his lost ship?"

Captain Henderson grunted. "Probably." The captain left her for his duties and Esme turned back to watch the people watching the ship being docked.

She felt very smart and fashionable in a burgundy traveling suit and a tiny matching hat perching on her glossy black curls. Her sophisticated ensemble proclaimed the height of Parisian fashion. A few men on the docks gave her admiring glances. She ignored them.

The ship was finally secured and the gangway lowered. Esme had been so young when she had been forced to leave everything she knew behind. First her mother had died, and then her father had insisted they go to school in Paris. Her father had carried her kicking and screaming up the gangplank followed by a subdued Luc and the au pair their father had hired to care for them. Their father had explained that they would be happier at school in Paris. Esme hadn't believed him. She had cried most of the way across the Atlantic, and Luc had remained stubbornly silent. Both of them knew, their father's wife had somehow caused their exile. Though she didn't understand why at the time. Since then, she'd grown wiser in the ways of women scorned.

The docks had been a bustling haven of commerce then. Esme remembered seeing tall bales of cotton stored in the warehouses and on the docks ready for shipment. Now the docks were sadly empty. A few warehouses, burned in the war, were in the process of being rebuilt, their skeletal remains a sad reminder of the hostilities.

The levee stretched out in both directions. A couple, arm in arm and accompanied by a nanny pushing a baby carriage, strolled along. The spires of St. Louis Cathedral rose into the sky. The intricate iron work of the Pontalba apartments bracketing Jackson Square reminded Esme of a childhood friend who had lived in the apartment and with whom Esme had played. They had pretend tea parties on the balcony and watched couples strolling about the square.

Before disembarking, Esme spoke to the purser and arranged for her twenty-two trunks to be stored for a few hours until she found place to stay. She hailed a cab and gave the driver her father's address.

As the open carriage moved through the Quarter, Esme thought about all she had left behind in Paris. Her beautiful house on the Left Bank, and her friends. With her lover dead, frankly, life in Paris no longer held any appeal. Her painting had become stale. She needed new artistic inspiration, and she wanted to get away because Paris was so sad for her.

The thoughts of her lover brought a small stab of grief. Not so strong any more, but still there. She owed Philippe so much. She would never forget him. She should have married Philippe. He'd proposed countless times. But she had prized her autonomy, her independence. Philippe had wanted a country wife and a country life, and she had wanted glitter. They'd had never been able to resolve the difference. So they had let things stand and now he was gone and she had a hole in her heart that her friends and her life no longer filled.

The Quarter appeared much as it had when she'd been a child. Though somehow it seemed smaller. Still, she felt as though she were finally home after so many years of wandering.

The carriage stopped in front of her father's house. This was her last task before she went on to a new life. She had brooded all the way across the Atlantic. She'd written her father of her decision to return home and hoped he'd gotten the letter. Since his quarrel with Luc, he had done little to keep his relationship with Esme alive. She wrote him faithfully once a month, but his return letters had trailed off and she had heard nothing from him in two years.

If she did nothing else while she was in New Orelans, she would do what she could to make her family whole again. She would find a way to heal the breech between her father and Luc.

"Wait for me," she told the driver as he helped her out.

He nodded and opened the gate for her. As she sailed inside, he climbed back up on the driver's seat, and in seconds his head drooped in a little nap.

Esme's father's home had an imposing facade. The house was not built in the style of most of the other homes in the Quarter which backed to the street with the front doors inside opening to the interior courtyard. Her father's home had an princely veranda bordered by Corinthian style pillars and a white railing surrounding it. A small green lawn, bordered by bright flowers, added a touch of rich green to the white pillars in the background.

As she walked up the front steps, Esme's stomach flip-flopped. The house had a neglected air about it. Fading yellow paint was worn off, bare wood showing through. The grand entry looked tired. The brass on the door knocker needed polishing. An closer inspection the flower garden had more weeds than it should. Esme gathered her courage and walked up the front steps. No back door for her. She pulled a bell cord and heard ringing deep in the house.

She waited, pacing back and forth, her mouth dry. Would he want to see her? So much had happened over the years. She wasn't a thirteen year old girl any more.

The front door swung open. Instead of the servant Esme expected, a young girl, maybe ten years old with her blonde hair in braids about her shoulders, smiled at Esme. The girl's dress was clean, but shabby and a touch too small.

"Hello, may I help you?" The girl's voice was soft with the cadence of New Orleans in her tone.

"I'm here to see Mr. Delacroix."

"You're very pretty." The girl smiled shyly, her hazel eyes moving rapidly up and down. She reached out to touch Esme's dress, but drew her fingers back shyly.

"Thank you, so are you." Except for the blonde hair, this girl could have been Esme's identical twin when she'd been ten. This had to be Lauren, her youngest half-sister.

Lauren bobbed in an abbreviated curtsey at the compliment. She held out her hand and drew Esme into the house. "Daddy's in the courtyard, but I don't know if he will see you. He's feeling poorly again today."

Again, Esme thought. Had he been ill? "You tell him Esme is here to see him."

The girl giggled. "Your name is pretty, too." She showed Esme into the visitor's parlor and skipped away her footsteps echoing hollowly as she bounced through the house.

Esme drew off her red leather gloves. The parlor was immaculate, the furniture gleamed and smelled of lemon oil. Her feet sank into the deep pile of a blue and red Persian rug. From the looks of things, her father had survived the war in a worse situation than Esme had feared.

A woman stormed into the room and glared at Esme. "Get out of my house."

Esme raised her chin defiantly. "I'm here to see my father." Esme had only seen Natalie Bruton Delacroix once in her whole life. She had stood on the docks with a smug smile on her face as Esme's father had forced her onto the ship. Natalie had changed. The chubby cheeks of her youth had whittled down into grooved hollows. Her mouth, at one time bow-shaped, was now pinched tightly. Wrinkles radiated outward from the corners of her dark brown eyes.

Natalie shook with rage. "How dare you appear on my doorstep without so much as a warning." Her eyes flickered over Esme's fashionable gown and a small light of envy appeared deep inside them. The she pursed her lips tightly and drew in a ragged breath.

Esme had anticipated hostility from her father's wife, but this way beyond anything she'd expected. "I can to see my father," she repeated.

"How dare you violate the sanctity of my home." Natalie's face grew red with blotches.

"Madam, I understand my father is ill. I wish to see him. Mayhap I can bring him some comfort."

"His real children will see to his needs."

Esme smiled. "You have always been bothered by the fact that Luc and I were his first family." Esme really didn't understand why Natalie should feel so threatened. Her father had married her.

Natalie spat at her. "You meant nothing to him then, and you mean nothing to him now."

"Really," Esme reached into her purse and drew out her father's last letter. Though it was two years old, it still contained his strong feelings of love for her. "Would you like me to show you how much I don't mean to him?" She held out the letter.

Natalie licked her lips. "You can't come in here with your fancy Parisian manners and demand anything from us. You'll never be anything more than a low-bred slave's bastard child."

Esme drew on all the haughtiness of the Parisian nobility. She looked down at Natalie. "My mother may have started life as a slave, but she died a free woman." Though the words my father loved her remained unspoken, Esme could see that Natalie was thinking the same thing.

A young woman flew into the room. "Mama, Mama, Lauren said there's a beautiful woman here to see Papa. Papa wants to see her right now."

Esme held out her hand to the young woman. "I'm Esme."

The young woman, an older version of Lauren, took Esme's hand and bobbed into a polite curtsey. "I'm Josette."

"Josette," Natalie said sharply. "Go to your room. Now."

Josette looked confused. Her gaze swung back and forth between Esme and her mother, but after a few seconds, bobbed a second polite curtsey and obediently backed out of the parlor.

Esme's temper flared. She hadn't liked Natalie when her father had married her, and she liked her less now. She walked firmly to the doorway. "No need to show me. I know my way to the courtyard." She headed down the long hall toward the courtyard.

What had happened to her father's beautiful home? Except for the parlor, the other rooms were empty of all furniture and the floors were filthy dirty. Dust and spider webs decorated every corner and hung from the ceiling in long strings. Water spots stained the walls where the roof leaked. The rooms smelled musty and moldy. Wallpaper had fallen off in strips revealing bare patches of plaster wall.

She stepped out into the courtyard appalled at the horrid mess. Last year's leaves still littered the corners. Weeds choked the flower beds. A door hung askew on the stable, and the servants quarters had broken windows. The fountain in the center of the courtyard held no water. The statue of the nymph Esme had so adored when she'd been a child was broken. She'd spent many hours drawing the nymph from all angles until she'd had three notebooks filled with drawings.

Esme's father sat in a broken chaise, one corner propped up by bricks. He wore a dingy robe over his pajamas. He coughed, a deep rumbling cough that shook his skeletal body. His cheeks were bristly with stubble, he hadn't shaved in days.

Esme choked back sudden tears. She couldn't let him see her crying. "Papa!"

His dark eyes snapped open. He stared at her for a long moment, his eyes blank, and then recognition slowly seeped into them. "Esme! Are you really you? What are you doing here?" He cried and held out a hand.

She took his hand. The fingers were long and bony and dark brown splotches showed on the paper thin skin. "Didn't you receive my letter."

He shook his head, white hair flying about his face. He badly needed a haircut. Where was the dapper man, who had been her father, gone? He'd been so handsome and strong. Now, he looked old with his scraggly white hair framing a too thin face.

Esme held herself steady and strong. She could not believe this was her father. He'd grown old and decrepit even though he was barely sixty-five.

When she'd been a child, he'd been the most fastidious person she'd known. He'd never left the house without shaving. His clothes had been impeccable, his shoes a brilliant shine. Soft leather gloves had covered his hands and he'd always held silver-tipped walking stick. He'd been a dandy and proud of it. Esme had inherited his love of fine clothing and refined European manners.

Esme kissed his cheek. "Mon Pere, you didn't shave this morning."

"You came all the way from Paris to tell me I haven't shaved." He grinned, a trace of his old, charming self showing in his green eyes that twinkled like jewels..

"That and a few other things." Esme sat down on the foot of the chaise. "Why didn't you write and tell me things were this bad? I could have helped. I would have been happy to help."

He touched her cheek with dry fingers. "Because it's my responsibility to take care of you." He caressed her cheek.

"You do, Papa. You always do." Tears welled in her eyes and she turned away.

On the second floor, a young woman in a tired dress ten years out of date stood with one hand holding back the drapes, watching Esme and her father. The woman's face was twisted with anger. That must be Simone, the eldest. Simone stepped back into shadow. The drapery fell back into position over the window.

Esme turned her gaze back to her father. "Well then, I guess I'll have to shave you. Just like when I was a little girl. Do you remember that? You always liked your morning coffee, your toast with a touch of cinnamon sugar and your shave, all in that order."

Her father nodded, smiling. "Those were the happiest days of my life. You and Luc, your mama and me, living in that cottage off Rampart street."

She touched his hair roughened cheek. "If only time would have stood still."

He shook his head. "So much has changed." Regret shone in his eyes.

"Papa, where's your shaving kit?"

He waved his arm toward the second floor. "In my bedroom on the night table."

"I'll be right back."

Esme returned to the house, her decision made. She would not go to a hotel, but stay here. Her Papa needed her in a way he had never needed her before and she would not abandon him.

In the dining room she found Natalie watching at one of the windows. "I'll be staying for awhile."

Natalie's face contorted. "No. I won't allow it."

Esme's voice was hard. "You have no choice."

"Then you sleep in the attic. You'll be right at home in the slave quarters."

Esme stared at the other woman for a long moment, and something grew in her. All her life, she'd been slightly fearful of Natalie because of the power Natalie had once wielded. She had had Esme and Luc sent far away. She had hammered a wedge between them and their father. She had stepped into the role that had originally belong to Esme's mother.

But time had changed things. Esme was now the one in control. She laughed as she stepped up to Natalie and looked down her regal nose at the petite southern woman. "Push me too hard, Natalie, and you'll be lucky to end up there yourself."

Natalie's face went ashen. She stepped back, hatred glittering in her eyes like a fever. Suddenly, she whirled and stalked away.

Natalie was a bully, and like a typical bully backed down when faced with someone who could stand up to her. As a child, Esme could never have stood up to Natalie, but time had changed their roles. Esme took no joy in her victory although she did relish the power to get back a bit of her own.

Esme turned toward the front of the house. She needed her trunks. As she walked through the barren rooms, she wondered if the furniture merchant was still on Royal Street. She would make a trip first thing in the morning. In the meantime, this house needed a thorough cleaning.

For the first time since Philippe's death, Esme felt as though she had found something to cling to. Her family was in tatters, and she was going to fix it no matter how hostile Natalie and her daughters were. The girls were still Esme's blood and she wasn't going to abandon them. Nor would she tolerate the rift between her father and Luc. Being with him would give her time to figure out a way to get them back together. She'd always been the peacemaker.

She gave the cab driver ten dollars and asked him to fetch her trunks. He stared at the money and saluted her. When he'd clattered down the street, Esme returned to the house to fetch her father's shaving kit.

⟞✦✦✦⟝

Luc sat on the ground next to his cot. He still couldn't believe that the boy, he thought Cal to be, was really a young woman. Now that he knew, he could see the woman in the subtle lines of her face. How had he missed something so obvious? He studied at her hands. Despite the calluses, her fingers were long and delicate, the hands of a pianist.

How could he have mistaken all the delicate beauty in her contours of her face for that of a fourteen year old boy? For beautiful she was. Now that his eyes were opened to her deception, he could see what she was much more clearly.

Cal's eyes fluttered open. "What happened?" she asked as she struggled to sit up. She groaned and closed her eyes.

Luc grabbed her shoulders, pushing her firmly back down to the cot. "You've been unconscious."

"The outlaws are getting away." She rubbed her hand against her forehead. "I have to stop them."

"Lieutenant Cooper will have them back in custody in no time," Luc assured her. "If not for your alertness, we wouldn't have known they were getting away."

She took a deep breath and opened her eyes again. Her head shifted from side to side. "Why am I in your tent?"

"I thought you needed privacy."

Her lips began to tremble. Her eyes searched the small space. "This isn't proper." She obviously figured her secret was still safe.

"Why not, Cal?"

"Because I'm black and you're white."

Luc almost smiled. "And I thought it was because you're a woman."

Her eyes went wide and her mouth fell open, but no words came out. A flash of panic crossed her face. She'd always had a ready come back for his statements, but for the moment she was wordless.

"I'm surprised," he said with a chuckle, "Have you nothing to say? This is a new side of you."

She eyed him suspiciously. "How did you know?"

Luc had had enough lovers in the past to know the female body inside and out. He figured it would only have been a matter of time before he discovered Cal's secret. "I'm not some callow youth unaware of the charms of a woman's body." And he had to admit, she had a fine body: supple, small and delicate, yet strong.

She clutched her shirt. "You touched me?"

"I was examining you. I thought you were hurt. You had blood all over you."

"That bastard hit me." She touched her head. "And he kicked me."

"You seem to be fine. I didn't find any broken bones." Though she would have bruises. One already was starting on her cheek. She'd have quite a black eye in the morning. He had actually enjoyed touching her, and had also been relieved to know that his feelings of attraction had a reason for being. He wasn't attracted to her because she was boy.

"Why are you watching me like that?"

She was an innocent. He wondered if his desire for her was so plain. He certain felt it very strongly. But her presence as his scout presented new problems. He couldn't have a woman as his scout. "You'll have to go back home."

She shook her head violently. "No. I want my land. You promised me forty acres if I worked for the Army. I'm not going home."

"Cal, you're a woman."

"I promised my mother I'd get that land. She deserves a better life than what she has. My people left Florida so we didn't have to be slaves. And now the white man doesn't want us because we're Indian. I know if I have a paper that says I own this piece of land, nobody can make me move. And I'm not letting anyone take away what I want. Not even you."

She sounded so vehement. He couldn't help but admire her strength of will. "You can't stay with me and my men."

"You can't force me to go." She grabbed his arm. "I signed a contract. And I intend to keep my word."

"I can't keep you here." He grasped her hand. Heat and fire caressed his skin. He wanted to let go, but he didn't seem to be able to. "You're a danger." She had no idea how much a danger she was, as much to him she was to the soldiers.

Snatching her hand away, she fell back on the cot. "I saved your life." Her tone was fierce. "You owe me."

For a second Luc tried to deny what she had done. He didn't owe her so much that he could deceive Major Adams. Why not? A small voice nagged at him. Luc had his own secret.

Shots sounded in the distance, startling Luc. He stood up and flung the flap of tent back to stare out into the darkness. The horses milled nervously on their picket line.

"What was that?" Cal asked from behind him.

"I don't know," Luc said, frowning. What was going on out in the dark? Recovering two unarmed outlaws shouldn't require gunfire.

He turned back to Cal. She lay on his cot looking tired and pale. Her eyes were huge in her small face and her hands plucked nervously at the collar of her shirt. What was he going to do with her?

Reggie suddenly flipped open the front flap. "All secure, Luc. Sorry, but the outlaws are dead. One fell off a rock and the other one resisted, trying to kill Sergeant-Major Parker. Must have found a gun a somewhere."

Tell Reggie, Luc ordered himself, that Cal was a woman. He glanced at Cal. She watched him closely, fear in her eyes. "Dammit, I wanted those men alive."

Reggie shrugged. "Couldn't be helped, Luc. They put up too much of a struggle. Better dead, than free."

He couldn't argue with that logic. "Has anyone found out how they escaped in the first place?"

"One of them had a knife. Must have had it concealed in his boot."

"I told you to take their boots away," Cal said. "No one can run far in their bare feet."

Luc glanced back at her wondering why Reggie didn't see the difference in her. "I don't do things that way," Luc said. At least he had the horses back and the rifles. The mission wasn't a total loss.

"How's the kid?" Reggie gestured at Cal.

"I'm fine." Cal flipped back the blanket and tried to stand. "I was just leaving."

"No, you're not." Luc pushed her down. His conscience screamed for him to reveal the truth. "We're going to have a little talk about what your duties are."

Cal swayed and gripped the tent post to steady herself. "I didn't do nothing wrong."

He could quote chapter and verse with what the little minx had done wrong. "You put yourself in unnecessary danger. You're a scout, not a soldier."

Cal glared at him defiantly. "I wasn't going to let that scum escape."

Reggie grinned. "Luc, I think I'll let you hammer this out with the boy." He closed the flap and Luc heard his footsteps as he walked away.

When they were alone again, Luc asked, "Is Cal your real name?"

"It's Callie. Callisto."

"Callisto, the she-bear. That's an appropriate name. You fight like an old injured grizzly."

Callie grinned. "Are you going to let me stay? I can take of myself." She reached into her boot and pulled out a wicked looking knife.

Right now, until he returned to the fort, he couldn't reveal she was a woman. Not with a group of men around. "For the moment, you have me over a barrel. But when we arrive back at Fort Duncan, I'll have to rethink your situation."

"You don't have to think anything. I'm staying. I've proven myself."

"I know, Cal, but you're still a woman."

Her voice was hard, but her eyes pleaded with him. "No one has to know."

She had proven herself several times over, but how could Luc expect to maintain any order with a beautiful woman on the trail with a bunch of men. She wouldn't be safe from them no matter how well she could take care of herself. He look at her soft, full mouth. Her lips were so kissable. Oh hell, he wasn't sure if she would be safe from him with lips so made for passion. "There's considerations about being a woman that you need to deal with."

"Nothing I haven't dealt with on the trail before."

What was he going to do with her. Now was not the time to make a decision. He had to get her back to the Fort and then decide. "You have a reprieve until we get back." He tunneled both his hands through his hair. He had to get away from her silky brown eyes staring at him like a wounded puppy. "If you're feeling well enough, you should get back to your own bedroll."

She grinned at him, a saucy come-on grin that he was sure she wasn't even aware of. He wanted to kiss her. Kiss her in a way he sensed she'd never been kissed before. He resisted the urge. He could almost feel the eyes of the soldiers on them and knew they were silhouetted against the canvas by his lamp.

She swung her legs over the side of the cot and pushed herself to her feet. For a moment she swayed unsteadily, but brought herself under control. She limped out of the tent and into the black night.

Luc let out his breath. The memory of his bath in the pool the night before burned through his mind. He had whipped off his clothes in front of her without once thinking about her. A hot flush crept up his neck. Suddenly, he was embarrassed that she'd seen him naked. And he wondered why he was embarrassed. Other women had seen him without his clothes.

But something about Cal, Callie, Callisto was different. Different in a way that intrigued him beyond measure. Women in his experience had certain roles, but Callie wanted to reach beyond her role, to accomplish something different. In a distant way, she reminded Luc of Esme who was always chafing at the boundaries society wanted to put on her. Like Esme, Callie was pushing at those boundaries. But then again, the West was a different place from Paris. If women weren't strong, they died.

Despite her strength, Callie had an aura of innocence. An innocence born of her lack of understanding about men. When Luc was around women, whether they were the daughters of his friends or grandmothers, he always treated them a certain way. He was more charming, more chivalrous, more on his best behavior. But he had treated Cal like a man, like the man Luc thought she was. He'd used no charm, he was blunt to the point, and he was hard on her. An attraction for her had still blossomed despite his treatment. His body had known what his mind had not.

With the exception of Esme, he'd never thought of women as his equal. They were something to be protected, cared for and shielded from the ugliness of the world. Cal had never been shielded from anything and she'd thrived. She knew a side of life not even he had experienced.

He lay down on his cot and extinguished the lamp. Did he have the right to take away her dream? To destroy her? She was running toward everything he wanted to escape. She wanted a home, a family, stability. He lived the life of a nomad to evade his past, his heritage, his father. He should feel contempt for her, but he couldn't. She had a dream. What did he have? Compared to her, he was a poor man indeed.

Revealing who she was would solve nothing. Her courage in the face of battle made him admire her. The other men admired her to. Maybe he could help her find her dreams. Other women had passed as men. He'd heard of women fighting side by side with their men during the war, hiding their sex the way he his hid heritage.

Luc didn't think any of the men even began to guess that she wasn't who she said she was. If he could bury his heritage, she could hide her sex. And he'd help her.

Oh God! He was being gallant and noble. All those qualities he thought he'd abandoned when he'd left Paris to fight the war. He chuckled and then broke into loud laughter. What strange and bizarre twists his life had taken. From the illegitimate pampered son of a Louisiana plantation owner, to a carefree young dandy in Paris, to a battle-weary soldier fighting against everything he'd been raised to respect. Now he was the keeper of secrets. How very, very strange. Life was so full of surprises.

He drifted off to sleep, but before he did he saw Callisto in his mind, her curls surrounding her delicate face like a glossy black halo, her golden brown skin as soft as silk, and cinnamon-brown eyes alight with mischief. In his daydream, she wore a red dress – a deep burgundy red – with her shoulders bare in the lamplight and her eyes bright and saucy. She would look magnificent with fire-red rubies resting against her dark skin. If given the chance, he suspected Callisto could be quite the seductress. But he would never know. Pity, he'd decided to do the honorable thing.

CHAPTER SIX

From deep in the underbrush Rafe watched the hollowed out log rotting on the ground near a cold stream. No one was around, but caution born of years of training keep him hidden even though he knew no one was around.

Finally, as the sun slipped down behind the horizon throwing the clearing into deep shadows, he made his move, approaching the log with extreme care. He couldn't take any chances the Fort was only a few miles away and he was a deserter. Some would say a traitor for fighting with the Comanche. If the Army found him, he would probably be shot for desertion. At the very least, he would spend a lot of time in jail.

He didn't feel like a traitor at least not any more. He'd felt like a Judas when he'd been with the Buffalo Soldiers killing other Indians. He kept picturing his mother and his sister in their peaceful village. He convinced himself he'd made the right decision. He was protecting them and his adopted people, his wife and son. For a price.

Rafe pulled a pouch of gold coin out of his pocket and inserted it deep into the log. Hopefully, the next time he returned, he would have the information he needed to keep the Army at bay.

He scuttled backward to his hiding place deep in the brush to wait a few more moments to make certain he'd been unobserved. As he waited, he sensed a movement behind him. Tensing, he turned his head as someone tackled him from the other side. He rolled, his knife out, but the soft laughter of his wife stopped him. He relaxed and returned the knife to its sheath.

"Would you make your son motherless, husband?" Willow said with a wry giggle.

"Willow." Her long black hair fanned across his cheek as he kissed her. Her skin was like satin. Her body soft and hard at the same time. Her name was so appropriate. She bent with the wind, yet remained firmly rooted in the ground.

"I made more noise than a buffalo." Her hand crept inside his shirt to caress his chest in an invitation he could not ignore.

"You're a very fetching buffalo." He thought of the fort so close and the danger, but the danger heightened his sense of risk. He untied the leather strings at the neck of her tunic, and reached into the opening to fondle her full breast. Her nipple was already hard. She shifted to give him better access as her own hand crept into his trousers.

"I will take that as a compliment, my husband," she whispered into his ear. She unlaced the rest of her bodice to expose her beautiful breasts. They were shaped like tears, the nipples large and dark.

"I love you, Willow. Everything I do is for you." He kissed her as he rolled her on her back, and reached for the waistband of her doeskin trousers and tugged it down. He caressed the contour of her hip, his fingers sliding between her legs as she wriggled free of her trousers.

"And I you, husband." She kicked her trousers away and lifting her tunic over her head, exposing the beauty of her small compact body to him. She was round in all the right places.

He reached for her. They had time.

—◗◖◗◖—

Callie was proud of herself. She had captured enough rabbits to feed everyone fresh meat for dinner. The rabbits hung from the pommel of her saddle.

Ahead, she saw the thread of dust that followed the patrol. She would be caught up to them shortly, but she was in no hurry. Ever since Luc had discovered her secret, she'd been on edge. She didn't think of him as Lieutenant Delacroix any longer. The discovery of her secret had created a new relationship between them.

How could she have been so careless? She should have just let the bandits go. The desert would have eventually killed them and her secret would have been safe. Luc knowing she was a woman left her feeling vulnerable and confused over what he was going to do. Would he reveal her secret and force her to leave, or would he keep it?

The plume of dust grew lighter. Luc would be calling a halt soon. The sun had dipped low in the west and soon they would have to rest the horses. In the ten days she had been with him and his soldiers on the trail, she had come to know understand how he managed things. In the morning he roused everyone before morning sun had even begun to light the eastern sky. They would roll out of their blankets and eat breakfast, then they would be on the trail.

The Buffalo Soldiers took great pride in their horses, grooming them nightly until their coats shone and feeding them the best grain. Once the animals were groomed and tied to their picket line, the men started setting up camp. A couple soldiers would set up Luc's tent, then Lt. Cooper's, while other started the fire and began preparing their evening meal. All in all, the whole procedure had an orderliness to it that Callie almost envied. She liked the structure of the Army.

She also noticed that the men under Luc's command respected him deeply, and she suspected they even liked him. The soldiers had little contact with her. The Seminoles were a tribe left alone. No one quite knew how to treat them, didn't know if they were black or Indian. So the Seminoles kept to themselves. And because she kept to herself, she had built sturdy walls to keep her secret intact.

She could see the horsemen in the distance. The sun had lost its brightness and the shadows had grown long. Callie urged her horse along faster, she needed to get the rabbits to the cook before he started their usual fare of beans and beef jerky with those terrible rock-like biscuits he called hardtack. How men could survive on such limited food she didn't know? She wanted to toss a chili into the cooking pot so badly, her hands trembled. Her mouth watered for her mother's home-made tortillas and the tartness of a fresh lime.

The unit had stopped, and as Callie approached the camp, the Luc issued orders and oversaw the outlaws. She skirted the camp, aware of the men horses watching her. Though they treated with a rough kindness, they showed little interest in her. They all had their own duties to perform and she had hers.

"Cook," she said as she reined her horse to a stop. She pulled the rabbits up and handed them to the man.

"Did you catch all these?" The cook held the rabbits up, admiring them.

She nodded. "We're eating good tonight." Callie turned her horse, but the cook stopped her.

"How's your ribs?" When he wasn't being the cook, he was the medic who took care of the men's wounds. "Need some more liniment for them?"

"I'm fine, sir."

He ran a hand through grizzled hair turning gray at the temples. "Don't call me sir." He chuckled. "I work for a living. The Lieutenant wants to see you."

"Which one?" Her stomach clenched at the thought that Cooper wanted to see her, though usually he had as little to do with her as possible.

"The good one." The contempt on the cook's dark face told her all she needed to know about how everyone felt about the blonde Lieutenant Cooper.

Everyone disliked him, except for Luc. And why he liked that blonde weasel, Callie didn't know. Lieutenant Cooper hated the Buffalo soldiers. He seemed to think that being in command of them was beneath him, or something. When Luc wasn't around, Cooper really took no pains to hide his hatred.

She turned her horse and headed toward Lieutenant Delacroix. Her ribs still hurt from where that bandito had kicked her. And if she took too deep a breath, a sharp pain would scissor through her. The Lieutenant had assured her nothing was broken.

The memory of his fingers examining her sent shivers up and down her spine. She had never been touched like that by a man before. For a second she had thought her skin was going to light on fire it was so hot.

Luc stood at the edge of the camp directing one of the soldiers in a task. Callie watched him remembering how much she wanted him to go on doctoring her. At night she lay in her bedroll remembering how his hands had touched her body and how gentle he'd been. Her stomach would get all jumpy and her breasts would ache beneath the bindings. Her skin would burn and she couldn't breath.

Why she was acting so silly was beyond her. She'd never felt so feverish about any of the young men in the village. She wished her mama were here to explain all the strange things going on with her. Her mama would know what was ailing her, and more importantly how to make it go away.

The hardest thing was to push Luc away, when she really wanted to kiss him and touch him. The memory of his bath in the sheltered pond haunted her. The silver moonlight on his body and the cool water caressing his skin invaded her dreams every night since she'd seen him.

Two men had pitched Luc's tent. The soldiers always attended to his needs first, despite Lieutenant Cooper's angry rumblings. Callie dismounted from her horse and waited behind Luc's tent. He saw her and walked up to her, his face creased with concern.

"How are your feeling, Cal?" His eyes searched her face as though looking for more than the answer to his question.

"I'm fine, sir," she assured him, though her whole body felt as though it was one huge bruise. "I brought some rabbits for dinner. We haven't had fresh meat since we started on the trail." She leaned in a bit closer so the other men couldn't hear her. "That stuff you and the Army calls meat hurts my mouth."

He chuckled. "Mine, too." He began walking away from the tent.

Callie gathered the reins of her horse. Shad no choice but to follow him and see what he wanted from her. "Did you want to talk to me, sir?"

He turned his head and looked over his shoulder. "Back in the village did you have a beau?"

"A bow and arrow?" She tapped her rifle in its scabbard on the saddle. "I been using this since I was five years old, sir. I could bring down--"

"I don't mean a bow and arrow. A love...." He shook his head. "I mean a companion that you love."

What was he talking about? Sometimes he could be so infuriatingly confusing. "You mean like my mama?"

A frown creased his mouth. Bluntly, he said, "Like a man you want to marry."

A flush burned her cheeks and necks. Why did he want to know about things like that? "I didn't have time for that kind of foolery. Why are you asking?" This was not the conversation to have with a bunch of other men hanging around, maybe listening in.

He shrugged. "Just curious. Every pretty girl I know, has a beau."

"I'm not pretty."

He stopped and faced her. "Yes, you are."

"Sir, you better hope no one notices that I'm pretty like you say or you're gonna have a hard time explaining why I'm here." She glanced around at the busy camp. No one seemed interested in her or Luc. Most of the men were busy tending the horses. Even Lieutenant Cooper was preoccupied as he watched his own tent being pitched.

"How old are you?"

She tilted her head up at him. "Why do you want to know?"

"It's bad enough you're a woman, but I don't need a fifteen year old girl running around."

"I'm nineteen. Old enough to know my own mind."

"I guess you are." He took his hat off and ran his fingers through his shiny, black hair. He looked tired and drawn. "Did you find any sign of the Comanches?"

She felt sorry for him. He worked so hard. As hard as his soldiers. It was almost as if he wanted to be like her and the rest of his troops. "Yes and no. Comanche bands are small. Five, ten riders. I found tracks, well-hidden, heading back to Texas. They're traveling fast which is why

I found their tracks. Otherwise, I wouldn't have known. Comanches are good at hiding when they want to." And other things.

So far, her village had avoided any conflict with the Comanches, but other Seminole villages hadn't. The Comanches were fierce and noble. At times, Callie admired them. They were fighting for more than their homes, but their future. And she understood how they felt at the loss of their homes.

"What do you think it means?"

"Comanches are sneaky. They have lots of tricks. I'd say they're just anxious to get home. After all, they got horses, rifles and ammunition from Valenzuela. So why not go home? As far as they're concerned, their business is over. They don't have anything to hide anymore. So they're making time as best they can." That's what she would do if she could.

"It makes no sense to split up. Safety in numbers."

She shook her head. "That's the problem with the Army. You don't think like Indians."

The Lieutenant crossed his arms. "All right, little one, explain it to me."

"The Comanche's not only pulled a fast one on the Army, but they pulled a fast one on Valenzuela. They had a hundred horses. Took maybe twenty or thirty for themselves and Valenzuela is short-changed. Army horses are the best horses. Grain fed for stamina and strength, and the Comanche prizes nothing more than a good horse. Valenzuela needs horses, too, for the army he's trying to raise. The Comanches ended up with some Army horses and Army rifles. Who do you think got the better deal?"

The Lieutenant sighed. "You put this all together yourself?"

"I'm smart, I think like an Indian." She laughed and walked away, tugging her horse after her. "Excuse me, sir, but I'm gonna check on those rabbits I brung to the cook. Don't want him burning them." She went about ten feet and then turned around to find Luc still watching her. He held his hat in one hand and banged it slightly against his knee. The last rays of the sun cast a glow over his face.

Her breath caught in her throat and then she grinned and headed toward the cooking fire. At that moment something occurred to her. This man was more of a danger to her peace of mind, than any Comanche to her body. That wasn't good. Nope, not good at all.

Luc watched her go. She had a sassy smile on her face and a light in her eyes that told him she was practicing her feminine wiles on him. He shook his head. Just what he needed, a nineteen year old woman, with no experience with men, loose in his command. Though he knew she would do nothing to jeopardize her position, he worried that someone might notice.

His soldiers treated Callie with a rough carelessness as though she were everyone's little brother. He had good men who believed in what they were doing. They were courageous fighters, good soldiers, and he was proud to be their commanding officer. For the most part they were gentlemen.

On the outskirt of the makeshift camp he saw the Private Vern Murdoch examining the leg of one of the solider's horses. Murdoch had escaped from slavery in Kentucky and set up as a blacksmith in Boston. When any horse lost a shoe, he set up on the trail and fixed it. There was no horse that man couldn't calm.

Sergeant John Sims was squatting next to the Vern. Sims had been with Luc for years. He was one of the survivors of the Fifty-Fourth Regiment and decided to make the Army his life after the war. He'd served under Colonel Shaw and his pride was a point of honor. Had Sims been a white man, there was no doubt, he'd be an officer.

Luc's pride in his soldiers reinforced his feelings that leading them was God's way of saying he forgave Luc his deception. He been raised Catholic, and he remembered all the lectures about God's testing his people. The lovely Callisto was a test. If he could survive her temptation, he could survive anything.

"Luc!"

He turned at the sound of Reggie's voice.

"You're daydreaming," Reggie said as he approached.

Luc threaded his canvas gauntlets through his belt. "Just enjoying the sunset."

"You're facing the wrong way."

Luc chuckled. "A man can only look into the eyes of the sun for so long." The memory of Callie's teasing smile returned to him. Yes, she was definitely a temptation, no matter how sexless she tried to make herself look. Now that he knew she was a woman, he wondered if she would be safe from him. "When we return these horses to the Fort, we're going after the Comanche. I'm tired of them making fools out of me."

Reggie shrugged. "They're making fools out of all of us. I don't know why the Army just doesn't do a massive campaign and wipe the heathens out. The settlers and the ranchers would be safe."

"And we'd be out of a job," Luc said. He studied at Reggie as a series of thoughts went through his mind. "Have you ever wondered how they know so much about us? As though they know everything we do before we do it."

Reggie shook his head and laughed. "You make it sound like they have a spy in our midst."

"Maybe they do." Luc frowned. "In the fourteen months since we arrived at Fort Duncan, we've lost a payroll, food and supplies, horses, rifles and ammunition. Every thing the Army needs to run properly. Every supply route has been compromised. And no matter what we do to combat it, the problem has only gotten worse."

Reggie patted Luc's shoulder. "I think you're imagining things. There's no spy, no ulterior motive. Who would be low enough to trade information with the Indians? And what reason would anyone have for such treason? Perhaps it's all a coincidence. Besides there isn't one man in this camp who would want to deal with the Comanches for any price."

Yet, the Comanches seemed to know when each shipment left San Antonio and what route it would take. Though some shipments arrived without incident, others simply disappeared never to be found again. Luc worried at the problem as he watched the men turn this desolate area of the desert into a camp.

He should write his daily report, but he found himself loathe to go into his hot tent. He wanted to find a place to bathe and possibly ask Callie to bathe with him. He shivered at the thought. Callie consumed too much of his thoughts, too much of the time he should be thinking about his duties.

Reggie wandered away. The enticing aroma of cooking rabbit filled the air. Luc shook off his thoughts and went into his tent to write the daily report.

His mind whirled with his suspicions. As he sat in his camp chair, writing by the light of a lantern, he couldn't forget Callie's face, the way she had teased him with her glistening eyes and the quirky lift of her lips. She was a natural-born seductress and he didn't know why the others couldn't see it. Did they not want to? Or were they so oblivious to her that they paid no attention?

He leaned against the canvas sling back of the chair, staring out the opened flaps of the tent. The noise had begun to die down and one of the men had brought out his harmonica and played a sweet, haunting tune reminding Luc of the war and how the hostilities had brought out the best in his men, and the worst.

Callie sat cross-legged, her back resting against a rock, staring up the sky. Her hat jammed down on her head hiding the contours of her face. Firelight flickered across the high crest of her cheekbones. Luc wondered what she found so engrossing.

He left his tent and approached her, standing over her waiting for her to notice him.

"The sky is pretty," she said.

"You can see it better away from the fire."

"I know." She jumped to her feet and headed off into the desert, away from the camp.

Luc found himself following her. He should stay as far away from her as he could, but the lure of her innocence drew him.

When was the last time he'd been so entranced by such a winsome face? The women he preferred knew the game of seduction and played it as well he did. Callisto, on the other hand, wouldn't even know the first rule.

A full moon cast a luminescent glow over the desert. Callie pointed and against the rocks he saw several shadows moving toward the camp in a slinking motion. For a second, he tensed, thinking the Comanches had found them, then he realized the shadows were coyotes. They stopped and raised their noses to sniff the air, and then continued their cautious approach to the camp pulled by the rich aroma of the cooked rabbit lingering on the air.

Some distance from the camp, she stopped him with a hand on his arms. Her touch burned through the fabric of his shirt. He couldn't move. Overhead, a hawk rode the wind, swirling and dipping with the currents. He heard rustling in the undergrowth. The hawk suddenly tucked its wings against it's body and dove to the ground. Luc heard a squeak and then all was quiet for moment before the muted sounds started again. They stood so still that a jackrabbit passed within a couple of feet of them.

He could make out her profile against the moonlight. Her Seminole heritage was strong in her face from the straight lines of her aristocratic nose to her wide-set eyes. He knew that the Seminoles had given harbor to slaves earlier in the century, and obviously had found no problem with intermarriage with the black slaves.

He couldn't believe she was a woman with her full, pouty lips begging to be kissed. He remembered the feel of her breasts, released from the binding. They had been small and round, fitting perfectly against his palm with dainty nipples that had poked against his palm. He wanted to touch them again, he ached to see her undressed, to separate the illusion from the reality.

Her disguise as a young man was almost perfect. If he hadn't known, he would never have guessed. She walked with the rolling stride of a man, and she used gestures and language that were vigorous and fluent. She showed no weakness, nothing to indicate in the smallest way that she wasn't what she appeared to be.

He wondered what she would look like with long hair cascading about her shoulders. Her hair was so black it had blue highlights in it, and he ached to touch it again, to feel the silken softness curling about his fingers.

What a magnificent mistress she would make. He could imagine himself taking hours of delight in teaching her the mysteries of pleasure. He imagined her body writhing beneath him with abandon. In a perfect world, he would set her up in a little house in Washington and visit her when he was on leave. He saw her tiny, delicate body swathed in blood red silk and rubies sparkling at her throat and ears.

"You're awful quiet, Lieutenant." Callie twisted to stare up at him. "You don't seem like the type to enjoy nature too much."

"I'm just enjoying the scenery."

"You're mooning over me. Stop that."

He knew that she didn't believe him one bit. But her low sultry voice sent shivers down his spine all the way to his toes. "I like looking at you." He hoped that last statement would let her know who was really in control.

She put her hands on her hips. "Did you like looking at me when I was a boy?"

Heat flared between them. She was enjoying his discomfort. What a tease she was turning out to be. His little innocent had a wicked streak after all. "Not that I would admit to anyone." Luc wanted to touch her so badly, his fingers ached.

"I don't think you looking at me in any way is proper." She sounded almost prim.

"Define proper, Callisto."

"Call me Callie, and proper is like being one of your soldiers. I'm not anything other than your scout."

"Do you want a lover?"

She turned on him. "No! I don't have time for such fancy notions. How can I have a lover and still pretend to be a boy?"

"I meant when you get to back to your village."

Her shoulders went back in a defiant stance as if she was preparing to meet her enemy head on. "I won't have time for that kind of silliness. When my mama and I have our own land, then maybe I'll think about marriage and babies. But right now, I can't afford to be bush-whacked."

"Bush-whacked?" How could she think love was like that?

"I can't afford love right now."

Interesting. Most women lived for love, lived for the conquest. Every woman he knew couldn't wait to find a man to call her own. What a mystery this young creature was turning out to be. "You think love can lead a woman astray?"

"Makes 'em crazy."

A laugh escaped from Luc. "Nothing is wrong with being a little crazy from time to time." Love made men crazy, too. Even he had done some outrageous things for the sake of romance. Giselle had been one of his sister's friends. She'd been high-class and beautiful. Luc had wanted her, but her parents had already engaged her to a German baron from Munich. Esme had painted her portrait, but Luc could have sworn Giselle had had eyes only for him. The last he'd heard she was the proud mama of a brood of fat children.

"Besides, being out on patrol is not exactly the best place to be courting." Her tone was firm, daring him to argue with her. "Then everyone would find out my secret and having you know is bad enough."

He touched her cheek with a finger. "I would be less than a gentlemen if I revealed a confidence. I know how to keep a secret, and your secret is safe with me."

She tilted her head up to study him. "What's the price?"

"A kiss." His answer surprised him. Until he'd said the words out loud, he didn't even know he wanted to kiss her. And now that the words were said, he bent toward her. She was so petite, so small and fragile looking, he felt like a big old lecher after a child.

She raised her lips to his. He could smell the fragrance of bayberry on her skin. He remembered he'd given her his soap to use. She must have kept some for herself. He'd always thought bayberry was a masculine scent, but on Callie it smelled delightful and seductive.

He kissed her. Her lips were pressed tight together, yet they were as soft as satin. He could feel her trembling beneath his touch. He groaned with a growing passion. He grabbed her shoulders and pulled her to him, pressing her against him. She stood stiff and still, her arms tight against her sides. He ran his hands down her arms and gently pried

76

open her fists.

He could taste her inexperience. He probed against her lips, but she refused to open to him. A jolt of lightning flashed through him. He knew one kiss would never be enough. She was intoxicating, sensual.

Suddenly, Callie pressed her hands flat against his chest and pushed him. He broke away, and she covered her mouth and bolted.

CHAPTER SEVEN

Esme sat on a bench on the veranda overlooking the courtyard, sipping a cup of cocoa, as she figured out what project she would tackle next. Natalie entertained a shriveled, decrepit old man in the parlor. Esme had disliked the man from the moment she'd answered the door. He'd leaned on his silver-headed cane, his tongue darting about his lips like a lizard, as he studied her in a way that was almost insulting.

He'd announced that his name was Jonas Ramsaye and that he was here to see Madame Delacroix. She remembered the man from the dock and wondered what business he had with Natalie.

His eyes had been flat and colorless, and he had looked at Esme as though she were a prize before transferring his gaze to Simone and Natalie who had come up behind Esme.

Esme had fled to the veranda. She didn't know the man and she didn't want to know him. Something about him had been slimy and unclean. She had to resist the urge to scrub her hands where he had attempted to touch her.

The sweet scent of the cocoa wafted upward and relaxed her. A cup of cocoa solved everything, especially all the unbridled unpleasantness Natalie had insisted on tossing at her these last few days. She settled back to smile at the progress she'd made in the courtyard.

The flower beds had been weeded and the wandering rose tamed along the stout pillars of the trellis. The fountain had been repaired and once more water cascaded over the smooth marble statue in the center. Esme had even found a couple goldfish for the pond to eat the mosquito larva and keep the water clean.

Simone blasted through the door. Tears streaked her pretty face as she stamped down the steps and stood in the middle of the courtyard, unaware of Esme on the veranda.

"Simone," Esme said in a soft voice. Her young sister was skittish as a colt and still difficult to get close to.

Simone whirled, panic on her face. "What are you doing here?"

"Having some cocoa." Esme touched the pot. "Would you like to join me?"

"Mama said to never be alone with you." Simone gave a haughty sniff, though her eyes seemed to yearn for something Esme couldn't name.

"Then go back in the kitchen and snivel." Esme waved her hand casually at the door.

Simone stood her ground, her head held eye, the tears still pouring from her eyes. "I won't marry him."

Esme frowned. "Marry who?"

"That old man. He smells of garlic and onions."

Esme brushed a leaf from the bench next to her. So her little sister was in trouble. "Come sit and tell me. If you didn't want to marry him, why become engaged to him."

"Because he's rich and we're poor. Because he'll take care of the whole family and he even promised modest dowries for Lauren and Josette. And because Mama said I have to marry him no matter what I feel."

"How generous of him." And Natalie, Esme thought. She couldn't keep the dryness out of her tone.

Simone plopped next to Esme and poured herself a cup of steaming cocoa. "I have no choice. I have to marry Mr. Ramsaye. Mama says I will save the family fortunes."

"Silly girl." Esme patted Simone's slender, elegant hand. "You don't have to do anything you don't want."

Her bottom lips trembled. "But how will we live without his money?"

"Is being poor so bad?" Not that Esme would want to find out, but she'd live in the streets before she married a man she didn't chose for herself.

Simone glanced at Esme's Paris made gown and then at her own thin cotton dress. "You're not poor."

"I'm not poor because I handle my own finances and don't depend on anyone."

"You're not Creole." Simone lifted her chin. "Creole women are supposed to be taken care of and treated with respect. We don't soil our hands with the worry about money. That's a man's job."

Esme rolled her eyes. Poor child, she had been bewitched by such silly notions of what was right, simply because society had already dictated to her what she could and couldn't do, or even feel. "Oh, yes, by men who are old, rich, and smelly husbands. Do you think they know us better than we do ourselves?"

Simone's tears started anew.

Esme felt like an ogre picking on a little child. She pulled a lace handkerchief from her pocket and handed it to her half-sister. "Be honest with me. Are you sure you don't want to marry this man?"

Simone shook her head. "I hate the way tries to touch me."

Esme put a finger under the girl's chin and lifted it. "Then you shall not." Carefully she handed the china cup to Simone, rose from the bench, and walked into the house.

The kitchen sparkled with cleanliness and Esme took a moment to smile at it. She'd hired a cook and a servant to help clean the house and they had done an excellent job. She walked up the back stairs that led to the second floor and stalked into her father's bedroom.

Her father had grown stronger in the week since Esme's arrival. Color had returned to his cheeks. The doctor had come and given Esme some hope that he might recover. Though her father would never been in the best of health again, the good food and the improved condition of the house had gone a long way toward making him more comfortable. At least he no longer looked like he would die at any moment.

Her father lay against a mound of pillows, half sitting up as he slept. Esme stopped at the door to study him. In her childhood he'd been tall and strong and filled with laughter. What had happened to that man? This one in front of her was a stranger, a shell of the man she'd once known. She'd already sent a letter to Luc telling him of the dire circumstances of their father, his illness, and his family's misfortune. She had outlined in detail what she planned to do to help them.

"Papa." Esme leaned over him and smoothed the blanket around his waist.

His eyes fluttered open and he stared at her for a moment with a blank look, then the look cleared, and was replaced by a glow of love.

Esme pulled a chair over to the side of the bed and sat down. She folded her hands almost primly in her lap because if she didn't control them, she'd be tempted to scratch Natalie's eyes out.

Her father reached for her hand and held it tightly. "Something is not pleasing you. I can tell by the war-like glint in your eyes."

"Are you aware Natalie has struck a marriage deal for Simone with a man old enough to be my grandfather."

Her father frowned. "But Natalie says Simone wants to marry him."

"Natalie told you this?" Esme pictured the girl crying on the veranda. Hardly someone running joyously to the altar.

"I wouldn't have allowed the negotiations to progress otherwise. Though I have to admit, I've never much liked the man. Already had a couple of wives and buried them. As bad off as we are, I will not barter my daughters against their future."

A white-hot rage built in her. "I just spoke with Simone and she is not at all happy about marrying this man. I wouldn't want to marry him. He's a toad." She repressed a shiver at the memory of his colorless eyes and thick lips.

"I must do something. If Simone truly does not want to marry him, she shouldn't have to."

He struggled to sit up, but Esme pushed him back against the pillows. "Papa, I'll take of this. You just rest." More than anything, Esme wanted to put Natalie in her place. Not so much for Simone's sake, but for all the past injustices Natalie had done to Esme and Luc. Having been in Natalie's company for the past week, Esme was beginning to think Natalie had been the reason for the trickling off of letters from her father. From what she could tell, Natalie had not mailed them, nor delivered the ones that Esme had written.

Esme walked down the front staircase and found Jonas Ramsaye in the parlor with a hand clasped around Lauren's arm while he studied her with appraising eyes. Natalie was nowhere in sight. Lauren squirmed and tried to wriggle away.

"You'll do for my cousin, Nathaniel," Ramsaye said in a wheezy voice. "He likes his women young."

"Let the child go." Esme snapped as she walked slowly into the parlor.

Surprised, Ramsaye let go, but a smile like a snake remained on his lined shallow face. "I'm just getting to know my new family better."

Lauren rubbed her backside. "He pinched me on my bottom. He stinks."

A look of rage clouded Ramsaye' face. He stood up and grabbed for the girl. She ran and hid behind Esme.

Esme touched the girl's cheek. "Leave us, Lauren, your papa is asking for you." Lauren fled and Esme stood in the center of the parlor glaring at Ramsaye. "Touch any woman in this house again and I'll personally break you in two. Which shouldn't be too difficult."

The old man laughed showing missing teeth in his mouth. He took a few steps toward Esme. "What are you going to do to me? You're a woman."

She reached into the deep pocket she had had sewn into all her gowns and grabbed the little dagger she kept hidden for emergencies. As she decided to prick him to show him she could be dangerous, then not to and let go of the dagger. If she was going to teach this man a lesson she preferred using her bare hands. "Laugh, old man, but I was taught my the finest fencing master in all France. Don't let my gender fool you."

He grinned. "You high-yellow ones were always feisty. I've missed having a mistress like you. Damn war took away too many privileges."

Esme raised an eyebrow. "As though I'd have a beast like you as a lover."

He tried to touch her and she grabbed his wrist and bent his thumb back until a wave of pain stirred in his eyes. "Don't ever attempt to touch me, again. I'll enjoy making you suffer."

"Let me go!"

"Stop struggling or I'll break your thumb and from the feel of it, it wouldn't take much. Now, get out."

"You can't throw me out. This isn't your home." He pulled his hand away and stood just out of reach, nursing his bruised thumb. "Who else is going to offer these church mice anything more than crumbs? They need me."

"Old man, I can buy and sell you without blinking an eye. You will not be marrying Simone. The engagement is ended."

"You can't do a thing. The arrangements have already been made."

She pushed him away from her. "Consider them unmade as of now. My lawyer will get in touch with your lawyer immediately."

He rubbed his wrist. "I will not be treated with such disrespect by one of your kind."

"My kind?" She stepped up to him. "I'm assuming you mean women who are strong enough, and rich enough, to know their mind. If you want a battle, old man, I would relish the opportunity to squash you like the ugly bug you are."

He slapped his hat on his head and picked up his cane. He headed for the front door. "This isn't ended."

"Yes, it is."

He opened the front door and stepped out, slamming the door behind him.

"What have you done?" Natalie demanded in a shrill voice.

Esme whirled around. "I just saved your entire family from a life of dealing with that odious man."

"He's wealthy. He said he would take care of me and my children."

"And you are willing to sell your own flesh and blood so that you can have pretty gowns."

Natalie glared at her. "What do you know?" she spat. "While we were scrounging for scraps at the market, you were eating fine Parisian cooking and dancing the night away wearing fine dresses and jewels. While we were fearing for our lives, you took carriage rides in the park."

"I offered you a home in Paris during the war. You chose not to live with me."

Natalie's face grew fierce with anger. "I'm not living with the bastard child of my husband."

"You're living with me now. And you allowed me to put food on the table and replace all the pieces of furniture you've sold over the last couple of years."

"Get out of my house." Natalie stamped her foot.

"You're wrong, Natalie. As of this morning, I've assumed the loan you took out against the house. One thing I learned long ago is to be kind to your landlord."

Natalie clutched her throat. "How can that be? The bank would never deal with the likes of you." Her eyes raked over Esme with scorn.

Esme smiled. The pleasure she received from besting Natalie was heartwarming. Not that this mouse was much of a challenge, but non-the-less it felt good. "One thing you Southerners have never learned about the North is that the color of money is much more important than the color of skin."

Natalie paled. "I will not have my home owned by a .... darkie."

Esme held up a hand. "Careful, Natalie. I would think nothing of turning you out on the street. If not for my father and sisters, you'd be on your backside in the gutter with a snap of my fingers."

Simone ran into the parlor. "Is it true, Mama? I don't have to marry him?"

Natalie whirled around, her hands curled into fists, her face twisted with fury. "Leave us. Immediately."

Esme grabbed her sister's wrist. "Tomorrow, Simone, I'm going to the bank, and I am setting up funds for you and your sisters to live on. But only under one condition. You will use the money to do what you please with your lives. If you don't wish to marry a smelly old man, then you will learn to take care of yourselves."

"Do you mean this?" Simone asked warily, her eyes flashing disbelief.

Esme put a hand over her heart. "Every word."

"I've always wanted to travel and have adventures, and ...." Her voice trailed off

Esme gently touched her sister's arm. "If you want to travel, I can arrange it. I have friends in China, India, Argentina, and Italy. They would all be delighted to have you as a guest."

Simone leaned toward Esme, a cautious look in her pretty eyes. "Are you really so wealthy you can help us like this?"

"Terribly rich." Esme whispered in her sister's ear. "I'm almost embarrassed by so much wealth." Wealth she would have been happy to share if she had only known had badly off her father had been.

Simone started toward the hall. "I have to tell Lauren and Josette." Before she left the room, she turned around and ran toward Esme to kiss her on the cheek. "Thank you," she whispered. She ran off, her footsteps ringing in the hallway as she called for her sisters.

"How dare you try," Natalie stormed, "to steal my daughters away from me." Her lips curled into a snarl. "You have my husband. Isn't that enough?"

Esme shook her head. "You're never going to understand. I refuse to spend my time here attempting to win your approval." Natalie didn't understand that the human heart wasn't restricted in who, or how many people a person could love. Esme felt sad that Natalie was so narrow-minded. If she could do one thing, she would make it possible for her sisters to know that there was more to life than fulfilling someone else's dreams.

Luc stood in the middle of the feed alley watching Callie as she cleaned Liberty's stall. Liberty, tied to a post in the alley, nibbling at Callie's pocket where she'd hidden a carrot scrounged from the kitchen. In all the years he'd ridden the horse, Liberty had never liked anyone but Luc and old Silas. Yet the old warhorse had taken to Callie as though she were a lump of sugar to be licked.

The post was buzzing with activity. They were expecting General Hammond who was coming straight from D.C. to hold a conference of all the area commanders regarding the Comanche problem.

Callie swatted Liberty on the nose. "You know the deal. You let me clean out the stall and you then you get your treat."

Luc smiled. Callie had made herself the darling of the post, willing to do just about anything to show him how important she could be and keep him from sending her back home. Very few people on the post didn't like her, though they all thought she was just a kid and treated her as though she were their kid brother.

After their kiss, Luc had vowed to keep contact with her to a minimum, but she kept doing little things for him, like cleaning Liberty's stall and exercising the gelding during long stretches of no activity. She mended harness for Silas. She ran errands for Major Adams, the post commander and even helped drive the enlisted men's wives into Eagle Pass for groceries.

She swept the floors of Luc's quarters, and had even done his laundry over his loud objections. Best of all, she knew how to track Indians and when she wasn't out scouting, she was teaching the kids on the post how to read sign out in the desert. She was like a funny little puppy that had followed him home and everyone loved.

If Luc had made any effort to send her home, he would have been lynched. He didn't understand how one small woman had managed to twist everyone around her little fingers. The wives on the post babied her and fed her telling her she needed more meat on her bones. The soldier had taught her to play poker. The only person who seemed to take her in active dislike was Reggie. But then Reggie disliked most everyone.

Callie had tried hard to please him, but after awhile just stayed out of his way. Reggie was so unhappy that Luc was thinking of requesting a transfer and sending him back to Washington.

A commotion arose and Luc slipped out of the barn to find a supply train arriving, a contingent of guards flanking it and a separate detachment at the front. Even from the barn, Luc could see that General Hammond had finally arrived and with him was a carriage. The General rode next to the carriage and talked to a woman hidden by a bright yellow parasol.

Luc smiled. General Hammond had been a rogue. Even during the war, he'd kept his mistress in style wherever he happened to be. The General considered himself a lady's man. And the ladies certainly seemed to enjoy his company.

An order to assemble sounded and Luc ran toward the parade ground. The men formed into parade rest and saluted as the General came to a stop. Major Adams stepped forward and addressed the General. Hammond nodded, dismounted, and held his hand out and a woman slid a slender foot out to the top step and lightly descended from the carriage to the ground. She turned, her laughter a cloud of merriment that floated over the parade ground. Even some of the men smiled slightly at the sound of her mirth.

Luc knew that laugh anywhere. Esme.

Luc could only stare at his twin sister. He hadn't seen her in several years and she looked incredibly beautiful in the afternoon sun.

How had she ended up with General Hammond? Acting as if they we're life-long friends. Perhaps it was safer if he didn't ask questions he didn't want to know the answers to. He'd only just received her last letter two days ago stating the problems with their father and his family. Luc had just finished a draft of the return letter telling her to do what she had to do.

What a flirt that woman was. How she managed to attach herself to the most important military man besides Ulysses S. Grant shouldn't have amazed Luc. Esme always did have a knack for placing herself in the right spot at the right time.

"Is that your sister?" Reggie asked as he joined Luc and they both walked across the parade ground. "She isn't supposed to arrive for another three weeks."

"She's early." Luc stoked his chin. "How novel." Esme hadn't even been born first, she came out almost fourteen hours after Luc. Despite being twins, their birthdays were a day apart. His mother said because she enjoyed her time alone being the center of attention. Luc speculated that when the time came she wouldn't arrive on time to her own funeral.

Esme turned and saw him. She winked. Luc grinned back. He couldn't help it.

General Hammond turned and waved Luc over to him. "Luc, look who I found in New Orleans."

Wandering the streets causing trouble, he wanted to ask. Luc approached and saluted. "General Hammond. It's good to see you again." He gave a sideways glance at his sister who was smiling at Major Adams. Major Adams turned to his wife and shrugged. His wife was going to have a talk with him later. Luc could see her standing in front of the suttler's store, frowning.

Esme smooth down her pale blue gown dotted with light yellow daisies to match her parasol. The General held out his hand to her and she curled her fingers lightly around his arm. "Lucien." She sounded like a cool refreshing brook. She walked up to him, tilted the parasol over his shoulder to hide him from the men on the parade ground and kissed him on the cheek. "You are well, big brother. The wilds of America seem to agree with you." She tucked her parasol back over her shoulder.

The General patted her fingers. "If I had known your sister was this pretty, I would never have let you leave Washington."

Esme chuckled and tossed him a flirty little smile. "Oh Monty, you have such a wicked tongue."

The General blushed. And all Luc could think was that she had him in the palm of her hand already. He couldn't believe anyone would dare to call the General Monty. He had met the General's mother once and even she had called her son, the General.

What was it about a woman that could turn a man into pudding with just a smile. "General, how did you find my sister?"

The General glanced fondly at his sister. "She was coming out of the Cathedral in Jackson Square and literally bumped into me."

Esme twirled her parasol smiling innocently. "I was at confession and this kind gentleman made me forget all about my transgressions."

Luc almost rolled his eyes. My God, was she laying on the helpless act. Not even Joan of Arc could wield her sword and erase Esme's many sins. Luc could see Callie hanging at the back of the formation watching Esme with huge eyes. Luc had to admit, Esme was the height of fashion and elegance. "I'm sure he was very helpful, sister dear."

"Son, you and I have a talk later. Why don't you take your sister to her quarters and get her settled in while I review the troops."

Reggie stepped forward. "General, it would be my pleasure to escort the lady. I can see you and Lieutenant Delacroix have a lot to talk about." He held out his arm.

Esme placed her hand on Reggie's arm and allowed him to lead her away. She turned once and wriggled her fingers at the General. "Until later."

While the General reviewed the troops, Luc couldn't get his mind off of Esme and why she was here so early. Esme didn't do anything early unless she had something on her mind. Luc cringed. When Esme was on a crusade nothing was safe from her efforts.

General Hammond offered Luc a fat cigar. They walked along the edge of the parade ground. The troops had dispersed the inspection completed. Fort Duncan received high marks as always. Major Adams was a stickler for detail.

Adams had gone off to see to some errands in regards to the officers' banquet to be held the next night. Reggie had been sent to see to the General's quarters.

"Esme is quite charming." General lit his cigar and puffed on it. He offered Luc a cigar from his pocket case.

Luc puffed on his cigar to light it. "Esme's stock and trade is charm."

The General chuckled. "She makes a man young again."

And young men old. Luc nodded. "General is this conversation leading somewhere?"

The General stopped to lean against a fence. The horses inside the corral milled restlessly. On the other side of the corral, Luc could see Callie talking to Esme. Even at a distance, he saw the hero-worship in Callie's eyes. He hoped Callie kept a hold of her senses and not get to friendly with his sister. For all her frivolity, Esme was an astute woman and no one ferreted out a mystery with such ease.

The General leaned a foot on the bottom rail. "Your sister is perfectly safe with me. A pretty woman makes an excellent cover."

Luc was startled. "Cover for what?"

"For why I'm here. The word is I'm just doing an inspection, an old General's last hurrah, but I'm here because I need to talk to you and you're the only person I trust."

"Sir." Luc couldn't even begin to understand why the General would put so much faith in him.

"The United States Army is the most powerful army on this continent and we cannot stop a group of heathens who have barely left the Stone Age behind."

"They aren't a bunch of savages, sir."

"You are correct." The General took a puff of his cigar. "They are smart enough to get information from one of our own men."

"A traitor?"

The General nodded. "I believe someone on this post is passing confidential information to the Indians."

"I don't believe it." Though his mind raced. He wanted to deny the General's allegations, but a niggling little thought kept surfacing. How else did the Comanche know when the supply train was due and what route it would take?

The General stared out over the post. "Every man can be bought with either money, women, or power."

Luc ran a hand over his face. "I'm every man."

"Lucien Delacroix, you're rich, you can have any woman you want, and if you wanted power you would have taken it. Don't you think I know you could have stayed in Washington, or been assigned to the embassy in London. But you volunteered to head this company of black men because you wanted excitement and adventure. I could have given you a desk and life filled with parties and beautiful women throwing themselves at you, but you chose this instead. Your price is loyalty to the cause and that's not corruptible. As I say, you're the only man I can trust with this information."

Luc glanced around at the post settling in for the evening. The smell of cooking wafted from the mess hall. Officers Row was filled with bustle as the wives set about grabbing children and getting ready for their own dinners. A laundress removed dry clothes on a line behind the barracks. Normal activity for a normal post in the middle of nowhere. "And you want me to do what?"

"Run this traitor to ground and hang him out to dry." A cloud of cigar smoke surrounded the General's head. He wiped a bead of sweat from his forehead.

"Any suggestions on where I should start my search?" Luc couldn't even begin to believe that someone on this post was a traitor. He knew them all from the lowliest new recruit to the Major and their families. He trusted them with his life when he was on patrol. Major Adams was the most loyal man Luc ever knew. He loved the Army. Even his wife loved the Army despite the rough life and the loneliness.

"The closest rock, my old friend, is always the best place to start."

Luc reeled with the shock of the information. On the other side of the corral, Callie struggled to drag Esme's trunk up to the front door of Luc's quarters. He should have assigned a man to help his sister unload her luggage, but had forgotten to tell Reggie.

"Now you know the truth." General Hammond rubbed his eyes. "I don't want to retire with this stain on my record."

"I still can't believe you of all people are thinking of retiring."

The General chuckled. "I think its about high time I find myself a wealthy young wife and start having myself a passel of kids before I get too old to enjoy them. Know anyone who might be interested in a old codger like me."

"You're forty-eight, sir. Hardly an old man." And Luc was only thirty-two, yet he saw his life stretching out in front of him with the same loneliness as the General. He hadn't given much thought to marriage simply because the type of woman he liked would never tolerate life on a remote army post. Somewhere down the path, he'd vowed not to marry.

The General clapped him on the back. "Spoken like a true soldier. Later on tonight, when the camp settles down, you stop by my quarters and I'll give you what I have. Once you read the dispatches, you'll know as much as I do and you'll probably arrive at the same conclusion. There's a traitor here at Fort Duncan and I want him bad."

CHAPTER EIGHT

Callie found her hand straying toward Miss Delacroix's silk underwear. The white mounds of silk and lace were a magnet. Callie had never seen anything so fine in her whole life. Not even her mama's best Sunday dress came close to such perfection.

A wonderful scent rose from the open trunk and Callie sniffed trying to identify it. She's never known a woman to perfume her underclothes before. Miss Delacroix's perfumed everything right down to the scalloped lace on her drawers. Callie thought that heaven must be like this, all pretty scents and beautiful clothes.

Miss Delacroix's gloves lay on the edge of the bed and Callie touched the buttery soft leather dyed to match the woman's traveling suit. She had gloves to match a dozen suits. Callie wanted to try them on, but comparing her hand to Miss Delacroix's already showed her that hers were roughened with calluses and wider in the palm. But what she wouldn't give to have such wonderful gloves.

Callie had never seen so many women's clothes before. Dresses and petticoats, matching shoes and hose, hats with silk flowers and long scarves that flowed like water over her fingers in a rainbow of colors. Callie hadn't known so many colors existed in the world.

Callie couldn't stop the pool of envy developing inside her. Back home in her village, she had two brown skirts and two white cotton blouses which she seldom had worn preferring her brother's trousers and cotton shirts. Frilly clothes didn't do her any good when she was on the trail.

Everything in Miss Delacroix's trunk drew Callie. Her mind was transported back to the night she had seen the Lieutenant bathing in the pond with his scented soap and pale skin. Callie lifted a while lace handkerchief to her nose and inhaled the subtle perfume. She closed her eyes.

"It's been a long time since a boy touched my underwear." Miss Delacroix's voice seemed to float across the room.

Callie couldn't move, mortified at being found with her hands on another woman's underwear.

"Turn around, little one," Miss Delacroix ordered.

Slowly Callie turned and faced the women. She dropped the hankie on the floor and stared at the toes of her boots. She couldn't believe she'd been so careless and hadn't heard the other woman's footsteps.

A small smile turned Miss Delacroix's lips up. Callie swallowed. "I'm sorry."

"When I was your age, I liked to touch pretty things, too."

Miss Delacroix picked up the hankie from the floor. She straightened and studied Callie. "What's your name?"

"Cal, ma'am."

Miss Delacroix flipped off Callie's hat and grasped her chin with strong fingers. She twisted Callie's face up and down. "Have you begun to shave yet. You're much too pretty to be a boy. Such long, lovely eyelashes. Some very smart woman in Paris would keep you for her own. She would teach you the ways of the world and you'd never have to work again."

Callie pushed away. She had no idea what Miss Delacroix meant. She tried to duck under Miss Delacroix's arm, but Miss Delacroix didn't let go. "I don't understand."

"Pretty little boys grow up to be pretty young man and are highly prized, especially if the young man develops certain talents."

Callie's face flamed with embarrassment. She was beginning to understand what Miss Delacroix meant. "No one would want me, ma'am."

"I don't know about that. I know some who would adore you."

Callie doubled her efforts to get away. "Ma'am, I don't think I should be listening to this."

Miss Delacroix laughed and Callie succeeded in getting away. She bolted out the door and ran right into her brother. He grunted under the force of her body hitting his and stumbled backward. He grasped Callie's shoulders and righted her.

"What's wrong?" He asked.

Callie shook her head. She tried to get away. Miss Delacroix was everything Callie would have liked to be. She was smart and men seemed to fall all over her. Callie needed to get away so she could control her raging feelings. She wanted to be like Miss Delacroix so that Luc would like her, too.

She twisted out of Luc's grasp and ran across the parade ground to the stables. Deep in a shadowed corner of Liberty's stall, she curled up on a mound of hay and lay there trying not to cry.

Old Silas peered into the stall. "You come out of there. I just cleaned this stall and I don't need your dirty boots in my clean stable. How come you shoot in here like a bullet, little man?"

Callie just shook her head. She was afraid if she said anything, she'd start to cry.

"Silence in good. Now you come out. Idle hand make for the devil's playground. I got lots of work. If you're sulking over something, you can do while your hands is cleaning harness."

Callie allowed him to coax her out and seconds later she was sitting on a stool in the tack room rubbing saddle soap across the leather and then cleaning it with a rag. "Silas, have you ever seen something you wanted bad."

"I used to think like that when I was young."

"How come you don't think that way now?" The measured movements of her hands soothed her.

"Because I'm old now. You can't go through life without learning a thing or two."

Callie wondered what she had to learn about life. "What did you learn?"

"That wanting something gnaws at your belly more than hunger."

"What did you want so badly?"

"A woman." His face took on a faraway cast as he dipped into his memories.

"Was she a slave?"

"Yes, she was a slave, but not like most of us. What she had to do was even worse. I worked the stables, but she had to ...." his voice trailed away.

"To what?" Callie asked intrigued.

Silas seemed to shake himself and the distant look in his eyes disappeared. "She was the Master's mistress. As beautiful as the sunset. Her name was Lorelei. But she wasn't for me."

"What happened?"

He shook his head. "The war. That bastard took her with him to Vicksburg and she was killed during the siege. He survived though."

"How do you know she died?"

"Because I tended the prisoners at Vicksburg and the bastard told me. I almost slipped a knife into his ribs. I could have, you know."

"Why didn't you?" Callie's hands stilled at the revelation of Silas' past.

"I had me enough killing, little man. Lorelei was dead, what good would it have been to kill the Master? He didn't have anything to go back to, didn't have anything left. He was a broken man and that was enough for me." A look dawned in Silas' eyes and he glanced knowingly at Callie. "I get it, little man, you got yourself a look at the Lieutenant's pretty sister and now you got yourself a hankering for her."

"No!" Callie jumped to her feet, dropping the harness and staring at him. "No!"

"Don't you get yourself all bent out of shape. It's natural. A man sees a pretty woman and he wants her, even if she is a white woman."

Callie shook her head violently. How could Silas even think Callie was hankering after Miss Delacroix? Callie wanted her clothes. All those beautiful, soft, scented things that women wore to be women. Callie wanted to wear those clothes for Luc. She wanted to be a woman for Luc. God, what was she thinking? She'd never owned soft, pretty things. She'd never known a man like Luc Delacroix. Callie didn't know anything about being a woman. She knew how to hunt and follow sign. She knew how to survive in harsh country. She knew necessary things. But just once in her life, she wanted to be frivolous, pretty and cherished by a Luc.

She picked up the dropped harness and hung it on its hook. "I promised cook I'd trap some rabbits for the banquet." She fled again.

She made her way on foot to a nearby stream and sat on a rock beneath the shade of a cottonwood facing the fort and trying to figure out how she was going to come to terms with her feelings. She couldn't afford to fall in love with any man, she had her family's future at stake. If she didn't fulfill the bargains of the enlistment contract, there would be no money and no free land. Her mama was counting on that land.

The sun disappeared beyond the horizon and the land began to darken into night. Lights came on in the different quarters and the barracks. Someone played a guitar accompanied by an harmonica. She should go back, no one was supposed to be off post at night without special permission. But she couldn't move.

Callie sat on her rock, her knees drawn under her chin, her arms wrapped around her legs. Darkness crept outward and still she sat.

After what seemed like hours, Callie saw a movement heading toward her. She tensed, wondering who would be wandering outside the post after dark. The shadowed figure slipped through the night and Callie's curiosity was piqued.

A man passed, not seeing her. When he passed, his face in darkness,

Callie slid off the rock and followed. Who would be so bold as to leave the post after dark? And from the stealthy way he moved, she knew he wasn't supposed to be there.

The man sidled through the underbrush and crossed the stream. He walked quickly and Callie wished she could see his face. Something about him told her he was up to no good.

She followed him for several miles along the stream until he paused at a rotted out log. The man kneeled in front of the log and put his hand inside. Callie squinted to see better, but the darkness defeated her.

And then man was gone, heading back to the post. She wished for a better view of him, but he moved quickly and she was interested in what he'd put in the log.

She crept toward the log and dug deep inside. She felt nothing was in the log, which meant the man had removed something. She patted the entire interior of the log and her fingers found something small and round. She pulled out the object, but couldn't tell what the object was. She slipped it into her pocket and then headed back toward the post.

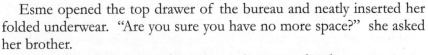

Esme opened the top drawer of the bureau and neatly inserted her folded underwear. "Are you sure you have no more space?" she asked her brother.

Luc sat in a chair across the room, trying not to laugh.

She rounded on him, hands on her hips, annoyance on her plainly face. "You knew I was coming. You could have made better arrangements."

He had toyed with idea of volunteering his unit to a long range patrol to avoid his sister all together, but he suspect Esme would traverse the desert just to find him and scold him for not having enough drawers for her. "I'm sleeping in the parlor for the duration of your stay." He smiled at her. "Which by the way, is how long?"

"I have just arrived and now you seem like you want to be rid of me. How rude you have become."

"You've never slept in the parlor." He was delighted to see her, but his bachelor quarters were small and cramped, hardly designed for her and her belongings. He eyed her eight trunks which filled every inch of floor space in the bedroom.

"I've made a new life plan." Esme sat on the edge of the bed and studied him.

"What's that?"

"I've decided to move."

Oh God please not to Texas. She'd start some revolution just to break the monotony. "To Texas?"

Her face contorted into an unattractive grimace. "My goodness, never."

"New Orleans?" He knew she'd visited their father, perhaps she longed for their childhood home. New Orleans was far enough away.

"No." Esme played with the lace collar of her neck. "I've decided on San Francisco. I've heard it's very wild and it's time I was wild again."

"Esme! San Francisco! What's possessed you?"

She shrugged. "There's nothing in Paris anymore. Philippe is dead and you are never returning to Paris. Why should I stay?"

"Because it's civilized." He couldn't imagine Esme anywhere in the world but Paris. She was made for Paris. She glittered as brightly as the city. He didn't know if he wanted her on the same continent as him.

Her lips quirked. "I'm bored. I can't paint. I can't breathe. I need something new, something exciting. I have put most of my life in order and I'm going to San Francisco and you should do the same."

He'd been to San Francisco and frankly it wasn't his type of city. He preferred the wilds of Texas. "I have no desire to live in San Francisco."

"No." She slapped his hand. "It's time you put your life in order."

"And, Sister dear, what do you mean by that?" Or did he really want to know.

She sat back and studied him. "I mean, father."

"Why did you see him?" Luc couldn't help the stiff anger in his voice.

"He is my father and I love him."

He'd known the relationship between Esme and their father had never wavered. Like everyone around her you either accepted Esme on her terms or not at all. She had been that way as a child and she certainly never grew out of it as a woman. But when you are the dutiful son, and transgress, there is no forgiveness. "And his wife and daughters? How did they feel about your visit?"

She waved a hand in the air. "Lauren will be joining me in San Francisco. Simone is going to London. And Josette will be visiting the Countess Duchand in Paris. The child is lovely, but she needs polish and the Countess will help her shine."

"You spoke to our half-sisters?" Luc could only stare at her disbelieving her.

She rolled her shoulders elegantly. "They love me."

"And our father? The subject was still painful for him to mention.

She drummed her long fingers on the mattress.

He could tell she was becoming impatient with him, but he didn't care. "What did he say?"

The fingers moved faster. "Lucien, I am not a stupid woman. I have always known, even Natalie has always known, that you were his favorite, his pride and joy. A man could not wish for a son more brilliant than you. And this feud between you two has gone on long enough. It's time for a reconciliation."

"As far as father is concerned I betrayed him and his precious cause."

"The war is over. He is willing to set all that aside if you will meet him half way."

"Really?" Luc gripped the arms of the chair. The war wasn't over. In a hundred years there would still be hate on both sides. Several months ago the his unit had raided a camp of Southern sympathizers. Texas had become a haven for southerners plotting to restart the hostilities.

"I don't care about your petty intrigues. Our father is dying."

Luc took a deep breath. He had never stopped loving his father, but in his heart he knew he couldn't defend an institution that condoned slavery after all the years Luc had lived as a free man in Paris. His father wanted to keep the old ways and seemed to see nothing odd in southern men indulging in their black mistresses and having children with them, while enslaving their mistresses' parents. Was Esme just lying to gain favor with him. "What's wrong with him?"

She glanced away. "The doctor says it's his heart. Of course, it didn't help that they were practically living in squalor." A tear rolled down her cheek and she quickly wiped it away.

Luc was jolted by shock. He knew she was telling the truth. His sister cried only in the most dire circumstance and hated herself for being weak. "What do you mean?"

"Father lost everything in the war. They have no money, no plantation. Nothing. All that is left is the house in New Orleans, and even Natalie tried to barter that away the same way she tried to barter her daughter."

"You helped, I know you did." Luc was proud of his sister. She saw things clearly, while his thoughts were muddied with feelings of anger.

"Of course."

"Then you must arrange for some of my money to be sent."

She waved her hand. "Whose money do you think I used?"

He grinned at her. "How generous of you."

"You gave me complete control of our fortune. I have amassed more money than you and I will ever use, so why shouldn't we be generous. After all, our father did arrange for us to have a very generous settlement. It wasn't his fault it was so much more than we could ever use. Now it's time for you to thank him in person. I spoke with Monty ...."

"How do you get away with calling General Hammond Monty?"

She laughed. "One afternoon at Antoine's I let him look down my dress. He's been very grateful ever since."

He had to ask. "Have you slept with him?"

"Although he enjoys looking at me, I fear his need is more centered on my financial attractiveness than my physical beauty."

Luc stared at her in amazement. "When did you become so mercenary?"

"When you left me alone in Paris to play soldier. And now you can make it up with me by visiting our father. I've arranged with Monty for you to take a short a leave of absence. He didn't want you to go, but I convinced him it was matter of life and death. I told him some of the truth, and that you needed to make your peace with our father, or you would never be able to live with yourself. Monty is understanding and I know he needs you here, but our father needs you, too."

"I have a job to do." Luc wasn't certain he wanted to visit his father. His father had disinherited him, had cut off all communication. What did Luc owe this man besides paternity?

"Please, Lucien." She grasped his hands. "I'm asking for one visit and three small words."

"What three small words?"

"I forgive you. Go to New Orleans, say I love you, and then return to your duties. You will only be gone a few weeks and the next supply train isn't due for several months. Monty has decided to stay on here while you are gone. He hopes his presence will deter the spy. And I will help him. Is visiting our father so little to ask? It need not be so taxing on your pride?"

"I'm not concerned with my pride."

Her lips pursed. "Than how long must you cling to your animosity?"

He didn't want to talk about his father anymore. "You're going to help catch a spy?"

"I will let you change the subject brother dear. And yes it will amuse me to strike a blow for justice."

"I see." Nobody was sneakier than Esme. If skullduggery were to be found, Esme would sniff it out like a hunting dog. Luc almost pitied the spy.

"Will you go?"

He'd faced death on the battlefield, seen men he'd called friends die in his arms, and survived a near fatal saber wound, but his sister terrified him. If he didn't go, she would keep at him like the dripping of a pump.

She would never let up and he would be subjected to a reign of silk-clad terror. That was how she worked. She would chip away at his resistance until he was worn down to nothing. He might as well give in now, but he couldn't he did have some pride after all. He needed to work a little bit. "I will think about it." He stood and started to leave.

She grabbed his hand. "No. Now that I've finished with my business, let us gossip."

"Esme, there is little to gossip about in Texas and I'm no longer interested in what is happening in Paris."

"But there is gossip in Texas, my dear brother." Her lips tilted up. "Very interesting gossip. Involving you."

A stab of fear went through him. What did Esme know and how did she know it. "What?"

She laid down on her side, propping herself on an elbow. "Let us start with your little boy, Cal. He's darling. And he's a girl. Did you know?"

Luc leaned against the door jamb. He shouldn't have been surprised, but he was. Esme was hard to fool over the most difficult things, one small disguise wouldn't distract her.

"Luc, I can see you know, as well. You paid for the finest art teachers in Europe to teach me. I have studied the human body for fifteen years. Trust me, dear brother, I know a woman when I see one. Nothing sneaks by me for long. Although this new proclivity surprises me."

"What do you mean?" He never could keep a secret from her.

"Do you remember Francois Picard?"

He did. He and Esme had a brief affair many years ago. "The Belgian ambassador!"

"We had a raging affair once until I caught him."

His curiosity was aroused. "Caught him doing what?"

"One morning, I went for my early ride, but my horse threw a shoe and I returned home to find him dressed in my best ball gown. I have heard of such sexual deviations, but I had no idea that you like your women to dress as men."

He could quite catch his breath. His heart raced with sheer terror. Did she think he was ... "What are you talking about?"

"This garb that she wears, is it for your excitement?"

"Esme." Luc couldn't believe what he was hearing. Wherever did she get such odd notions?

She sat up. "Don't 'Esme' me. It's perfectly acceptable. Except for Francois. I kicked him out, he ruined a whole season's worth of clothes for me. Nothing fit me correctly after that. Not that I didn't enjoy replacing everything, but the man was not honest with me. If he had been, I would have arranged for his own wardrobe. My colors did not suit his fair complexion and blond hair."

He crossed his arms. "Esme, every conversation always seems to turn back to you."

She stood up and walked over to him. "Is there a more interesting topic?"

"I need some air." He tried to bolt through the door, but she stopped him.

"Don't force me to follow you forcing me to question you about your little camp follower. Sit here." She patted the mattress. "And tell me everything about her. She's beautiful. I think I want to paint her."

"I have not bedded her. I have no desire to bed her contrary to what you might believe. As far as she is concerned, she is just trying to earn money to help her family. This is a secret and it will go no further than you or I. If you will excuse me. Good night." He walked away. The only way to end a conversation with his sister was to simply leave and hope she didn't follow.

She may tease him, or taunt him, but he knew that any secret she possessed of his would go to the grave with her. If Esme loved you, she protected you with the fierceness of a she-wolf with her young.

He stood out on the veranda and smoked a cigar. The parade ground was empty. Horses milled in the corral. Someone played music in the barracks and the smell of cooking emanated from his neighbor's kitchen.

Down the row of officer's quarters, several of the officers' wives sat in rocking chairs and were probably gossiping. More than likely, the subject of their gossip was Esme. When Luc had told her there was no gossip in Texas, he'd neglected to tell her that an Army post was a hot bed of rumor. She'd find out soon enough. Esme had the ability to put even the most stand-offish woman on her side. Luc was never certain how she did it. For all her outrageous behavior, Esme had the ability to create friendships with the most unlikely people.

In the post headquarters lamps were lit, and Luc figured General Hammond and Major Adams were talking about the Comanche problems. The news that the General had laid in his lap, still left him shaken.

Across the parade ground, Old Silas closed the stable door and secured it. Then he limped toward the barracks.

Callie darted out of the shadows of the stable. She slid so quickly from shadow to shadow, Luc almost didn't see her. She crossed the parade ground toward the mess hall.

As she passed him, Luc stepped out of the darkness and grabbed her arm. "What did you tell my sister?"

CHAPTER NINE

Rafe sat cross-legged just outside the entrance of his tee-pee. He held his son on one knee. A few feet away sat his wife working on a new pair of moccasins for the boy. The boy seemed to grow out of his moccasins every day. At two years old, Proud Horse, was growing so fast Rafe always expected to come home and find a stranger in his place.

The War Chief, Night Feather, approached and gestured Rafe to accompany him. Rafe handed Proud Horse to his mother and followed the old chief across the compound to his teepee. In side, Rafe found all the elders.

Night Feather gestured for Rafe to sit. "You have done well, Black Fox. We have many fine horses and rifle."

Rafe simply nodded. But he could see that something was bothering the elders. "What is wrong?"

Night Feather half smiled. "Can you trust this blue coat who betrays his own people?"

"No, but I can trust his greed. He promises new maps with the new supply routes. And then we will be able to kill all the white men who disturb our way of living and be done with them for good."

Night Feather shook his head. "Do you fight for us, or do you fight for your own demons?"

Rafe was surprised. "Does it matter?" He glanced from face to face. Each man in the teepee represented the combined wisdom of the tribe. He could see that despite their wish to keep their way of life intact, the white man had wiped out so much of what the Comanche prized.

"You saved my first daughter from being spoiled by the white blue coats." Night Feather banged his fist on his knee. "Yes, it matters to me."

"And you let me live." Rafe's muscled tensed. "You gave me your daughter."

Night Feather nodded. "But you were a buffalo soldier. You counted coup many times on us, but now you are one with the Comanche. You brought us the ways of the blue coats. Because of you, we're still free. Many of the tribes to the north, east and west of us are gone. Is my daughter the only thing that ties you to our people?"

"Quannah Parker has white blood and no one questions his loyalty to the Comanche. Many have questioned my loyalty, but never you. Why now?"

Night Feather looked at each of the elders in the circle. "The elders have been talking about just leaving this land behind and going to Mexico."

Rafe was surprised. He'd never thought that Night Feather and the others would ever consider giving up and moving away. "Why?"

Night Feather glanced around again. Several of the men nodded. "Too many of our young men are dead. Mothers and wives still wail their grief. The tribe suffers. In Mexico we have a chance to survive."

Rafe thought about his own mother. Did she still cry for him? He didn't want his adopted family to go to Mexico, but he could understand their desire. But he also didn't want them coming into conflict with his own people. "Why should you give up your land? You were here first. My people, the Seminole, have been moved time after time. Our tribe, once large, is now small. The white man is the enemy. They take what they want and then they accuse us of greed in wanting to keep what we had. Eventually, the Americans are going to want Mexico and then we will fight all over again. We must stop it now."

Night Feather took a deep breath. The depths of his eyes showed sadness. He glanced around at the other. "Our adopted brother speaks in wisdom. He knows the ways of the white man and the blue coats. Do we stay, or do we move."

One of the old men spoke. "How do we continue the fight, when our bravest men are dead? If we leave this place, we can grow new warriors to take up the fight again."

"I am not going to run like a scared rabbit." Another of the old men said. "Why should we give up what is ours so easily? Black Fox is right. Eventually the white man will look to the South and they will come again. Where will we run to then? I know of no place beyond Mexico."

The other men glanced at each other, nodding.

"Black Fox," Night Feather said, "has shed blood for us. For the moment, I think we should stay and continue to fight as he wishes."

102

Another of the elders said, "What will happen when there is no one left to fight but old men, women and children. Will we surrender then?"

Night Feather shook his head. "I have no taste for surrender. I will fight until my blood spills on the ground. So will my sons and daughters." He patted Proud Horse's dark hair. "So will my grandchildren."

Rafe had left behind everything of who he was in Mexico. The Comanche were his family now. This was his way of life and until he was dead, he would fight too.

Luc dragged Callie away from the mess hall to a small grove of trees. The night air was fragrant and Callie had been so caught up in her thoughts of what she'd seen by the stream, she hadn't seen Luc until he'd grabbed her.

Callie shook her head. "Nothing. I didn't say anything."

Luc glared at her, hands on his hips. "My sister knows you're a woman. Do you know what kind of risk you're putting yourself into, not to say me?"

Callie was dumbfounded. They had spent all of five minutes in the same room. The Lieutenant's sister had looked at her with all-knowing green eyes as though she could see all the way inside to Callie's soul. But she hadn't thought she'd guessed Callie's secret. "I know the risk better than you." Callie risked her whole future.

"Stay away from my sister," Luc said roughly.

Her eyes narrowed. Just what the hell did he expect of her? "I was ordered to move her trunks. That's what I do. I follow orders."

Luc laughed and Callie was struck by how his hair glowed silver in the starlight.

"If you followed orders," he said, "you would have stayed in your village, and I wouldn't have this problem."

He was so close she could smell the bayberry on his skin. "I'm not the one kissing on you, staring at you, touching on you."

"I only kissed you once."

Callie tilted her head up to study him. Just the thought of kissing her again sent shivers down her spine. She couldn't forget what it was like to be touched by him. "Yeah, but I can tell you think about it a lot. And I don't like that you're thinking about me."

"I've been trying to leave you alone."

"I'm not going to be any man's fancy woman. Just because I work for you doesn't mean you can take advantage of me." Besides, he was a white officer and she was a Negro-Seminole, that meant they didn't mix. As much as she wanted to be in his thoughts what right did he have thinking about her? Nothing could ever come of it.

"This argument isn't getting us anywhere. Just stay away from my sister."

"I didn't go out of my way to make her talk to me." But she had touched the lacy underwear and for the first time regretted her masquerade. She wanted to be soft and feminine and have the men look at her like they looked at Miss Delacroix. Or at least have the Lieutenant look at her like she was a desirable woman. Even though it was wrong in every aspect. He was her commanding officer. He was handsome and refined and she was a desert brat with no education, not much good for anything but hunting and tracking. They came from such opposite worlds. They could never be together no matter what she might want. Yet she couldn't stop wondering what it would be like to be hungered for by him. The way she hungered for him.

"I know this isn't your fault." Luc ran a hand through his hair. "I have no one but myself to blame. I let you talk me into allowing the charade to continue and now I'm stuck with it. If I report you to the Major, he'll ask how I found out and then I'd have to reveal that I've known for weeks. And half the post will skin me alive. The Major, there's no telling how the Major will react to this piece of news. For all I know I could be digging ditches for the rest of my career, if I even have one left."

For the first time, Callie realized what an awkward position she'd put him into. Guilt washed over her. Her plan had been so simple. Why was it getting tangled? "I didn't think about the way you could be hurt by my actions."

He grabbed her shoulders. "Then start thinking." His voice was harsh. "I'm as much at fault. All I had to do was march straight to the Major and tell him about you, but I didn't. I listened to your pleas and kept your secret."

"Why didn't you say anything?"

"If there's one thing I understand, it's about secrets."

"What kind of secret would someone like you have?" Callie couldn't imagine anything bad in his past. Except maybe if it involved a woman. She could imagine a woman risking everything to be with him.

He leaned down, his lips brushing against her cheek. "It's a secret."

His breath was warm on her skin and she turned her mouth toward his and his lips touched hers. His arms slid around her and pulled her close. Callie closed her eyes. She couldn't resist him. She liked the feel

104

of his body next to hers. The way he smelled. His hands seemed so knowing on her body. She'd had boys fumbling at her before, but Luc knew what he was doing. His skillful touched begged for a response and she felt a spiraling heat shoot through her. A heat that set her body on fire.

Luc broke away and Callie staggered back. Her cheeks burned and she wanted nothing more than to pull him back, to have his arms encircling her.

"Get away from me." Luc turned and stalked off.

Callie stared after him. Tears started in her eyes and she fought them, rubbing her fists against her eyes. She wouldn't cry. She wouldn't give him such power over her.

Callie had no idea where her feet were taking her, but when she stepped up on the porch of the Lieutenant's quarters, she found his sister leaning against the rail smoking a cigarette. The light from the window framed her. Smoke curled about her hair.

Callie just stared at Esme, and broke into tears.

Esme slipped an arm around Callie and drew her inside the small house. "Come inside, you can't stand on the porch and cry, being a soldier and all." She led Callie into the bedroom and sat her down on the bed. Esme drew up a chair and sat in it, her green eyes searching Callie's.

"I'm sorry for blubbering."

"So tell me, little one" Esme said quietly, "what makes you cry?"

"He kissed me." Callie was uncomfortable in the Lieutenant's bedroom, though she had to admit, his sister had totally transformed it.

"Who?"

"The Lieutenant?"

"Do you mean my brother?"

Callie nodded.

Esme hooked a finger under her chin. "So what is wrong with that, little sister? Many women have enjoyed my brother's kisses."

"He's not supposed to kiss me. He's an officer. He's white." Remembering the softness of his lips brought fresh tears to her eyes. "And then he told me to get away from him."

She sighed. "Men are all alike. They want their little kisses and then they don't want to take responsibility for them. My brother is no different. I had hoped I'd done a better job with him, but obviously not."

Callie swiped a hand across her cheek. "But I'm not supposed to be a girl."

Esme patted her hand. "And you've done a good job with your masquerade. How do you feel about my brother?"

She handed Callie a hankie bordered with white lace and Callie wiped her eyes. "He's a real good officer. His men respect him. He treats them good. He fights good. And he has courage."

"How dry and boring all that sounds," Esme said. "I meant, what do you think about him as a man? Do you think he's handsome? Do you think he's charming? I'm not interested in how he sits on a horse, shoots his gun or commands his ever so loyal troops."

Callie stood up. "I don't think I like these questions and I don't think it's proper for me to say anything like that about your brother."

"You came to me, dear. And I'm dying to know, and I will ply you with my best French wine until you answer all my questions." Esme opened one of her trunks and removed a bottle. She rummaged through the trunk until she found a corkscrew and while Callie fought to regain control, Esme opened the bottle with a pop, found two wine glasses and poured them both a generous amount.

Callie sipped the wine. It had a sharp, fruity taste that puckered her lips and slid down her throat like liquid fire. She took a deep breath and stared at the glass. "I've never had wine before."

"Have you had enough to sufficiently loosen your tongue and your inhibitions, my dear?" Esme sat back in her chair and sipped her wine delicately, her long narrow fingers twined around the stem of the glass as though she were holding the most fragile object.

"I'm feeling kind of hot, but I was feeling that way before." Callie took another experimental sip. "I wish I could be more like you."

Esme chuckled. "Blazing a trail in a gown would be a trifle difficult."

"No, I mean, you're smart, beautiful, and refined. I can't even read."

"There are many people in this world who don't read."

"The Lieutenant does. He reads all the time." Callie pointed at the wall with his shelves of books. He read them over and over and Callie envied him the knowledge in those books.

"When you are with me, you may refer to my brother by his Christian name."

Callie was horrified. She'd never called a white person by their first name. Ever. "No, ma'am. I can't. He's my commanding officer."

Esme waved a hand. "The Army is too silly for women to be involved."

Callie laughed. Sometimes she thought the same thing. So many rules and regulations and ways of doing things. She didn't understand how things got done. Who cared if all the saddles were lined up by rank. First the Major's, then the Lieutenants and then the Sergeants, and finally the enlisted men. She was so junior in rank her saddle was always the last in line.

"So you want to read." Esme reached for book on the bedside table. "I can teach you. You're very smart and will learn in no time at all."

For a second, Callie was shocked. She glanced against at the books lining the shelf.

"I don't know. I can't afford to pay you." Life in her village had been difficult enough without her taking the time to learn things like reading. She had to save all her money and send it home to her mother.

Esme tilted her head to study Callie's face. She pursed her lips. "If you let me paint you, I will consider that payment enough."

"Paint me!"

"I'm an artiste. I am one of the most important up and coming painters in all of Europe, I will have you know. My portraits are in the Louvre." She winked. "And in the bedrooms of some of the most influential people in government."

Callie had no idea what the Louvre was, or why someone would put a painting in a bedroom. But if Esme were willing to teach her to read, Callie would do it if all it cost was to get her picture painted. Until the offer had been made, she had no idea how much she thirsted for knowledge. If she could read, she would be able to take care of the land she would be getting after leaving the Army. That way no one would be able to trick her. And then she could teach other people in the tribe to read. Maybe she could open a school. Suddenly, the idea of reading truly excited her.

"Why are you being so nice to me?" Callie hated to be suspicious but everything came at a price and she wanted to make sure she was willing to pay before she made a deal. "You don't know me."

Esme smiled. "You're forging ahead in a man's world and making your own destiny. That is what I think I admire about you. You're not afraid."

"How did you know I wasn't a boy?"

Esme put finger under Callie's chin and tilted her face toward the light. "I caught the way my brother looked at you. I know my brother better than anyone else in the world and he has no attraction for boys no matter how lonely he may be. And when I caught you in here holding my underwear, I saw something in your face that no boy would ever have. I put two and two together and came up with four. Though I have to say, your disguise is excellent to the untrained eye."

"Are you saying I'm not pretty like a girl."

"Mais non," Esme said with a grin, "you have beautiful skin and your eyes flash." She took Callie's hands in her own. "Your hands are rough from work, but no man could have hands so beautiful and delicate. If you were in Paris, you would be one of the most sought after companions by wealthy men. They would kill to spoil you and keep you in silk and perfume just for one of your smiles.

Callie didn't know how to accept her words. "Aren't they all white in France?"

"In all Europe, a beautiful woman is a beautiful woman no matter the color of her skin."

"Does your brother feel that way?"

"My brother has had many mistresses. One was even the illegitimate daughter of an Indian Rajah. Another woman, feted, as the most beautiful woman in all Europe, was from Brazil and she was much like you in coloring. Her mother was Indian and black and her father was Portuguese. And there have been the odd blondes, redheads, and brunettes."

"Is the Lieutenant very experienced?" Callie could never measure up to his idea of a woman.

"Since he was thirteen, women have fallen all over him. But he has always been very particular." Esme gave Callie a sly look. "I'm not surprised he is attempting to make a conquest out of you."

Callie blushed. Her entire body warmed at the thought of being the Lieutenant's woman. She was torn between envy of the Lieutenant's many women in the past and her desire for him now. She would never have the experience to satisfy him. And she felt sad that his interest in her was so casual. She suspected that if a more suitable woman arrived, his interest in her would evaporate like rain on the desert. She didn't know if that would be a good thing, or a bad thing.

Luc sat on a bench outside Liberty's stall. The horses were restless. They moved back and forth in their stalls the same way his emotions moved back and forth in his head. How could he be attracted to Callie? She was nothing like the women he was used to, yet something about her called to him. She had a vulnerability in her eyes that brought out his need to protect her. But he knew she didn't need his protection. She was one of the best soldiers he'd ever commanded. She was fearless, courageous and he suspected that if he tried gentleness with her, she'd run away.

How could he manage to stay away from her during the duration of her enlistment? Every instinct demanded he do everything he could to help her satisfy her ambitions. He admired her stead-fast approach to obtaining what she wanted. What she wanted wasn't about greed or power, but family and her duty to her tribe. With the exception of Esme, he had forgotten the power of family. His life had been about what he wanted, what he desired. If he wanted a woman, he did what was necessary to get her. If he wanted to win a battle, he did what was necessary to win.

Callie disturbed him in a way no other woman had ever done. She touched some place inside of him, he didn't know existed. He was torn between allowing her to be herself and folding her in cotton and keeping her safe.

Liberty nudged at his shoulder and he absently rubbed the horse's smooth nose. The action was soothing.

When was the last time he'd done something selfless. He hadn't reported Callie because he thought he was attempting to save his career that was built on a lie anyway. He wanted her to succeed and obtain her dream. He wanted her to be happy. And his honor demanded that he help her. His help was against regulations, but he would do so anyway. In his heart, he knew a rightness in his decision, and didn't that supercede any of the Army's regulations?

He felt caught in a moral dilemma that had no solution, except to let it play out in it's entirety.

"You acting like you have the world on your shoulders, Mr. Luc."

He was surprised to see the old man up and about. "Silas, what are you doing up this late?"

Silas shuffled into a patch of moonlight streaming through a window. "When a body is old, it doesn't need much sleep. My horses is fussing and I came out to talk to them, hoping they'll settle."

"I think I'm the one disturbing them. They sense my uneasiness."

"You and the boys going out tomorrow hunting for those Comanche who been attacking our supply trains?"

"No." He shook his head. "For the moment, I have to entertain the General."

"And your sister. She's got the whole fort a-buzzing. She sure is a pretty one."

"She's a hand full, at best." Luc loved Esme, but she turned the whole world upside down and remade it to suit her purposes. He didn't know if the United States Army was ready for that.

"Well, maybe you'll find her a husband out here. A couple of those young officers wouldn't mind finding themselves a rich, young wife."

Luc laughed. "And Esme would eat them alive. After five minutes in her company they would rather face the Comanche with nothing to defend themselves but their good intentions."

Silas settled himself on a bench opposite Luc. "Well she sure had young Cal wrapped around her finger. I was passing your quarters and I heard the two of them giggling like a couple of young girls."

Luc jumped to his feet. He had to rescue Callie. No telling what Esme would do. "Silas, I'm going to leave you to the horses and see what I can do to rescue Cal."

"I don't think the young 'un needed rescuing. He's a good boy and if Miss Esme is anything like you, she won't hurt him on purpose."

Luc wasn't too sure about that. He already felt out maneuvered. The last thing he needed was for Esme to team with Callie to make his life even more miserable than it was at this moment.

CHAPTER TEN

The officer's mess hall had been transformed to accommodate the General's banquet. Streamers hung from the ceiling and the good linen and company china and silver had been pulled out of storage. A small band, made up of the company's enlisted personnel, sat in a corner providing the music.

The officers wore their dress uniforms and the women wore ball gowns in a rainbow of colors with their hair pulled into intricate styles and aflutter with ribbons and lace.

The cooks had outdone themselves with an array of dishes to tempt even the most jaded palettes including a selection of Mexican delicacies. The meal was a feast to behold and Luc was stuffed as willing to taste everything as all the others present.

The General, at the head of the table, beamed at Esme who sat on his right. Esme sparkled in a black lace gown with her hair swept up into a ring of curls and diamonds encircling her neck. She looked every inch the sophisticated example of Paris fashion, and Luc could see the muted envy in the eyes of the officers' wives as they studied the lines of Esme's gown. The Major sat at the foot of the table with his wife on his right. All the other officers sat in between their position depending on rank and length of service.

Behind the general, Luc could see the curious faces of the post children as they stared in the mess hall windows at the festivities with Callie in the background her eyes as big with wonder as any child's.

The conversation flowed around Luc. The topics included the Comanches, the price of beef, Indian policy and the President's ever-present conflict with Congress. Reggie sat across from Esme and down a couple seats. Luc noticed Reggie hadn't taken his eyes off of his sister. Luc had seen that predatory gleam in Reggie's eyes, he recognized a man on a hunt and Esme was the prey. A small smile spread across Luc's face. Esme was no mouse, and Reggie was in for the shock of his life if he thought she was going to simper and flirt with him like some Boston Belle hoping for a man of breeding and money. Esme would chose her own man, and he wouldn't be a poor second Lieutenant.

The General stood and the conversation fell off as people realized he wanted to speak. The General smiled at everyone and the Major's wife dimpled.

"Ladies and gentlemen, I have a announcement." He pulled a small box from his pocket. "I hate all things formal, so I'm just going to say what I need to say. A man's speech should be like a battle – short, sweet and to the point. Lieutenant Lucien Francois Delacroix, it is my great pleasure to announce that you have been promoted to Captain." He handed the box to Esme. "If you would be so kind, my dear."

Luc stumbled to his feet. Captain! He was a Captain!

Esme grinned and stood. She worked her way around the table to Luc and kissed him on each cheek before handing him the box. He opened it and found his brand new Captain's bars residing on a pillow of velvet.

"Luc, I'm so proud of you." She removed his Lieutenant's bar and inserted the Captain's gold bars on his shoulders.

Out of the corner of his eye, he saw Callie her face pressed against the window, a look of pridein her eyes.

The Major stood and raised his wine glass. "A toast to Captain Delacroix, the finest officer I've ever had in my command."

Everyone stood, their wine glasses raised. "Here. Here," they chorused.

Luc almost flushed with pride and pleasure he didn't know what to say.

"Captain," the General said after the toasts were completed, "I have known you for many years, and I must say that no officer I have known more deserves to be recognized. Captain, you are to be congratulated."

"Thank you, sir." Luc replied.

"Business is over." The General clapped. "I think we should get to the dancing." He held an arm out to the Major's wife. "Madame, if you would, please." He led her out onto the dance floor to open the dancing.

The band burst into music. Reggie almost pushed Luc out of the way to get Esme.

Esme nodded at him. "Reggie, mon cherie."

"May I have this dance?" He held out his arm.

Esme gave him a brilliant smile. "I would love to dance with you, but I do think my brother should be my first partner for the night. It's only proper."

Reggie's face went dark as he glanced at Luc, his eyes flicking over Luc's new bars. He bowed at Esme and backed away. "Another time, then."

"Of course." Esme tucked her gloved hand around Luc's elbow and tugged him onto the dance floor. "You know chivalry demands that you save me from that worm, little brother."

"You don't like Reggie." Luc was surprised.

She nodded smiling. "I think he begrudges you your good fortune."

Luc slipped his arm around Esme and twirled her in step with the music. "You don't understand. There has always been a friendly rivalry between the officers."

Esme tilted her head. "He looks at me as though I'm a morsel on a plate, and his for the taking should he lift a finger."

Luc chuckled. "Esme, has there been a man born who doesn't want you? You are simply used to men who play games, who understand the rules of seduction like you do. Reggie doesn't understand. He comes from a much different social background."

"He's poor."

"Most officers are poor. That is why they marry rich wives."

Esme laughed. "Brother, I would never tolerate a man who was more concerned with my finances than ... the other treasures I have to offer."

"Esme," Luc said, "I believe it to be improper to speak to your brother of such things. Let me have my illusions that you are as fresh as morning dew."

Esme shook her head. "You've been away from Paris far too long. As a matter of fact, you have your own little morsel and you haven't taken a bite yet."

His spine stiffen. He hoped no one was paying attention to their conversation. "Esme, not here."

Her eyebrows arched. "Why not here? When did you become so moral?"

"Morality has nothing to do with my feelings. Perhaps I'm thinking of my 'morsel's' well being."

After an exaggerated pout, she sighed. "It would be inconvenient, wouldn't it? I will have to think on that to make this work?"

Luc needed to change the subject. He didn't want to talk about Callie or his desire to bed her. "Aren't you leaving for California?"

"That is my ultimate destination. For the time being, I've decided to stay. The scenery around here fascinates me. I think I would like to do a series of paintings."

"This is a dangerous place. Your charm is not going to stop a Comanche arrow."

She smiled again. "You underestimate my ability to take care of myself."

"Fort Duncan is not Paris."

"And Paris is not Fort Duncan," she retorted. "This place is very raw, visceral, filled with such forcefulness. I think that is what my painting has been lacking lately. I need a challenge. I've painted flowers, and vases of flowers, and gardens of flowers. I'm tired of flowers."

"What about all the portraits?"

She tossed her head. "I'm tired of milk-faced aristocracy. They all want to look the same. I want faces with characters, with scars and wrinkles, with life in them. I want to paint Callie."

Luc jerked back. "What?"

"I want to paint Callie. She has character and fire. She's beautiful in an tempestuous and uninhibited way."

Luc stared at her. "I have never heard the words beautiful and tempestuous in the same sentence before."

The music ended and they walked to the edge of the dance floor. Esme flicked open her lace fan and cooled her face. "My dear brother, you are not an artist." She whirled away from him and stood for a moment. All the junior officers made a mad dash for her, but the General parted the waves and claimed her for himself.

Reggie touched Luc's arm. "Congratulations, Captain." Though the look in his eyes told Luc that he was jealous.

"Thank you." Luc watched as the General whirled his sister around the floor to the strains of a stately waltz.

Reggie gestured at Esme. "Do you think I'll ever get a chance?"

"No. Save yourself now while you still have a chance." Luc left the mess room turned ballroom for the cool air of the veranda.

Callie couldn't take her eyes off the women. Their gowns were like pretty flowers; yellows and pinks and blues. The folds of the fabrics sparkled like stars. But no one looked more beautiful than Esme in her black silk that flowed about her like the night sky. No one looked more handsome than her new Captain in his dress uniform with all the gold buttons shining in the lamplight. His broad shoulders filled out his uniform. He looked so tall and proud with his boots spit-polished to a high shine and his gold insignias glowing.

A huge lump in her throat wouldn't go away. Her palms sweated when she remembered how he'd kissed her and how strong his hands had been on her arms. The image of him bathing in the pond returned and she remembered the muscled look of his naked body and the way he appeared in the moonlight.

Her breasts swelled painfully beneath the cotton bindings and her nipples felt on fire. If he kissed her now, she'd willingly surrender. Even though he wasn't for her. She cursed herself for lusting after a white officer. How could she let herself become so entangled in her feelings for him?

He was the last man on earth she needed to be in love with. She couldn't even think about being with a man until her family was settled on their own land. And here she was mooning after her commanding officer.

She knew she didn't mean anything to him. When the time came for her Captain to chose a wife, he'd chose from the types of women who were like his sister – sophisticated and beautiful – and not some uneducated half-breed like herself who was better at being a boy than she would ever be at being a woman.

She turned away from the window. Tears welled up in her eyes and she brushed them away impatiently. She left the group of wide-eyed children and stepped down onto the gravel. Footsteps sounded on the wooden planks of the veranda and a flame flashed. In the flare, Callie saw Luc as he lit his cigarette.

The smoke of his cigarette was a fragrant cloud about his head. Callie stood in the shadows and watched him. He leaned against a post of the porch railing, the smoke billowing around his head.

Was he happy with his new promotion? Callie was mystified by the ranks in the army and had no idea if being a Captain made Luc a more important person. She wanted to congratulate him, throw her arms around his neck and tell him how proud she was of him. She wanted to kiss him. She started toward him and he glanced up from his contemplation and saw her.

"Cal," he said.

"Congratulations, Captain." She hated when he called her Cal. She wanted him to call her by her real name. She wished she could be a woman for him.

He flicked his cigarette away from him and stepped down on the ground. He grabbed her by the elbow and pulled her away from the banquet hall for a secluded spot under the oaks near the corral.

Under the spreading branches of the oak, Callie found herself sitting on a low branch watching him. He paced back and forth, the moonlight shining on his hair, reflecting from his eyes.

He paused and studied her. "I wanted to say good-bye."

Her heart sank. "Where are you going?" She willed herself not to cry.

"I'm leaving for New Orleans in a few days."

Callie's throat went dry and her voice cracked. "Are you coming back?"

"Yes, I should only be gone for six weeks."

Relieved, the tightness in her chest eased. He would return. "What about the Comanche?"

"That problem isn't going away. They'll be here when I return."

"Will Lieutenant Cooper lead the unit?" She shuddered. Cooper didn't like her.

"Are you telling me if I leave for six weeks, I'll return and find everyone gone?"

"Lieutenant Cooper isn't like you. He doesn't like ...." Her voice trailed away.

"We can be honest with each other." Luc stopped pacing and smiled at her.

"He's not fair like you are. He doesn't like the colored soldiers."

Luc shrugged. "He'll be fine. Lieutenant Cooper may be difficult, but he's fair, too." He touched her cheek running his fingers down the line of her chin. "Just stay out of his way."

"How can I stay out of his way? If he's in charge while you're gone, he's my commander."

"Other than routine patrols along the river, I doubt that you'll see any action that will put you in danger. Lieutenant Cooper isn't a man who craves excitement like me."

His fingers on her cheek were like fire trailing along her skin. She leaned into his touch. "I don't think you should do this, sir."

"Do what?"

"Touch me." She nearly choked on the words.

"I think of touching you all the time. At night when I'm alone, I dream about it. The way you smell, the way you look at me. You're making me insane."

She knew she should run, but her feet couldn't seem to move. "Lieutenant."

"Captain," he corrected her.

"You can't talk like this. I'm a lowly scout and you're an important officer."

116

He laughed. "You're wrong. I'm as much of a pawn of the Army as you are."

She stood facing him. He was so close the heat of his body scorched her skin. "You can't be dreamin' about me. I won't let you." She started to walk away, but he stopped her and she faced him again knowing if she didn't leave now, she would never leave him.

"Won't let me!"

"Captain, you are ...."

He stopped her next words with a kiss that cut off her breath and sent her blood flaming through her veins like hot liquid fire. She almost stopped breathing. His lips were soft and demanding. She didn't want to respond, but found herself kissing him back with the same intensity.

She should stop this, but couldn't. The kiss went on and on until her knees grew weak and her skin tingled. Her breasts swelled and her clothes felt tight. She wanted to rip off her shirt so he could touch her more intimately.

"I'll miss you," he whispered against her hair, his breath fanning across her ear and cheek.

She braced her hands against his chest and pushed with all her strength. Her breath came in struggling gasps. "No." She didn't know what else to do except run away.

Luc watched her run toward the stable. He fought not to run after her. He sat down on the branch Callie had sat on earlier. The bark was still warm from her body.

He didn't understand why he was so attracted to a shy young woman who had no sophistication and whose whole world was wrapped around her need to provide for her family. The women in his past had been sophisticated, charming and as sexually adventurous as him.

The women he'd frequented knew he wasn't interested in marriage, and family, but only in sexual fulfillment. They understood the rules of the game. Callie was an innocent and he wanted her more than any woman he'd ever wanted in the past. They were as different as night and day. So what about her intrigued him so? What was it about her that made her worm her way into his brain?

She could live in a soldier's world as an equal. She understood the demands of the life and could fight at his side without thinking about her role as a woman. She didn't faint at the sight of blood, and was just as likely to pick up a gun and use it as he was.

He liked the solitude and figured that Callie did, too. She was a woman who could take of herself. So why was he attracted to her? She wasn't the most beautiful woman he'd ever known, yet she was beautiful with her soft curly black hair and chestnut brown eyes. Callie was a true innocent. She had no idea of the allure she could have if she weren't pretending to be a soldier.

Major Adams' oldest daughter Gloria was a pretty enough woman with her red hair and comely figure. She understood his life as a soldier. She would have made him a fine wife and Major Adams would have been thrilled, but frankly she bored Luc to tears. Even though she was well-suited for his lifestyle, deep in his heart, he knew he couldn't marry a white woman born in the United States. In Europe his black blood didn't matter. In Europe, he would have been considered exotic and desirable. French and Italian women loved the exotic. But those women wouldn't have understood his life as a soldier.

So why Callie? She was as far removed from the women he knew as France was from China. Yet he couldn't still his burning attraction for her. He fought it, he bargained with himself, yet his thoughts were consumed with her. Maybe this six weeks away from her would be a good thing. Maybe then he could control the fire in his belly and return to his normal life.

Reggie approached. "Well, Captain Delacroix, I didn't get a chance to congratulate you."

Luc could tell that Reggie's words came stiffly. "Thanks, Reggie." Reggie was jealous and Luc didn't blame him. Reggie had been in the army as long and performed with the same dedication, but Luc had managed to move ahead while Reggie was still mired in being a second lieutenant. Reggie didn't deal well with people because he looked down his nose at everybody. Luc doubted he'd go much beyond full lieutenant. He might even make Captain, but he'd be a long time making the grade.

"I hear you're off to New Orleans for a few weeks." Reggie leaned against the trunk of the tree and looked toward the distant Rio Grande, moonlight glistening off the water.

"Some personal business."

"You're taking your sister with you?"

"Esme has decided she needs to paint Texas and has decided to stay. She wants to try her hand at being a school marm."

Reggie's eyebrows rose. "I beg your pardon."

"She's going to open a school for some of our recruits. She thinks everyone needs to read."

"Darkies don't need to read. If they can even learn."

"Reggie, remember when you're on patrol that those darkies stand between you and a Comanche bullet. Perhaps, you shouldn't be so vocal about your bigotry."

Reggie glanced at him. "Why do you care so much about them? You weren't even raised in the South, but in Europe."

Luc frowned. Why did he care? He'd never lived his life as a black man. Only a handful of people knew that his mother had black blood. Even in her, the black blood was so muted, that if she hadn't been required by law to wear a turban, no man would have known her background much less cared.

"Europe is different, Reggie. I man is judged by who he is, not what he is. Character, not color, is more important."

Reggie started to laugh. "Are you telling me you've met black men in Europe who acted as equal to you or I."

"Some of the most prominent scholars in Europe have black blood. And you would be amazed at what they've accomplished when they don't have to deal with bigotry."

Reggie waved his hand and snorted. "Captain, I'll believe that when I see it. Now if you'll excuse me, some of us have to work for a living and I have an early morning patrol. Major Adams says he's received another complain about missing cattle from one of the ranchers. I have to make us look like we care." He headed toward his quarters.

That in and of itself was Reggie's main problem. He simply didn't care. Maybe Luc's problem was that he cared too much. Caring too much lead him to living a lie. A lie that he'd perpetrated for so long, he'd forgotten. When was the last time he'd thought about being a black man. According to the law in the United States, but one drop of black blood made you black. He didn't feel black, didn't look black and didn't have to live black, and yet one law condemned him to second class citizenship forever.

He glanced at the stable. What would Callie say if she knew the truth about him? Would she embrace him, or castigate him for hiding who he was? Would she understand?

CHAPTER ELEVEN

Esme watched as Luc and Callie ride off together side by side. Callie took the lead and little puffs of dust rose from her horse's hooves and drifted off with the wind. Luc turned and raised his hand and Esme waved back. She was sorry to see him go, but he had to make his peace with their father. Esme had twisted General Hammond around her little finger until he had agreed to allow Luc a furlough. When Esme wanted to, she could bend any man to her will.

Insuring that Callie was ordered to accompany Luc had taken a mountain of manipulation on her part, and she was tickled at her success. Once they were together then nature would take its course. Then they would realize they loved each other. Incurable romantic that she claimed herself to be Esme thought her time at Fort Duncan would be deary and boring. Oh how she hated being wrong.

She stood on the porch twirling her yellow parasol, the wind rustling the matching silk of her gown. Ivory gloves encased her hand and she wore a broad-brimmed hat with a veil to shield her face from the burning sun. Despite a generous lathering of glycerine and lilac lotion, her skin felt tight. She wanted a bath with the water treated with the special oils she'd had created for her in Paris. Maybe then her skin would feel less dry. Frenchwomen were prized for their beautiful, luminous skin, and Esme had made a study of the women she knew and distilled from them their beauty secrets and then had her own lotions made to her exact specifications. She prided herself on her flawless skin. She might be thirty-two, but she knew she looked barely twenty-one.

As the riders left the Fort, Esme shaded her eyes with her hand.

General Hammond joined her on the porch "My dear, you have the most sly smirk on your face."

She gave him a coquettish look over her shoulder. "Monty, my sweet general, whatever do you mean?"

"I think you are plotting something. Does your brother have a sweetheart in New Orleans that you want him to marry? Was this trip was just an excuse to get him there. Not that I mind, he's one of my best officers and he needs a good wife if he is to rise further in the ranks."

"Perhaps he will find love in New Orleans, but our father is more important." She slid her arm around his. "But let us talk of more pleasant things." On the overland trip from Corpus Christi, she had almost told the general the truth about her and Luc, but didn't. Luc had built a life he wanted in the army and Esme would do nothing to harm him, and everything to aid him. If the General thought he needed a wive, that maybe it was time she put her mind to that, as well.

The General's weathered face looked hurt. "I would have been willing to speak to your father."

She patted him on the arm. She liked this man and would have taken him as a lover in a minute if not for the fact he was Luc's superior. "How sweet of you? You are so gallant, but this is something Lucien must do alone."

The General took a cigar from his pocket and glanced inquiringly at Esme. She gave her permission for him to smoke. "I'm surprised, you didn't try to do something yourself. You're very determined."

She grinned at him. "I'm just a poor woman, weak and defenseless, subject to the winds of fate." How she hated woman like that. Early in her life she had determined to be strong and powerful for herself and to let no man use her. She would use them and she had learned how blind men could be when they thought they were getting what they wanted from her when the reverse was true.

He laughed. "Pardon me for being so forward, but there is nothing defenseless about you."

The General was such a good-looking man. But he saw through her a little too easily. She had to try harder to keep him dazzled and unaware of her true motives. She put a finger to her lips. "Sh! You must guard that secret with your life."

He laughed as he lit the cigar and puffed on it for a few seconds. "Marry me."

For a second, she was startled at his boldness, although not surprised by his question. "You are much too young for me."

Fragrant smoke enveloped him. He puffed for several more seconds and then stared at the end of the cigar. "I need a wife who is astute and savvy. With you at my side, I could go as far as I want, maybe even be President."

His ambition was showing. He wanted to retire because he'd seen a future for himself in politics. Esme burst out laughing. "I would not be the type of First Lady who would be embraced by American society."

"Who could not adore you."

"I am very scandalous."

He studied her with a serious expression on his face but a glint in his eyes. "I know. That's why I want you."

She tapped him gently on the arm. "Monty, trust me. I would eat you alive. If you are searching for a wife, I will find one for you." How she loved match-making. She thought for a moment. "You seem to be very enamored of French women. I have a friend, Maud Lafayette-Deavers who resides in Baltimore. She is a widow, and also rich, titled and very passionate about soldiers. She has a great sense of adventure and is more than your match. When you return to Washington you will contact her. She is young and beautiful and from what I understand, quite skilled in many things."

"Skilled at what?"

She smiled. "The womanly arts, my dear. Trust me, you will adore her and forget me in a second." She snapped her fingers. "I will write you a letter of introduction today. When you return to Washington, you will post to Baltimore immediately and make an appointment to meet her. And when you have swept her off her feet and she is ready to surrender, you will send me a note of thanks and then invite me to the wedding."

He kissed her hand. "You are a scheming, manipulative, shrewd, and much too intelligent woman." His tone was admiring. "I would be forever in your debt." He winked at her. "But a man must think of his legacy."

"She will give you the most beautiful intelligent children. Trust me."

His frowned slightly. "So what do I owe you for this favor?"

Ah! A man who understood the technique of give and take. She thought about what she wanted, of how Callie thirsted for an education. "I would like a room in order to hold classes for your soldiers."

He frowned. "Classes. What type of classes?"

"Reading, writing, arithmetic. Your soldiers would be much better soldiers if they had some skills. And what better way to sniff out information about your ... little problem with confidential information. Trust me, your soldiers are not stupid. They know something is going on, they just don't know they know it. And as you already know, men want to tell me everything." She knew he hadn't intended to tell her about the spy at the Fort, but the information had leaked out. "I will find out who is your spy and relay the information to Luc to send on

122

to you. Don't you think that an adequate compensation for finding you the perfect wife?"

"I don't know." He shook his head. "I don't want to put you at risk."

"It would be an honor to serve you." She ran her hand gently up his arm and tilted her head at him with unspoken promise. "I won't take any chances. And I shall be a model of discretion."

"But a school!"

She pouted at him, twirling her parasol. "Monty." She touched his cheek with the tip of her gloved finger. "I'm asking such a little thing in exchange for your legacy, for the woman who will keep your bed warm on cold Washington nights and give you little children who will carry your name and your legacy into the future."

He looked grave as though he still wasn't convinced. "I'll talk to Major Adams."

"Make it happen for me, darling." She turned and cast a look back over her shoulder. "If you'll excuse me, darling, I'm going to ... bathe." Let him think about her naked, water sluicing down her bare skin, touching places he would only dream about.

She walked toward Luc's quarters. Using her parasol to shade her eyes, she glanced back and saw the General rushing toward Major Adam's office.

Men, she thought. She might not be able to lead a horse to water and make it drink, but men were an easy task. One had to wonder who was the stupid beast.

She walked toward Luc's quarters, her mind working at a furious pace. She owed a favor to Monty, though he didn't know it. He'd made it possible for Luc to go to New Orleans even though Monty could ill spare him considering the problem of the traitor. So Esme would start the groundwork and she would do her best to find the spy and hand him over to Luc.

She shivered with delight. She loved intrigue. She would make a good spy herself. Not that she would admit such a thing to Monty.

The spy could be anyone. As she passed the Post Store, several soldiers lounged on the steps, one eating from a can of beans. One of the men smiled politely at her. She studied them. Was the spy of these men? If not, then who?

Her whole body tingled. She was going to be useful to Luc. And if she were successful, Luc would be a General within ten years and she would be able to say she had helped him up the ranks and he owed his success to this moment. She loved having her brother in her debt.

A day from Corpus Christi, Luc sat near their tiny cooking fire, staring into the cool night air. A heavy sprinkling of stars lit the night sky and as he watched a shooting star raced across it. The small fire crackled merrily, a counterpoint to his sour mood. Behind him, the horses stamped restlessly on their picket line as though in agreement with his mood.

A week in Callie's company had left him with his nerves jangled and his blood hot. They had hardly spoken to each other. Each day, Callie would disappear and return with a rabbit, or a quail for dinner. Once she found some wild onions and cooked them with their rabbit. She was the most resourceful woman he'd ever known and he envied her. She knew who she was while he struggled to understand who he was.

In the distance he could hear the sound of running water. Callie had gone to bathe. Luc imagined her in the water with her skin bare to the stars and slick with wetness. He wanted to splash in the water with her and make her laugh. He wanted to caress her beautiful body and make love to her on the shore; to show her what her body was capable of and hear her groan with passion. He felt on a collision course with her.

The minute they'd left the Fort, she'd told him in no uncertain terms to leave her alone or she'd gut him. That threat stilled his hand when he wanted to touch her, kept him staring straight ahead when he wanted to look at her. The quiet threat in her voice had sent shivers down his spine. He'd never before known a woman who was as dangerous as Callie. Unlike other women who would attempt to intimidate with words, Callie had the means to make good on her threats. Luc never doubted she would do exactly as promised.

Each moment in her company was agony. He felt like a boy in the throes of his first infatuation. Esme was going to pay for this. Luc had expected to leave Callie behind and somehow, the next he knew, Esme was announcing that the General had approved an order to allow Callie would accompany him on the journey.

Esme was a calculating, conniving, duplicitous woman. If she had been anywhere near him, Luc would have told her. He knew what his darling sister was attempting to do. She wanted him to have a love affair with Callie, no matter what the risk would be for the both of them.

While her motives, whatever they were, were admirable. Only her means were suspect. Esme moved people around like pieces on a chess board, sometimes for no other reason than a whim. He was surprised General Hammond fell for such an obvious ploy. The General had the ability to see right through a man's excuses, yet was totally blinded by a beautiful woman. A woman who was his sister.

He shifted and pushed to his feet. Callie was taking too long. He squinted into the dark. For all he knew she could have been attacked by rogue Indians or dragged off by wild coyotes. Maybe, he would just take a little peek to make certain she was unharmed, and then he would return to camp and attempt to sleep. Even though sleep came harder and harder each night.

Just a little peek.

He eased through the underbrush. A small deer, startled by his passage, bolted. He was making more noise than a herd of circus elephants. The sound of running water came closer and he topped a small rise to stare down at the river.

He felt a sharp blow to his belly and he fell to the ground staring up at the stars. Callie straddled him, a knife to his throat. He stared up at her shocked that she would attack him. He started to tell her that she was guilty of striking an officer and that was a court martial offence, but the words never formed on his lips.

"I told you, if you spied on me, I'd gut you." The knife pressed tight against his skin. He felt the point jab into his skin and small trickle of hot blood oozed down his skin. He could smell his blood in his nostrils.

He gulped. "You were gone too long."

She pressed harder against him. "A bath takes as long as it takes."

She smelled wondrously of bayberry and wild flowers. Her skin shone moistly in the starlight. Her hair had curled up into a riot of black tendrils framing her slender face. She reminded him of a water sprite. A very dangerous water sprite.

"I don't know what kind of game you're playing," she said, "but you need to leave me alone. I have more important things to do than be your fancy woman."

"Callie, I was just worried. I'm your commanding officer and I'm responsible for your safety."

"I can take care of myself." She shifted back and returned the knife to its sheath. "You have to leave me alone. Stop looking at me. Stop undressing me in your thoughts. Don't you understand black and white don't mix ... ever."

Her words sent a thrust of pain through him so intense he gasped. If only she knew how close they were. "Callie, you don't know anything." He had almost decided to tell her when she shook her head.

"I know plenty." She slid to the side and stood up, staring down at him. "You let me let me." And she was gone, disappearing into the dark as though she were a part of it.

Luc sat up and rubbed his throat trying to gather the threads of his dignity. He stood and scanned the ghostly landscape. She was nowhere to be seen. He wouldn't be surprised if she left him. He was behaving less than honorably. But he couldn't seem to stop himself from making this situation intolerable for her.

During their long ride, he'd watched her, the way she swayed in the saddle, the way her legs dangled on either side of the horse. The way her hands gripped the reins.

They'd barely said a hundred words to each other, and despite her threat, he couldn't stop watching her. He wondered what she would look like in the finest silk with her hair fluffed and ribbons flowing from the curls. He envisioned her in a gown of ivory silk to set off her tawny skin. If she would let him, he would purchase the finest rubies money could buy. The thought of the blood red jewels against her swelling bosom sent a shock of desire through him so strong he almost groaned.

He knew she wanted him despite her hostility. He was a man of the world. He understood a woman's needs and despite her masquerade, Callie was a highly desirable woman. She was the type of woman who could inspired a man's destiny as well as inflame his heart.

Oh my God! Where the hell did that thought come from? He didn't have a destiny. Hell, he didn't want a destiny.

He thought he knew what he wanted from life, but Callie had upset the balance. She made everything that he wanted seem trivial. She had made him examine his own motives and what he saw didn't make him feel as though he'd made the right decision all those years ago.

He'd made a promise to himself that he would help her get her land and make her tribe self-sufficient. Seducing her was not helping. He had to get back on track and start thinking like a soldier. Stop thinking about her.

He made his way back to the fire. Callie had taken her blankets and bedded down as far from him as she could without being in another country. He threw dirt over the fire and then poured the leftover coffee on the ashes. He rolled up in his blanket and closed his eyes.

Sleep wouldn't come. The memory of his father putting him and Esme on the ship bound for France returned to him. What was he going to do about his father? Esme had painted their father's plight as desperate, his health precarious. Luc couldn't let the man who had given him life die without seeing him one last time. They were adults now, they should be able to speak to each other like civilized people.

He tossed and turned restlessly all night. Soon he and Callie would take a ship across the Gulf to New Orleans and then he would be faced with more problems than just Callie.

———⟨∅∅∅⟩———

Callie was amazed. From the moment the paddle wheeler had docked, she couldn't take her eyes from the women in their fancy dresses and the men in their elegant suits. As she watched them stroll down the banquette, she felt a thirst to be one of them. Callie wanted to be a lady.

She sat back in the carriage and stared at the Cathedral and the fancy buildings around the park that the Captain had called Jackson Square. Corpus Christi had been a rough border town compared to New Orleans. Callie had been enthralled by Corpus Christi. She was enchanted by New Orleans. New Orleans was exotic and different with a sophistication in the architecture the people Corpus Christi would never have. That Callie would never have.

Carriages drove down the street, the harnesses of the horses jingling with bells. New Orleans was crowded and smelled of sewage. She couldn't breathe because the air was heavy with moisture.

The carriage halted in front of a fancy hotel with ornate ironwork on the outside and arched windows with white fabric covering them. Captain Delacroix descended the carriage and motioned Callie to follow him. He told the driver to wait and then entered the hotel. Callie stayed as close behind as she could without stepping on his heels.

Tall pillars in a pinkish stone held the roof up. The floor was covered in carpet so thick, she didn't want to step on it. Huge pictures of people in strange forms of dress hung on the walls. A white stone statue stood in the center of the lobby spouting water out of a jar. Callie stared. The statue wore no clothes and it was a boy. Her cheeks grew hot.

Red and white fabric hung at the windows, and the chairs were covered in a nubby blue fabric with a floral pattern. Callie stopped in the middle of the carpet and stared, unable to move. Was she in a palace? Her mama had told her stories of people in other countries who lived in huge buildings with lots of statues and fountains with water. She felt like she was caught in a dream.

A woman, wearing a hat that bounced with long curling feathers and dressed a beige gown, pushed past Callie and she bumped into a chair and tried to look like she belonged. She realized Luc wasn't with her. She panicked and whirled around searching for him.

Luc stood at the reception desk speaking to a man in a fancy grey suit.

127

Luc motioned to Callie, who sidled up to him trying not to ogle all the fancy people and the fancy room. She didn't belong here. Not the way her Captain did.

Luc spoke to the man behind the desk, "I want a suite with two bedrooms and servant quarters."

"Yes, sir, Captain Delacroix." The man pushed an open book toward Luc. "If you just sign in we'll get you situated immediately. Best room in the house with a little room off the main parlor for your boy." The man gave Callie a hard, unfriendly look. "Your boy can take your luggage around back and bring it in the servant's entrance. Also, in the future, Captain, things may have changed here, but not that much. Please make sure your little darkie uses the back entrance at all times."

Callie swallowed. Back entrance! She'd never walked in anyone's back door. Now she knew why her mama had stayed in Mexico instead of heading back to Florida. In Mexico she was treated like a person. She had told Callie stories of how black people were treated in the South, and the man behind the desk had just confirmed those stories. Callie felt a spurt of anger in the pit of her stomach.

"My little darkie," Luc said, his voice tight, "as you so crudely put it, is a commissioned soldier in the United States Army and will be treated with respect."

The man looked her up and down. "Excuse me, sir." The man smiled at Luc. "My mistake."

Luc signed the register.

"I'll get the luggage, Captain." Callie stepped back.

Luc stopped her. "The hotel has porters for that."

"But, sir..."

Luc shook his head. "One of the benefits in being the conquering army in this city is that we get to go wherever the hell we want." He started toward the stairs.

Callie watched him, unable to make her feet move. Then he stopped and turned to look at her. He raised one eyebrow and Callie jumped forward to follow him up the stairs. She glanced back at the man at the desk to find him scowling at her.

Callie couldn't believe the room Luc had taken for them. The furniture was fancy and looked so fragile she didn't think it would hold her much less the Captain's big body. The porter had arrived with the luggage and stood in the center of the room.

"Captain Delacroix, sir. I'm Cornelius Jardine and I'm in charge of this floor. Anything that you need, please let me know."

Captain Delacroix opened his wallet and flipped the man a ten dollar gold coin. Callie was amazed the man had received so much money for just carrying their bags and packs up to the room. The way things were done in cities was a lot different than out in the desert.

After Cornelius left, Callie wandered around the suite pretending she was the lady of the house. Her imagination took flight. She turned and found Luc sitting in a chair watching her, a slight on his face.

"I want to be a lady," she blurted out.

A look of surprise swept over his face. "I ..."

She put her hands on her hips. "Don't laugh at me," she warned.

"I wasn't going to laugh. I'm just surprised."

"Why? Because you don't think I can do it." She glanced out the window at the street below.

"You're a smart woman."

"Then what?"

His eyes seemed to roll upward. "I just don't understand why."

"What do you need to understand. I'm just asking for your help. Will you do it? You're the only person here I know who help me."

He pulled off his gloves. "Esme can help you."

"She's not here and you are. Besides, I'd look pretty odd taking lady lessons at the Fort."

"You have a point." He tossed them down on a nearby table. "Do you have any idea what being a lady encompasses?"

"Pretty dresses and perfume and hats with lots of feathers." She wanted everything.

Luc looked her up and down. "Being a lady means more than just fashion. But a new dress is a good place to start."

"You'll do it."

"Yes." He stood and jerked the bell cord to summon Cornelius. And when the man arrived, Luc said, "Do you know a dressmaker, who's quick with the needle?" Luc tossed him another coin.

Cornelius glanced at the gold coin in his palm. "My sister, Eloise. I can have her here in half an hour."

"Do it," Luc ordered. "And tell her to bring her finest fabrics. This is a rush job. I'll give her a bonus." The Captain opened the top on a fancy bottle and sniffed then replaced the plug. "Also, send up some decent brandy and food. The best food this hotel has."

The porter touched his black cap. "Yes, sir. Is that all, sir?"

"You tell everyone in this hotel that Captain Delacroix pays generously for exemplary service."

Cornelius' eyes grew round. He stood straight. "Yes, sir. I'll tell them, sir. I'll tell them all."

After the porter had left, Callie said, "Does everyone in the town get paid to bring up luggage?"

Captain Luc walked around the room, glancing out the windows overlooking a huge courtyard. "It's customary to tip for service. I tip better than most because I expect better service."

"If I'd known you'd given me ten dollars, I would have carried up your bags, too." That ten dollars represented a lot of money to Callie. That was almost a month's wages.

The Captain laughed at her. He sat down on a chair and extended his booted foot. "Help me off with my boots."

Callie rested her hands on her hips and tilted her head at him. "Are you going to tip me?"

The Captain started laughing. "You learn quickly, I'll give you that. But since you're already employed by the army, I don't think so."

Callie found herself joining in with his laughter. "I had to try." She had to admit living in a city had some advantages. Money seemed easy to come by and except for the man at the desk, people minded their own business.

A knock sounded at the door and Callie opened it and found a young woman with curly black hair and lively brown eyes standing in the hall with a pile of towels in her hand. "I came to prepare your bath and Cornelius thought you might like extra towels, sir."

She cast a flirty smile at the Captain and Callie fought the urge to slap her and she didn't know why she felt the way she did.

"Thank you," the Captain replied.

Callie watched as the woman walked through the parlor to a door which she opened and stepped inside. A second later she heard the sound of water running. Callie stared after the woman realizing that she was jealous. How could she be jealous? Her mother had once said that being jealous of a man only meant one thing....

CHAPTER TWELVE

Rafe checked the hollow log. Nothing was inside. He blew his breath out in frustration. The maps he'd paid for a week ago had still not been delivered. He sat back on his heels and stared at the rotting log. Damn it. If he knew who the man was from the fort who was giving him all this information, he'd lay in wait for him and throttle the man. He agreed to the conditions that went with the payment of gold and he wasn't delivering.

The sound of horses filled the air. Rafe whirled and headed for shelter in the middle of a dense thicket of bushes. Coming to complete stillness as the sound of horses moved closer to his position.

Two riders stopped in the shade of a grove of oaks and dismounted. One of the riders was a woman dressed in a bright green dress and the other rider was a General, the brass insignias on his uniform reflecting the bright sun.

Rafe tensed.

The General dismounted from his horse and then helped the woman down. She leaned against him and Rafe saw the playful look on her face as she smiled up at him. Rafe couldn't take his eyes from the couple. What a coup if he could kill himself a General of the United States Army. He slipped through the underbrush intent on his quarry, checking his knife in its sheath. A General, he thought. His wife would so proud of him.

The sound of more horses stopped him. He faded back into the shadows and crouched as still as he could. He could hear the woman laughing as several other officers rode up and dismounted their horses.

"General," one of the young officers said, "you shouldn't ride so far ahead of us."

The General laughed. "What man wouldn't want to be along with a beautiful woman?"

The woman laughed. "Oh, Monty. You are so droll."

Rafe shrank back as silently as he could. He'd missed his opportunity. For now.

"Monty," the woman said, "Hold still. Stop charging around like you own the place."

"But my dear, I'm a General. I practically do."

"Mon Dieu. If you keep babbling I will lose the light. How can I paint a portrait then." The woman opened a box and unpacked a book which she opened and glanced at.

Rafe watched eagerly wanting to understand what she was doing. She seemed to have little tubes of something in the box along with another pad of paper. She picked up black sticks and sat cross-legged on the ground. "Sit on the rock, Monty. And hold still. I want you to look your best for Maud." She started scribbling on the paper and Rafe's curiosity was piqued. "I have so much to do before the light fades."

The other officers dismounted. Rafe studied them all. One of the officers inched away from the group and melted back into the brush. Rafe watched him fascinated. He slid through the underbrush, disappointed at losing his chance to kill a General and eased back toward the rotting log.

The officer knelt down and thrust a bag into the log. Rafe grinned. The information he'd been waiting for had finally been delivered. The officer slipped away and Rafe found a place to wait until everyone had left. Still and silent, he watched them through the leaves of the bushes. The woman laughed and flirted with all the men.

She was beautiful with rich black hair and dancing green eyes. Her skin was like ivory and Rafe found himself admiring her. Not the way he admired his wife, but the way a man admired a pretty woman. A pity she was one of them. Someday Rafe would kill her, too.

✦✦✦

Callie glared at Captain Luc. "I only need one dress and you told her five."

Callie stood on a stool while Eloise pinned up the hem of an ivory silk dress that Luc had to admit looked stunning on Callie. He rubbed his throbbing temples. After a good night's sleep and a long bath, he'd awakened to a thick, humid day with storm clouds filling the sky. Though the day had started out well, the moment the woman, Eloise, had arrived, Callie had changed into a stubborn mule, balking at the idea of so many new clothes. She'd dug her heels in and argued with him until a headache raged behind his eyes.

132

"What will I do with five dresses at Fort Duncan? Muck out the stables." She held up her hands. "Scout for Comanche with my hem flapping around my ankles and scaring my horse half to death. Some scout I'd be."

He counted on his fingers. "Not Fort Duncan, but later, when you own your own farm and you become part of a community. Then you will need more than one dress. You need a dress for dinner engagements, another for day wear, and a morning dress. You said you wanted to be a lady. Being a lady means having a gown for every occasion." A request that so surprised him he was still trying to comprehend the scope of his actions. That Callie had no idea what being a lady entailed was obvious from the way she was reacting to a wardrobe to fit the dream. But that she wanted this made him realize how lovely she was and how much a lady she already looked in the ivory silk.

"A lady yes." Callie slapped her thigh. "A fashion doll, no. I just wanted one dress and a hat with lots of feathers." Callie frowned at him. "I can't pay for more than one dress." She glanced at the tall dresser where a small leather pouch sat.

Eloise stopped and glanced up from her hemming and her eyes met Luc's.

"Callie, just consider the extras to be my treat. Unless you have a way to earn money here in the city." Callie was like a prickly cactus. Luc felt worn out trying to follow her shifts in thought and logic. Yet he couldn't help admiring the way the ivory silk clung to her slender body. He'd had no idea under all those disguising clothes how womanly she looked.

"If you give me a generous tip like you've given everyone else in this hotel, I'd have money. You cough and seven people are holding out a hankie."

Luc glared at her. The woman, Eloise, tried to hide the smile on her face, but she kept giggling. She was being extremely well-paid for the wardrobe to be completed in three days.

"Do not force me to make this an order."

"You mean I'm still a soldier?" She stood in a shift and held up a fistful of fabric. "A soldier don't need five dresses."

"Scottish soldiers fight in kilts."

"What are you talking about?"

He shook his head. He was on the losing end of this argument. He ran his hands through his hair. He doubted he'd ever win anything with Callie. *I give in to her and she's not happy. I don't give in to her and she's not happy. How the hell was he supposed to make her happy, and dammit, why did he care?* "Miss Eloise, could I have a few minutes alone with you?"

"Let me finish this hem and I'll be out."

Luc stalked to the bedroom door and slammed out. In the parlor, he poured himself a generous serving of brandy and swirled it in the bowled glass. He needed some more.

Eloise opened Callie's bedroom door and stepped into the parlor, a smile on her face. "I don't envy you. She's a feisty one, Captain."

"Too feisty." He couldn't decide to throttle her or kiss her. "I assume Cornelius spoke to you about the need for discretion and that you'll be well compensated." He reached for his wallet.

"Captain, please." She held up her hands. "You've given me quite enough. I understand your need for privacy. I used to work as a dressmaker for Madame Nadine. I realize you aren't from around here, but Madame Nadine was notorious."

Luc knew exactly who Eloise was talking about. Madame Nadine had run the finest brothel in the state for nearly fifty years. Not that Luc had ever had occasion to visit it, but he'd heard about it from his friends when he was young. "Do you have enough information about her size to finish the dresses without her?" He gestured at the closed bedroom door.

Eloise nodded. "Don't worry. I know what I'm doing, but can I give you a little piece of advice from a woman who's seen her fair share."

"Yes, please." Anything to help him with Callie. He'd thought she'd be tickled to have the new dresses and be a lady for awhile. But Callie wasn't like any other woman he'd ever known.

Eloise moved close to him and gently patted his arm. "She thinks that by accepting the clothes that she'll be your fancy woman and she doesn't want that."

Luc didn't know what to think. He just wanted to help her realize her dream. When had he become the villain. "Thank you. You've given me something to think about."

"That woman is a beauty. But be careful, Captain. She's not the kind of woman you can trifle with. She doesn't understand the rules of the game. She's the kind of woman who holds out for a wedding ring, and I don't think you're in a position to offer her one."

Luc knew how innocent Callie was and he had no intention of hurting her in any way. "I'll remember what you said."

Eloise dimpled at him. "I know you will. And when you tire of your innocent little back-country girl, come see me. I understand the rules." She turned back into Callie's bedroom. The door opened and he caught a brief glimpse of Callie standing in a borrowed shift, her breasts unbound, her silken hair a tangle of curls about her face. She looked unhappy. Maybe he should just get away for a couple of hours. Eloise seemed competent enough to handle Callie. Even though Callie insisted she didn't need new dresses, Luc remembered the look of awe on her face when she'd helped Esme unpack her trunk. He'd work something out with her. In a couple years, she'd be out of the army and probably a landowner. She'd need dresses then, to be a lady when she wasn't being a farmer.

He knocked on the door and when Eloise answered he told her he was going for a walk. She smiled and closed the door and Luc felt as though he'd been removed from some important decision and he didn't know what it was.

The city was much as he remembered it as a boy. The bustle of people on the banquette, carriages in the street, the heat and the sultriness of the air. His feet took him first to his father's house and he stood on the street and looked at the huge structure he'd remembered from childhood.

The house had a new look, fresh paint, new slate shingles on the roof and fresh flowers dotting the sidewalk. Esme hadn't been able to completely erase the years of neglect, but she'd done a good job. With a little more care, the house would look as good as new. A man walked up, a bag on his shoulder. He paused at the front of the house and then slung the bag onto the ground. He opened it and pulled out gardening tools and started attacking a thick bush that was overgrown.

Luc approached the gardener. The man looked at Luc, his dark face crinkling with sudden smile. "Mornin', sir."

"Morning." Luc saw that the fence still needed repair. One small area had come loose from the frame.

The gardener stared at Luc, suddenly frowning. "Pardon me for being so nosy, sir, but you are you any kin to Miss Esme Delacroix?"

"I'm her brother. We don't look a lot alike, but we are twins."

"I've known twins who were spitting images of each other, and twins who weren't. You look like her around the eyes and the mouth."

"I've been told that." Luc glanced up at the house. As a child, he'd lived on Rampart Street with his mother while his father lived here. Luc had been inside this house several times and remembered it as gracious place filled with old furniture and paintings on the wall. He remembered one painting of a fierce looking man who turned out to be his great grandfather. "I see you're getting things in shape."

"Yes, sir." The gardener looked up from his weed-pulling. "Gonna be a wedding here in two weeks. Oldest girl is marrying Old Jonas

Ramsaye, meanest man in New Orleans. Already buried himself three wives. Bred those poor things until death was their only escape. Not a one could give him a boy. And here he is taking on another one who's a good twenty years younger than his oldest girl. Old lecher." The gardener laughed and continued his work.

Esme had said the wedding was off and that Simone was going to Paris. She'd made all the arrangements. Josette was supposed to go to England and eventually Lauren would be joining Esme in San Francisco next spring. What had changed?

Luc thanked the old gardener and left. Luc walked briskly down the street, crossing over to Bourbon. He didn't have time to waste on Natalie's betrayal. She had agreed to Esme's conditions and if Luc hadn't arrived, Natalie would have married her eldest daughter off before anyone could stop her a second time. Esme had left too soon. She should have stayed behind to make certain that Natalie complied and all two oldest girls were sent off to their respective destinations.

Esme snapped her fingers and expected things to be done. She never believed anyone had the fortitude to deny her wishes. Unlike Esme, Luc didn't rush in. He planned things. He needed more detail and he certainly needed to find out more about Jonas Ramsaye and why the wedding was back on after Esme had stopped it.

Cornelius. Luc needed to talk to Cornelius. He would know what was going on and if he didn't he would know how to find out.

Luc returned to the hotel. He asked the desk clerk to send Cornelius up to his room. He sprinted up the stairs and flung open the door to his suite and stopped.

Callie and Eloise sat at the dining table, food spread out between them. Callie was dressed in a wrapper of fabric so fine it clung to her slender body revealing all her curves.

Across from Callie was Eloise with a fork in the air. "This is a salad fork."

Both women turned startled eyes at Luc. Callie looked guilty. She jumped to her feet. "Captain, sir. We weren't expecting you back so soon."

Through the open door of Callie's bedroom, Luc could see a woman hunched over an sewing machine with yards of fabric running through it as her feet moved up and down over the treadles. Another woman stood behind her holding up a bodice.

"Obviously." Luc smiled. Eloise was schooling Callie on the fine points of dining. He picked up a tiny shrimp, popped it into his mouth and ate it shell and all.

136

"You're not supposed to use your fingers," Callie said.

Luc chuckled. "Once you know how to eat food properly, you can use your fingers. That's a rule, you know."

"I'm never going to have those little pink things again."

"Shrimp," Eloise stated.

"They are good." Callie studied the array of food before her. "Do people in cities eat like this all the time."

Eloise opened her mouth and Luc held up a hand. "Let her have her illusions."

The door to suite opened and Cornelius stepped in. "Captain, sir, you want to see me."

Luc sat down at the table and helped himself to a piece of bread. "Eloise, could you and Callie go into the bedroom, please, Cornelius and I have something to talk about it."

"But what all this food?"

Luc handed her a plate. "Fill it up and take it all with you."

Callie and Eloise filled their plate. While Cornelius waited, Eloise made several trips into the bedroom with the utensils she needed to continue her instructions.

When Luc was alone, he filled up a plate for himself. "Cornelius, if I wanted to find out something about a man in the city, who would I talk to?"

"You're talking to him, sir. And if I don't know, I can find out who would."

"So you know Jonas Ramsaye?"

"Yes, sir. That man still has the first penny he ever stole. I hear he's getting himself married in a couple weeks to a young thing from an old family." Cornelius shrugged. "It's a shame when a man can't be happy with what he has. Six daughters and a pack of grandchildren and my cousin, Milo, who works in his house, says he's still trying to get himself a son so his name will live on. Like the world should be a special place for someone with the name Ramsaye."

"Can I talk to Milo?"

"I will arrange something."

Luc stroked his chin. "The sooner the better."

Cornelius nodded. "I can have him here tonight right after dinner. According to Milo, Mr. Jonas likes to have his nightly thing at the whorehouse down the street and Milo usually has himself a couple hours free."

"Excellent." Luc mentally rubbed his hands. "And thank you."

Cornelius left and the door to the bedroom opened and Callie walked out wearing an ivory dress. She held matching shoes in her hand.

She held the shoes out toward Luc, a look of disgust in her eyes. She lifted the hem of her dress and Luc saw she was wearing her boots. "I had to take the shoes off. They hurt my feet."

Luc burst out laughing. She stared at him and then stamped her feet. When he didn't stop, she threw the shoes at him.

"Don't you laugh at me." She stormed about the room.

"In ten years, Callie, you are going to be a force to be reckoned with in the state of Texas."

"I changed my mind, I don't think being a lady is worth the pain."

"Nothing worth having should be so easily obtained because then you don't value it."

She stopped. "Does Esme have to work so hard at being a lady?"

Luc nodded. "Esme knows what being a lady is like, but she also knows when to smoke and drink like a man. That is her most devastating talent."

"Why are you doing this?" "Are you making me all these extra clothes because you like me, or because you want to bed me?"

Luc's throat went dry. He realized he didn't know the answer to her question. Or maybe he did know, but was afraid of the answer. "Because you might need them."

Her eyes narrowed. "I don't need a party dress. I'm a black woman. No one is going to invite me into their fancy homes."

The gown was devastating on her. She looked fashionable and sophisticated. "There is a world beyond Mexico. There are towns with no one but black people all over the west. In California, Oklahoma Territory, Kansas, even as far away as Canada. Towns where people go to school, go to teas and have city council meetings. You want to fit in with those people. I'm trying to help you."

"Excuse me." She stood tall and stared at him. "Why would a big city man like you bother with a desert rat like me?"

She had too many questions in her today. He had no answers. "Callie, trust me. I can help you get everything you want, everything you dreamed of. I want to help. Isn't that enough for you?"

"No."

Luc drew back, startled. What the hell was he going to do with her? Why couldn't she just be grateful and be quiet? Why did she have to be so different from every other woman he had ever known?

"Soldier," he said, "you're dismissed."

She took a step back. "You can't treat me like a soldier when I'm in a dress."

Luc didn't think he was ever going to get out of the hole he'd just dug for himself. He stood and put his arms around her. "You're right. You're not a soldier." He kissed her.

She stood still in the circle of his arms, her lips pressed together tightly. He nibbled on her lower lip and stroked her cheek. She smelled of flowers, soft and feminine. He pressed her tight against him. Her lips moved.

His heart raced and he body reacted to her. The door to his bedroom stood open and his bed an invitation. How could he get her in his bed? He touched her breasts and she jerked away, slamming him across the face and ran into her bedroom, slapping the door behind her.

CHAPTER THIRTEEN

Callie sat across the table from Luc, covered food dishes between them containing their dinner. The windows of the suite were open to the courtyard and a cool breeze ruffled the hems of the curtains as the sun slid down toward the horizon. A headache had woven its way through her head and she tried to take deep breaths against the hard edges of her corset.

Luc had barely said a word to her all afternoon. He seemed to be ignoring her. That was fine with Callie. She could ignore him as easily as he her.

Callie wore the ivory dress and felt constricted by all the items she had to wear. She had thought that binding her breasts had been uncomfortable, but the corset Eloise had insisted she stuff herself into was worse--much worse. She was not happy. Every breath she took was such an effort she'd exhausted herself in less than an hour.

Luc had chosen a brown suit to wear for dinner and he looked strange in it. Callie had never seen him in anything but his uniform. And his birthday suit, a small voice said and she remembered the sight of his naked body in the moonlight.

The array of silverware in front of her was still confusing despite Eloise's efforts to teach her. And the glasses terrified her. She had a glass for each type of wine served with the meal. And she still didn't know which one was which. The plates were all sizes and shapes and filled with different foods that tempted her with their smells. She ached to try them, but one bite seemed to be all she could manage.

"You've hardly touched your food." He pointed at her full plate. "Don't you like it?"

Like it? She lusted after it. "Captain, I want to eat. I just can't. I don't know how. I don't even know what fork to use." She couldn't breathe, she couldn't eat. She was surprised city women survived their

140

city life. Being a lady wasn't working with her. "Do all city women wear corsets?" She nibbled at the piece of chicken in front of her.

Luc dropped his fork. "Underwear, is not a proper dinner conversation."

"Captain, I..."

"And I think it's time you started calling me Luc. I won't take offense."

Soldiers didn't call their commanding officers by their first names. She lifted her chin. "Who's gonna hear us talk about underwear? I've been cooped up in this room for two days now. I've been pinched, poked, hemmed in and fussed over. I've earned the right to talk about my underwear." Her hand strayed to smooth the silk fabric over her leg. She'd lusted after clothes like Esme's and her new dress, as beautiful as it was, made her feel like a painted doll. She felt out-of-place and awkward.

"It must be the sea air, you have turned into the feistiest shrew I've ever known."

"Captain, are you calling me a rat? Because if you are, I have my knife. Just because you're a man and bigger than me doesn't mean I can't gut you."

Luc hit the table with the open palm of his hand. "Call me Luc. I insist on it for the time being. Just say Luc."

"I..."

"Luc," he repeated.

She took as deep a breath as her corset would allow. "Luc, you started this by making me wear this stupid corset." Just the effort of talking left her breathless. "I can't even take a deep breath because I'm afraid my ribs will crack."

"You don't seem to be running out of air anytime soon."

She glared at him.

"Don't you stare at me like that," Luc said.

"Like what?"

"Like you hate me."

She sat back, startled. "I don't hate you. I think I'm just mad at you now. Or maybe I'm made at myself for wanting to be something I'm not."

"You can be anything you want." He gave her an odd look, and Callie thought she detected pity in his eyes.

"You're playing with me," she said.

"I don't play." He took a deep breath. "Maybe I just enjoy being nice to you."

"I may not be city-wise, but I do know that everything has a price." She leaned forward. "Captain, sir, what is the price for all these new gowns that I can't afford to pay for?"

Luc drew back, his eyes going wide and his eyebrows arched in surprise. "I understand that you feel you must pay me back in some way, but a simple thank you is enough. You've lived in the desert all your live. If you hadn't come to Fort Duncan, you would still be in the desert. I thought you'd like to see that there is more to life than an adobe hovel and forty acres of land."

The window gave a tantalizing glimpse of the city and Callie was anxious to see some of it, to store the sights and sounds in her memory to tell her mother about later. "Show me the city instead of keeping me cooped up here. I don't need fancy clothes for that."

"You have a uniform you wear in the army and you need a uniform here."

She shook her head. "I don't understand. People aren't going to notice me any more here in my old clothes, than at Fort Duncan."

Luc laughed. "You're a beautiful woman and where else in the world would you be most appreciated than here. New Orleans has worshiped beautiful women for over two hundred years."

She eyed him suspiciously. "But your sister said the same thing about Paris."

"If Paris were closer, I'd take you there. Maybe someday I will, but for now, New Orleans is going to have to do."

"But we can't walk around here. Because people will stare at me. Because we're...you're...I'm, you know."

"Callie," Luc said sternly, "you've spent a sheltered life. New Orleans has places I can take you where it is acceptable for a white man to be seen in the company of a beautiful black woman. Restaurants, theaters, walking in the park. I can even take you to Mass if I chose to, and no one would bat an eyelash. If ever a place existed in this country where I could take you out, New Orleans is the place."

"Why do you want to take me out?" The very idea of going to dinner in a restaurant terrified her. She'd never eaten something she hadn't grown or killed herself. Who even knew where the food came from and who had touched it. "I don't think want to go to a restaurant."

Luc looked surprised. "But you want to be a lady. Ladies eat in restaurants."

She was having trouble choosing the right forks to use in the privacy of her room. She couldn't conceive of going out in public and embarrassing herself. "I don't think we should be seen in public together."

"But I already explained to you that being seen with you will raise no eyebrows."

"Maybe, but I don't think I could be at ease hanging on to your arm. I can't walk like a real person in these clothes." Though she had to admit, the women she studied in the lobby seemed to handle themselves without tripping over their hems.

Probably because they didn't have to get anywhere in a hurry. Somehow chasing rustlers in a silk dress ticked her funny bone. She could see herself sitting in the saddle with the skirt hiked up around her waist showing off everything she owned. Suddenly she giggled.

"What's so funny?" Luc asked.

"Me." She covered her face with her hands. Boy, was she rude. She was throwing a gift horse back at him. Whatever his motives were, he'd been nice to her. He'd taught her to read, to be a lady. He treated her like a person, not a black woman. When they'd been on the trail, he'd asked her opinion as though it mattered. He was trying to do the best for her. And she knew she should show more of her appreciation, she was just beginning doubt her motives.

When she had first asked him to help her, deep inside herself she knew the real reason. Not because she really wanted to be a lady, but because she wanted him to be attracted to her. She didn't know any other way to draw his attention to her. He was a man who could have any woman he wanted. And she wanted him to want her.

A chill traveled up and down her spine. Her stomach clenched with a roiling fear that left her mouth dry and her heart thudding tightly in her chest.

"Callie, what's wrong?" Luc asked, his eyes showing concern.

"Nothing." She stared down at her plate trying to make her face and eyes empty so he couldn't read into her soul. Her throat closed and she found breathing almost impossible.

"You look like you've eaten something that didn't agree with you."

"I'm fine." She shoved herself from the table.

"If you would like, we could go for a walk after dinner."

He was offering her a treat. She shook her head. "I don't think so." She pushed away from the table and stood. "I think I'm going to bed." She glanced at the window and realized that the light had faded to a dusky purple streaked sky. "If you'll excuse me." She opened the door to her bedroom and went inside.

Callie sat on the edge of the bed. She took off the shoes that so offended her feet. She stretched her toes out and flexed her feet, relieved to have them free of the cramped shoes. She stood and pulled her hem up over her head and tugged and tugged and tugged. How the hell was she supposed to get out of the dress?

She stood in front of the mirror and twisted and turned trying to see how the back was fastened. When Eloise had draped the dress over her head, Callie had been too enchanted to see what else she was doing. Faced with her back, she could a row of tiny buttons, so dainty she didn't think she'd ever be able to loosen them.

Callie reached for her knife and slipped it into the bodice and stopped, staring at herself in the mirror. Her short hair was a cap of wild curls about her face and her eyes were wide and frightened looking like a deer at night stumbling into camp.

She couldn't cut this dress off. Luc had paid for it and it wasn't hers to destroy. How was she going to get undressed? She glanced at the door and knew she'd have to swallow her pride and ask Luc to help her.

Her steps dragged all the way to the door. She opened it to find Luc still sitting where she'd left him. He'd refilled his wineglass and had lit a cigar. A fragrant cloud of smoke encircled his head. He eyed her as she entered the parlor. He'd removed his jacket, opened the top buttons of the shirt and rolled up his shirt sleeves. His arms were muscular with the skin tanned from years in the sun. And she found herself staring at his skin.

"I need help." Her voice came out sulky and angry.

"What do you want me to do?" He stood and waited, the cigar clenched between his fingers. He raised the wineglass to his lips and took a long drink.

"I can't reach the buttons."

"You seem to have found yourself in quite a dilemma." His lips quirked.

He was teasing her, and Callie's frustration level rose another notch. She wanted to stamp her feet, but worried he wouldn't help her if she did. Her mother had hated her temper tantrums, and Callie worked hard to control herself. But the look on his face made her want to scream at him. He was so composed, so self-assured, nothing ever rattled Luc's feathers. Which was probably why he was the officer and she was the scout.

She gritted her teeth. "Could you please help me?"

"What's my name?"

"Captain."

"No."

She bit the inside of her lip. "Luc." The name was foreign on her tongue and she stumbled over it.

144

He smiled. "I'll be happy to help you."

"I thought officers were supposed to be gentlemen."

He tilted his head at her. "Why would you think that?"

"You should have offered to help. You knew I couldn't get out of these clothes by myself."

"But you didn't know that."

"Please."

"My pleasure. It's been a long time since I've played at being a lady's maid."

She wondered how many women he'd actually undressed. From the tone in his voice, more than she wanted to know. What would his fingers feel like against her skin? What kind of lover would he be like? Not that she'd ever had a lover before, but she'd let Jimmy Red Bear kiss her. The kiss had been sweet, but uninspiring. Of course, she'd been thirteen years old at the time.

He took another sip from his wine and put the cigar down. Then he sauntered toward her, a small smile tipping up the ends of his mouth.

Callie backed away from him.

"Don't run away little rabbit, I don't bite." His voice was silky smooth and seductive.

Callie couldn't swallow. She trembled. She back up until she bumped into the wall.

Luc touched her cheek. His fingers left a blazing trail of heat as he slid his hands down her shoulders to her arms. Then he turned her around and placed his hands flat on her back and ran them downward from shoulders to waist.

Callie's knees went weak and she pressed her hands against the wall to steady her.

His fingers touched the back of her neck. "Such tiny buttons. This could take me awhile."

Her spine stiffened. "I'm sure you've done this before any number of times."

"My fair share, but never with someone so delectable."

His voice was a caress, and Callie felt the deepest purr start in her throat. She had to fight the urge not to lean back against his broad chest. Never in her life, had she felt such raging emotions. She didn't want his hands to stop with the buttons. She wanted him to continue down to her skin.

When the dress was loose, he swept her curls back and she felt the pressure of his warm lips on the back of her neck. His breath was a flame that heated her in radiating waves down her spine. She could barely stand. Every part of her wanted to turn around and experience his lips on hers.

He nipped at her skin and her back arched. Her breasts grew tight against the constriction of the corset. Heat grew in her until she couldn't breathe.

"Don't do that," she said.

"Why not?" His voice was husky and harsh.

Callie could barely control her trembling. She didn't know if she were excited or frightened. Each tremor that shook her sent her pulse racing. "When we return to Fort Duncan, I have to go back to being who I was. I don't want be your fancy woman."

His fingers touched her waist. "I haven't asked you yet."

"Not with words."

He slid the dress forward down her arms. He tugged at the corset until it loosened. Callie found her breath.

"How old are you?" He asked.

"Nineteen."

"You're hardly a woman yet."

She turned around and looked at his face. Then her eyes strayed downward and she saw the bulge in his trousers. "I'm woman enough for you now."

He cupped her face with his hands and tilted her face up. "I can't hide anything from you can I?"

She shoved him away. "I can finish, thank you." Holding her bodice to her chest, she ran into her room and slammed the door.

She leaned against the cool wood and stared at the opposite wall. What am I going to do?

Luc buttoned his shirt and cuffs, grabbed his coat and opened the door to find Cornelius with his hand raised as though he were about to knock. A second man stood with him, bearing a slight resemblance. Luc decided the man was Milo, Cornelius' cousin.

"Mr. Delacroix," Cornelius said, "I was just coming to find you. This is my cousin, Milo, servant to Mr. Jonas."

Luc held out his hand to Milo and Milo stared at it. Then he wiped the palm of his hand on the back of his trousers and shook Luc's hand. "Evenin', sir."

Cornelius slapped his cousin on the back. "You need to know about Mr. Jonas. Milo here knows all there is to know about Mr. Jonas. Don't you, Milo?"

146

Milo simply shrugged. "I just drive the carriage, Cornelius. He says I can trust you, sir."

Luc smiled at the man. "Where can go go. I want to ask you about Mr. Ramsaye. And then I want you to point him out to me."

"Yes, sir. I'll meet you outside in five minutes." Milo turned and hurried down the hallway, Cornelius following.

Milo led Luc down a side street toward a simple looking building with a white facade and an emblem embedded in the corner. A line of carriages waited and Milo opened the door of one and gestured for Luc to step inside. "Mr. Jonas inside here, sir. He'll be occupied for a few hours. But you and me, we can talk in here for a bit."

Luc stepped into the carriage and Milo followed him. He left the door opened and seated himself across from Luc in a position so he could watch the front door.

"How long have you worked for Jonas?" Luc asked.

"From just after the war. He pays good. Course not many people like Mr. Jonas. Myself included, if you don't mind my saying."

Luc hid a grin. Milo was a talker. All Luc had to do was ask one question, and he would get the answer for the next three, too. "What don't you like about him."

"That man is pure evil." Milo shook his head. "He's mean. He'd work a body to death if he could get away with it and it was easy enough to replace it. I'd a left long ago if I didn't have so many mouths to feed. But then again, Mr. Jonas don't pay no mind. I drive the carriage and take care of the horses. I like the horses better than Mr. Jonas. And they like me better."

"How is he mean?"

Milo clicked his tongue against his teeth. "He don't pay no never mind to his children. He treats those girls like they was trash. All he can think about is getting them all married off and that's going to cost him. They is not pretty. And then his wives. I don't know how he can get such ugly children from such pretty girls. I think they take one look at them ugly babies and keel over. Mr. Jonas has lost himself a pack of wives. Not a one of them twenty yet. And they get younger and younger. He's got his eye on a pretty little thing and she's sixteen if she's a day. Don't even want to be in the same room with him. Took them for a carriage ride and all she did was sit back here and cry. How her mama wants to make her marry a man she fears. I understand Mr. Jonas though. He wants himself a son to leave all his worldly things to. Like all those worldly things matter. Mr. Jonas, he wants a legacy. If he could make himself king, he would."

The outpouring of Milo's information, exceeded Luc's imagination.

Luc pulled a gold piece out of his pocket. "Thank you, Milo."

"But this is twenty dollars, sir. Way too much for..." Milo attempted to hand the coin back.

Luc waved the coin away. "You have children to feed."

"This is will feed them all the rest of the year. Thank you, sir."

Luc pushed out of the carriage. He had to get away, to think. Luc had to find a way to break up this marriage. He couldn't go back to Esme and tell her what had happened. Esme would walk herself back to New Orleans and kill the bastard. And Luc wasn't too sure he wouldn't be at her side.

CHAPTER FOURTEEN

Luc woke the next morning with the sun streaming through the window. He had tossed and turned the whole night trying to figure out what to do about Jonas Ramsaye's marriage to his half-sister. No seventeen year old girl deserved to be saddled with a husband old enough to be her great-grandfather even worst one who wanted to use her as a brood mare.

He decided the only option he had was to confront his father's wife . Esme had made the marriage a moot point, he didn't understand why Natalie insisted it continue.

He stalked out of the room to find Callie sitting on the table eating her breakfast. She wore her old pants and a plaid shirt two sizes too big for her. Despite her clothes, he was stuck by how beautiful she was. As beautiful as she was in her feminine garb, the sight of her in men's clothing was more intense.

"Captain," she struggled to stand, "good morning."

"Good morning, Callie."

"City life is making you soft. Look at the clock. It's already after nine. The sun has been up for hours."

Luc frowned. "What do you think I'm going to do so early? Hunt Comanche in the Garden District, or trail some cattle rustlers through Jackson Square."

Red stained her cheeks. "Sorry, sir. I wasn't thinking." She sat down again.

"At ease, soldier. We're on leave. Before I joined the army, I rarely rose before noon. So enjoy the leisure time. It may not come again for a long while."

She smiled. "What are we going to do today? I'm tired of being cooped up in this room."

"I hired one of Cornelius many cousins to take you on a carriage ride through the city while I take care of some business."

Her lips drooped in a frown. "Can't I come with you?"

"No," he replied in a firm tone she knew from the past meant he was issuing an order.

Her eyes narrowed. "Why not?"

At this moment she reminded of a very unhappy five year-old, but a battle test solider. "Because I said no. This is personal."

"I see." She glanced down at her place and fiddled with her fork.

He could tell from the stiffness of her body, that she didn't see. He knew all her secrets, but she had no right to know his. Her secret was not life or death. If anyone found out what she was, they'd send her home. But his secrets had a whole a different set of problems attached. But with him who knew what the army would do, he could face either a simple discharge or a firing squad. He doubted the army would know what to do with him should they find out his secret.

She slanted a glance at him. "I thought you wanted to spend time with me."

"I have a surprise for you. Something that includes lots of people, music and food. You can wear your prettiest gown."

Her face brightened. "What?"

"It's a surprise."

"But I want to know now." Her eyes sparkled.

He shook his head. Now that he'd made the promise, he'd have to consult Cornelius on how to accomplish his promise. Cornelius was certain to know where Luc could take Callie. "Tonight." He picked up his hat. "I'll see you later."

"Don't you want your breakfast?" She gestured at the array of food dishes on the table.

He shook his head. "I have business and I want to get it over as quickly as possible." Not that he wanted to face Natalie at all, but he had to take care of Simone. He opened the door and stalked out into the hall. He would stop for beignets and café du lait at Café du Monde. As he walked down the stairs and out onto the street, he catalogued what he was going to do. See Natalie, go to the bank to withdraw funds since he was running low on money, and take a moment to visit his old home.

He hadn't seen the home he'd grown up in since he and Esme had been sent to Paris. After the bank, he found himself standing in front of his mother's cottage amazed to find it so well kept up.

Magnolia trees shaded the house. Azaleas lined the pathways through the garden. His mother had loved flowers. He remembered the day she'd planted the hibiscus in the corner. It was huge now, dominating the area of the side yard like a sentinel. His mother had never allowed anyone to touch her garden. She planted each rose bush, every flower herself. His happiest memories were of her weeding while he swung on the swing tied to the overhanging branches of the ancient live oak in the back yard.

A gardener knelt in front of a flower pulling at an errant weed. Luc stepped around the white fence and approached him. The man had a familiar look to him, but Luc couldn't place him.

"Don't I know you?" Luc asked the old man.

The gardener turned his wrinkled brown face to Luc. "Might have met my brother, at Mr. Delacroix's home."

"That's it."

"Yes, sir."

"Is anyone inside?" Luc pointed at the front door. He ached to enter to retrace the steps of his childhood.

"What's your concern, sir?"

Luc paused. "I'm thinking of purchasing the property."

The garden smiled. "I don't think so, sir. Mr. Delacroix wouldn't part with this place for nothing. Told me it had happy memories for him."

Happy memories for Luc, too. "You take good care of the place."

The old man nodded. "Before Mr. Delacroix took sick, he visited most every week. My wife, usually she cleans the house but she's ailing today, says he hasn't changed a thing on the inside. His lady's clothes are still in the closet and her brushes on the vanity. Even kept all the children's clothes here."

Luc stared at the cottage. Esme had said she had found the family in dire circumstances. Why hadn't his father sold this house? The Delacroix's were not known for their sentimentality. Esme certainly had inherited that trait. But their mother had been sentimental. As a young boy, Luc remembered finding a golden mother-of-pearl box. Inside were locks of hair tied in ribbons, two baby teeth, and silver rattles with his and Esme's initials on them.

"Can I see inside?" Luc asked.

"Don't seem much harm in that, seein' as how you're planning on offering for it. Land speculation is big in this part of the city." He reached into his back pocket and handed Luc a key.

Luc stepped onto the porch. The scent of the magnolias took him back into his past. He imagined his mother on her porch swing, swinging back and forth while she cleaned a bowl of snap beans. Their cat, Rags, has curled up at her feet. Esme had liked to sit on the railing and watch the street.

Luc opened the door and stepped into the parlor. His mother's possessions sat around the room as though she had just left them. A book half opened on the sofa. Lacy curtains waved gently in the breeze. A portrait of Esme and Luc hung on the wall. Another one of his mother and father on another wall.

The furniture was delicate, feminine. The only out of place piece was a huge black leather chair at an angle to the fireplace. Luc touched the chair, the leather was soft and supple beneath his fingers. His father had sat in this chair with Esme and Luc on his knees while he read to them. A row of children's books sat on a table near the arm. A carved horse rode on the fireplace mantle.

The first bedroom on the right had been his mother's. Crystal perfume bottles decorated the vanity. He picked up one of the bottles and uncapped it. The fragrance of the bottle was long gone, but he remembered the scent of spring flowers and summer rain on his skin. A silver brush and ivory combs rested on an etched mirror tray. His mother had had blue-black hair down to her waist. He had enjoyed running his fingers through her silky waves. She used to let Esme and Luc take turns brushing her hair. He still remembered the soothing rhythm of the brush.

Two earrings sat on the tray, ruby red jewels winking in the morning light. The earrings would look beautiful on Callie with her long graceful neck and small ears. His father had bought those earrings to celebrate Luc and Esme's birth. Their birth stones.

Miniature portraits of Esme and Luc as babies, painted by their mother, decorated the dresser. Esme had inherited their mother's talent and their father's drive.

The bed was turned open waiting for his mother. Luc's most painful memory was of her death in this room, in that bed. He remembered the painful breathing that had stilled the laughter which had filled his childhood. Her laughter had been like music. Her death had been a stillness in his heart that still hurt him eighteen years later.

Luc wished he could share the idyllic memories of his childhood with Callie. He'd been happy in this cottage, at peace with himself. A peace he hadn't experienced again until he'd gotten to know Callie. She would like this cottage. She could be happy here with the garden and the flowers, so different from her desert home.

He wandered through the rest of the house, but the memories were so overwhelming he had finally had to leave. As he locked the door behind him and handed the key back to the gardener, he realized that he had never thought of himself as a sentimental man, almost as though sentimentality was a weakness. When he'd broken with his father, he thought he'd broken with his past, but he'd been wrong. He had locked all his memories away, the same way his father had kept that house in such an unchanged manner.

He thanked the gardener and hurried down the street. He paused at the corner and turned, his glance sweeping over the house. For a moment, he had the odd feeling someone watched him, but he shrugged the odd feeling away.

He turned a corner and headed toward his father's house. He couldn't shake the feeling that he was being watched. He wasn't a superstitious man, but he couldn't help feeling that the eyes of the past followed him, that the ghosts of the Quarter judged him as he hurried down the banquette, rushing away from the confrontation from his past.

His father's house was bathed in late morning sunlight. The fresh flowers, so recently planted, raised their colorful bloom to the sun. Luc paused at the street to stare at the windows, preparing himself for the confrontation to come. Then he walked up the steps to the front door and knocked.

The door swung open and a young girl, maybe ten or eleven years old stood in the hallway staring up at him.

A smile grew on her lips. "You look like my sister Esme."

Luc felt a smile growing in on his own lips. "That's because I'm your brother, Luc."

She rushed at him and threw her arms around his waist. "Did you bring Esme with you?" She glanced around him. "She said she would take me to San Francisco when I was older. Well, I'm older now."

Luc started laughing. He leaned over and kissed her on the cheek. "Before you can go to San Francisco, a lot of arrangements have to be made. One of which, I have to speak to our Papa." So this was Lauren. What a charmer she was and even in her childish features, he could see the beauty she'd be some day.

"Papa's upstairs." Lauren took his hand and tugged him into the house. "I was reading to him, but he was tired, so I let him sleep."

"What were you reading?"

"Sir Walter Scott. Ivanhoe."

"That's an interesting story." As Luc walked through the house, he saw empty places on the walls where paintings had been sold. Esme had told him how she had attempted to recover the furnishings, but many had not been found. "Is your Mama at home?"

"She's out having lunch with Mr. Jonas." Lauren tugged him up the stairs to the second floor. "Mr. Jonas is marrying Simone. Simone hates him. He's old and pinches her. But he has lots of money. Mama says we're poor, but Esme is rich and if she's rich then you're rich, and Simone shouldn't have to marry him."

She prattled on and on, but was a wealth of information. She led Luc down the hall toward his father's bedroom. When he approached, he hesitated. So much anger between them, would he be able to repair the damage?

His father lay on the huge bed, a small shrunken man, shriveled and gray. What had happened to the tall, strong man who had been Luc's father? Luc stopped and stared, a peculiar grief filling him at the lost years between them.

His father's eyes were closed, his skin almost translucent. Luc recognized the smell of death lingering in the room. His years on the battlefield had taught him about death. He bent over to whisper in Lauren's ear. "Would you leave me alone with our father, please?"

"Can I bring you some iced tea? I make good tea, but Mama says I put too much sugar in it, but I like my tea extra sweet. Don't you?"

"Tea extra sweet would be nice, but don't bring it for a full fifteen minutes."

"I can tell time. Esme gave me this watch." And she showed him a small watch pinned to her bodice.

He smiled at her and patted her on the head. He wasn't quite sure what to do with his voluble little sister.

After Lauren left, he entered the room. He tried to summon the anger that his father's animosity had planted in him, but it wouldn't come. He had no room in heart for last recriminations. This was his last chance to make peace with his father, or else just leave without waking him.

Luc licked dry lips, and then sat down in the chair at the side of the bed. He gazed at his father for a minute before he gently rested his hand on his father's. The fingers were chilled and his skin felt like paper. His father's lids fluttered open and he stared at the ceiling for a moment before turning to gaze at Luc.

"Lucien. I'd hoped you'd come."

"Papa."

His father sighed. "You're a man. I missed seeing you grow into a man."

"No regrets, Papa. Promise me, no regrets."

"I don't have much time."

"I know." The words stuck in Luc's throat.

"Take care of your sisters. Like I should have taken care of you."

Luc nodded. His father needed absolution. What right did Luc have to pass judgement on him, or ask him to change? His father was old and dying. He didn't need to take the burden of his actions into the next world.

"Please," his father whispered.

A huge lump closed his throat. He felt the unaccustomed heat of tears. The weight of all the years fell away from him. He was amazed that the anger was gone. Some childish part of him wanted to cling to the anger. "There's nothing to forgive." Luc bent close and kissed his father on the lips, relieving his father of the burden. Tears overflowed and dripped down Luc's cheeks.

His father smiled. "Don't cry over me, Luc."

But Luc didn't brush the tears away. "Papa, I love you." And with the words, he felt his own burden and guilt fall away. He thought about all the years they'd missed loving each other.

"I love you, Luc. Don't leave me again." He closed his eyes, his breathing stilling.

Luc felt a moment of fear, but he saw the slight rise and fall of his father's chest and realized he was only asleep. Luc reached up to tuck the blanket securely around his father's frail shoulders. When he turned, he found Natalie standing in the doorway, glaring at him with such hatred, Luc winced. What had he done to this woman to so earn such scorn and ire?

"Get out of my house," she hissed.

Luc stood and walked softly from the room. In the hall, he faced her. "You live in this house at my sufferance." Esme had told him she'd purchased the mortgage. The house belonged to them.

She turned stiffly and started toward the stairs.

Luc caught up with her. "I'm not finished with you yet."

She drew in a harsh breath. "You have no rights here. You are not a legitimate heir."

"This pauper's palace. I already own it."

She stamped down the stairs, her body unyielding. "I want you out of this house now."

"I'll leave, but not before I finish with you."

She turned on him and gave a brittle laugh. "You forget your station."

"This is a brand new world. Tradition is dead, the new god is money. I have money. You don't."

"I'll have it."

"No, you won't."

She laughed at him. "We'll have this discussion again."

"I can buy and sell Jonas Ramsaye without lifting a finger. You're potential son-in-law lives in a house of cards. I am not going to let you sell my sister."

She went pale. "You don't know her."

"She is a Delacroix, that is enough." He glanced up at the top of the stairs and he saw Lauren, and she had a look of such relief on her face that he gave her an encouraging smile.

Natalie flung open the front door, but Luc made no move to leave. "Name your price," he said, "what is my sister's freedom worth."

"Simone is not your sister. She will never be your sister. All you are is an accident of blood."

Luc knew that he had to retreat for the moment. He'd won, and a wise victor gave the vanquished mercy. "I'll be back later in the day." He stepped out onto the veranda.

"You have no authority in my house."

"You forget, it's my house."

Her face contorted. "I will not allow my husband's pickininny bastard any quarter. You may look white. You may talk white, but all you are, deep down, is nothing but a darkie. Do you understand me, darkie?"

He put his hat on. "Perfectly. Good day, Natalie."

She recoiled as though slapped. Then slammed the door.

Luc walked down the steps and turned the corner. He bumped into Callie.

Her face told him everything. She knew.

CHAPTER FIFTEEN

Luc's hand spanned her neck and tilted her head back. Looking into her sherry brown eyes, he saw her want for him. The same desire that burned in his belly. "I don't have the words to tell you how much I want you. Wanted you since I found out you weren't a boy."

She giggled.

His other hand settled on her small waist. The material felt soft under his hand. He tired not to think about the silk dressing gown hiding her bare skin. "I haven't had a woman laugh at me in a long while."

Callie licked her lips. "I'm not sorry."

"Don't be." His knees wobbled. "I think its might be good for me." Dear God how he ached for her. His thumbs twitched coming into contact with the knot of the robe and unwrap it from her body. One little tug and she would be naked. This moment was better than Christmas morning when he was a boy, anticipating the loot he would get that year. She was the best present he'd ever received.

"Kiss me."

This time he laughed. "Usually you're telling me no."

Her finger touched his bottom lip. "Tonight you need me."

Luc kissed the tip of her finger. "Callie, you know where this will lead."

"I'm not a child."

Part of him knew he had to stop this no matter how much he might want her. She wasn't ready for the risk becoming his lover would entail. "Compared to me you are."

Her face flushed. "What if I tell you I want you to" She stared at his chest. " ... make love to me."

"You can barely say the words." His heart thrilled at the words, but his mind told him that it was wrong. He would be taking advantage of her. When they crossed this bridge there would be no going back for either one of them. He hooked a finger under her chin and forced her to meet his gaze. "Almost like you've never said them before." He had no doubt she was still a virgin.

She stood on her tip toes. "Maybe I have. Maybe I haven't."

He lowered his head until his lips were nearly on hers. "Little girls shouldn't play with fire. They are likely to get burned."

"I can start a fire with two rocks and a stick. I'm not afraid risk." She raised up higher and brushed his mouth with hers.

A sweetness overwhelmed him. How long had he felt that particular emotion when he been with a woman. The touch sent heat through her. This kiss was different than any other they had ever shared. The others seemed born out of desperation, but this kiss was born out of mutual desire. Of a want as old as time itself. This was how the dance between men and women was supposed to be played out. How could he be expected to resist the temptation so close at hand. He was only made of flesh and bone.

"Luc ..."

"Oh God, Callie." He deepened the kiss. Her lips were soft and yielding under his. He could feel the strength of her passion down to his boots. At this moment it didn't matter that his father rejected him, or that he was living a lie. He needed Callie. She made everything tolerable. Everything right.

Callie tugged at his shirt. Under her hurried touch he felt the shirt begin to give way to her fingers. Luc had to get her to the bed. He refused to let her first time making love be on the floor. More than anything he wanted to give her the pleasure he knew he would have.

He wanted to take care with her with tenderness that every first time should be. He wanted to be gentle, but the need to consume her completely rage in his head. He couldn't quite quiet the voice whispering in his head that he was stealing something precious from her. Or that this was wrong.

The cool air night air blowing in from the open window hit his bare chest. His nipples hardened as her fingers glazed over their tips. For an innocent, she was a fast learner or a natural seductress. He didn't care.

Callie opened her mouth under his.

Her tongue slipped inside his mouth dancing with his. Luc could taste her inexperience, and it unnerved him. He couldn't shake the fear of eternal damnation at ruining an innocent. He pulled his head back breaking contact with her.

Her eyes shined with passion and bewilderment. "Did I do something wrong?"

Cupping her face with both hands, he stared into her eyes. "God no."

Her lips trembled. "Then why did you stop?"

Luc dropped his hands to his side. If he was going to control himself he had to stop touching her. "You're a virgin aren't you?"

Her brown eyes pleaded with him. "I've never been with anyone."

He couldn't stop a smile from forming on his lips. "I suspected as much."

Her eyes widened. "Is that bad?"

He palmed her cheek. Her satin skin warmed under his palm. "No."

"You don't like virgins?"

"I've never been with one."

"You don't know what to do?"

In all her innocence he just questioned his prowess. He couldn't remember a woman who did before. Not even when he was an untired boy. He wasn't sure if he should be insulted or not. "I know perfectly well what to do with a woman, my sweet. It's just that ... that... well--"

"You think I won't be any good at it."

Laughter rumbled in his chest. How did he explain to her that he knew between them making love would be perfect.

Her brown eyes pleaded with him. "You aren't saying anything."

"You are a natural enchantress."

Callie stiffened. "Is that good?"

"Too good."

Callie thrust her body against his. "I want you. Please make love to me."

A shudder of pure desire washed over his body. He could feel her breasts crushed against his chest. Her hand massaged his chest. She slithered against like a cat. He could hear the rustle of silk on skin. This was madness. Luc lost all control at this moment. He grabbed her upper arms and took her mouth with an ungoverned need. She was so willing, so warm, he could no longer resists. His brains screamed for gentleness his body demand wildness. He plundered her soft mouth. His tongue ravaged her mouth. But Callie only matched his ardor. He wanted her to run and hide from him. But she didn't.

The dye was cast. Nothing between heaven and hell would stop them from making love. A calmness settled over him.

Luc torn his lips from Callie's. In one swift motion he bent over and picked her up. Her arms went around his neck. She opened her mouth. He shook his head, if she spoke she might ruin the spell that had woven around them.

He took long strides until he came to the master bedroom door. Fumbling for the handle he didn't want to drop her. That would have put a quick end to the seduction. The door swung open on quiet hinges. He entered the room and headed straight for the bed.

Carefully he lowered her to the soft mattress.

"You are so beautiful."

A hot flush crept up his neck. He didn't know how to take her compliment. From her they sounded so sincere, so honest. "Men aren't beautiful."

"You are."

Why she was here was beyond him. In her innocense, he knew she wanted him, but in a way he'd never known. He had left his childhood emotional long before his body did, but part of Callie still lingered in hers. "Thank you." He smiled. "But I will never match your perfection."

She lowered her eyes hiding her embarrassment. "Thank you. No one ever told me I was pretty, but you and Esme are."

Luc walked across the room and put out the lights bordering the door. "I don't want to talk about my sister at a time like this."

"Alright, but are you going to turn all the lights out."

"How can I see you in the dark?"

She scooted further up the bed. "The only person who has seen me with no clothes on is my mother."

Why she needed to talk about their family was beyond him. He couldn't think of anything more that would kill a seduction. "I don't want to talk about your mother either."

"If you say so."

He walked over to the bed. Looming over her, he put his hands on his hips. "I do."

She sat up and started to untie the knot of her dressing gown.

"Stop."

Her hands dropped to the mattress. "Was I doing something wrong?"

"I would like to undress you." He held out his hand.

"Oh."

Slowly she raised her hand and touched his fingers to his. Her skin was warm to his touch, but he couldn't help but notice her hands shook. "Are you having second thoughts?"

She stood then shook her head. "No. Are you?"

"I can't count that high."

"I want you."

He squeezed his eyes shut. Her words echoed in his head. How could he be worthy of such trust, when he had lived a deep dark lie for so many years. Luc had no idea her trust in him would effect him. "I need you."

Callie slipped her arms around his waist and tilted back her head. "Kiss me."

For a second he could only stare at the perfection of her young face. Candlelight flickered off her smooth skin casting her cinnamon colored face in softness. This was not the same woman who could read a week old trail, shod a horse, or catch a rabbit with her bare hands. No this was a desirable creature who stirred his imagination and gave life to his barren soul. He had no idea how truly bankrupt he was until Callie pushed her way into his existence. "What man couldn't give into such a demand." He lowered his head and kissed her. As their lips met. Luc found the knot of her dressing gown and slowly untangled the sash. He heard the rustle of silk over bare skin. Or maybe the sound was the rush of his blood through his veins, he wasn't sure.

The shirt fell off his shoulders and her hands moved over his skin. Her hands were callused. He never thought the feel of calloused skin would feel so seductive on his skin. Her unschooled touch inflamed him.

Her mouth opened his. She tasted sweet of wine and chocolate. Their tongues entwined and he felt his knees go weak. How could this untired girl bring him such pleasure.

Her skin smelled of vanilla and exotic flowers from the soap he bought her. Her skin was soft like hot satin. He could feel the muscle of her back contract as he caressed her skin. He couldn't seem to get enough of the feel of her.

She touched his stomach. So potent was the impact, he heard himself moan. Her hands dropped to the opening of his trousers and she began to unfasten them. He wanted to help her but that would mean he would have to take his hands away from her skin, and he was addicted to the supple tone of her body. And he had to admit to himself he liked that she was a desperate to have him as he was to have her. He made his guilt seem less that he was taking advantage of her inexperience.

She broke the kiss. "Help me."

Luc grabbed her wrists and guided her hands down to her side. He took a moment to notice her. Her small breasts were firm and chocolate tipped. She had a tiny waist that flared into gently rounded hips. How had he mistaken her for a boy was beyond him. This was the body of a goddess woman. Luc reached out and touched the tip of her breast with his finger. Her nipple beaded on contact. He heard her sigh. Luc completely cupped her breast. They both trembled.

He raised his other hand and cupped the other breast. The feel of her was sublime. Perfect. "I want to give you pleasure, but the first time for a woman isn't ..."

"Then the second time will be perfect."

How could she sound so logical? The child woman who knew nothing about the art of making love was trying to ease his mind. He wanted to laugh at the irony.

"So are you going to talk or are you going to ..." She inclined her head toward the bed.

Luc pushed on her shoulders until she was seated on the bed. Callie scooted over until she was nestled against the snowy white pillows. Luc sat on bed and quickly removed his boots. When he was done he stood and removed the rest of his clothes. He could feel the slow heat well up inside him. He was already hard and ready for her. He had to keep reminding himself that she was a virgin. He couldn't just leap on her and do his business he needed to take time to make sure she climbed slowly up the ladder to pleasure.

Callie pushed herself further back on the nest of pillows. She been dreaming of this moment since she first laid eyes on Luc. Only she didn't know it. Somehow finding out the truth about him only made her love his more.

The mattress sagged beneath his weight and the bed springs creaked. He slipped an arm around her waist and brought her to him. He crushed her to his chest. Every muscle of his chest pressed to her. He stroked her body with his hands leaving trails of excitement all over her. Callie whimpered. The need for him was almost painful.

"So beautiful," he whispered.

His words thrilled her. "Love me, Luc."

His head lulled back for a second. The muscles in his throat constricted. He took a harsh breath than lowered his gaze to her meet hers. "After this there is no turning back for you or I. Are you sure you will risk the consequence?"

Looking into his green eyes, Callie nodded. "I think I waited all my life for you."

The lamp light glowed on his white skin making his features sharper, his shoulder wider. Callie slid her fingers into his silky hair and brought his mouth back down to hers. He rolled slightly on her and their legs entwined She could fell his erection jutting into her belly. A thousand

162

new sensations attacked her all at once. She pressed closer to his body wanting to feel every bit on him next to her.

Luc groaned. "Callie,"

She liked the way he said her name as his lips moved to her neck. He smelled like of smoke and musk. Callie head was light and she couldn't seem to grab on to a single thought. Her body had taken over and was doing all the thinking for her. She like the sensation.

Luc began to nibble at her earlobe. He gentle nips tickled and she forced herself not to laugh. An ache knotted her stomach. She closed her eyes tight stunned by her powerful reaction. His hands seemed to roam all over her body. His fingertips drew small circles on her hips. She liked the roughness of his palms on her skin.

His mouth slipped down and his lips closed over the tip of her breast.

Callie's back arched at the moist swirls on her breast. Blood rushed from her head. She felt her fingers push his head down and she sunk her nose into the darkness of his head. She turned her head and rubbed her cheek in the springy softness of his hair. She lifted her head and watched him suckle her. His body was so white against her dark skin. The contrast was perfect as if it was meant to be.

Her hands fell to his broad shoulders. She could feel the strength and vigor just below the skin. He was a powerful man who could be so gentle.

His mouth moved to her other breast.

Callie was in heaven. This is what she always hoped what being in love would feel like. She didn't want to think of love. Love might ruin her plans for the future. She couldn't afford to let the that happen.

Luc's hands grazing the skin of her inner thigh brought her away from her thoughts of love. Callie parted her legs hoping for more of the sweet sensation of his hands on her delicate skin. Callie's head lulled back against the pillows. This was more than she hoped for.

Luc hand moved over her secret place. He stroked her and she could feel a damp heat deep inside her. Her heart was racing. She was light headed. He buried his fingers in her curls dipping his finger inside her. Shock went through her at his subtle invasion.

"Relax. I want to give you pleasure."

Did it really get better than this? She didn't know if she could stand it if her body felt any better than this.

He began stroking the tight bud at her core.

Callie bit her lip to stop from crying out. Her hips arched up as she tried to fight the sensations racing through her body. She was almost ashamed that she could be so easily swayed by his skill.

"Do you like that?"

Callie opened her eyes and stared at Luc. She nodded her head.

"Good."

His eyes were full of passion and craving it almost made her cry. No man had ever looked at her with such emotion before. He continued his stoking. An increasing pressure built inside her.

Callie wanted to close her legs and trap his hand there. He increased his friction as if he knew that's exactly what she wanted. Her inside grew tighter and tighter until she thought she would explode. He murmured words she didn't understand into her ear. French she figured. She didn't care if she didn't know the exact words, she knew that he was talking about what they were doing. This only heightened her enjoyment. Her body stiffened. She ascended higher and higher. This what it must be like to be an eagle racing toward the sun. Her body began to twitch. Callie tired to stop her body from acting so strangely, but it seemed to have a mind of its own. Luc didn't seem to mind. His voice got huskier, deeper more insistent. Finally she could hold back the tide and her body erupted. She heard herself cry out unable to stop herself. She seemed to float on air for endless seconds. Then she went limp.

Luc chuckled in her ear.

Callie drifted back to earth. "What did you do to me?"

He smiled. "That is why men and women make love."

She had a hard time trying to catch her breath. "Now what do we do?"

He pushed a curl off her forehead. "That was only the beginning."

"Is it always like that?"

"No." He kissed her lightly on the mouth. "Sometimes its better."

"What do I have to do to you?"

"Tonight is just for you."

"But what about you. I want to make you feel what I did."

He smiled. "Trust me I will." He touched her thigh again. Every time I touch you ... I enjoy myself."

"No one has ever talked to me like you do."

He bent his head and nipped her breast. "I glad. I'm honored to be your first."

Callie didn't know what to say and not ruin the moment, so she remained silent.

Luc shifted her body until she was lying completely on the bed. He positioned himself over and began to rain kisses over her body. Callie giggled as he stuck his tongue in her navel. She grabbed a fistful of his hair and pulled his head up, but he was to strong and she couldn't make him stop. Not that she really wanted to. His lips moved down her body until they reached the juncture of her thighs. Callie squeezed her legs closes, but he didn't stop kissing her there.

"Open for me." He didn't look up her.

Curious to experience how his mouth would feel on her there she gave into his demand.

He lifted himself and positioned himself between her legs. Callie closed her eyes and he put her legs over his shoulders. She felt so exposed. Her nerves were on edge and her stomach was tight.

Again time stood still as she waited for his newest way at pleasuring her. He placed a kiss right at her center and a wanton shiver went through her. His tongue slipped inside her. Callie groaned and arched her hips. His tongue did wondrous things to her body and she was helpless to stop her reactions. Honey hot heat washed over her as he caressed her. Callie made herself relax and let the sensations wash over her. The now familiar tightening built in her body and instead of fighting it she gave herself over. Her hips wriggled as she wanted him further inside her. Her back arched and she fisted the bed covers. Her body exploded ans she cried out Luc's name.

As she came back down to earth, Luc moved over her. He braced his hands on either side of her. She looked up at his handsome face, his green eyes glittering like jewels. His powerfully muscled chest heaved with every breath.

"Put your legs around my waist."

She did as he commanded. She lifted her hips until his erection was nestled on her stomach. "Love me. Now."

He laughed and lowered his body over hers. His eyes smouldered. Carefully entered her.

With a slight thrust he broke though the barrier of her virginity.

Callie bit her lip to stop from crying out. A look of pure guilt colored his face. She reached up and touched his cheek.

Oddly enough her body seemed to adjust to him inside her instantly. Her muscled conformed to his length as if she was made only for him. He began moving in slow steady strokes.

Callie threaded her fingers through his black hair. She brought his mouth to hers. Their kiss was sweet and lingering. Again he spoke to her in French. Softly and lovingly. She didn't understand the actual words, but she knew the feeling behind them.

Sweat trickled down his back as her hands spanned his back. He felt so hot and alive. The light from the single lamp illuminated his body giving his a slick look of ivory. His movements increased. Callie could feel herself moving closer to the edge. She chanted Luc's name urging him on. He dropped his head into her neck. The first wave of pleasure washed over her and her whole body tensed. Luc must have sensed her readiness, he began to thrust deep inside her. Callie cried out his name as a surge of ecstasy crashed over her.

He moaned her name and went still on top of her. Their bodies melted together. They lay like that for long seconds, she was to afraid to speak to end the moment. The one thing she knew they could never go back to who they used to be.

CHAPTER SIXTEEN

Esme sat at Luc's desk making a list of all the possible people on the post who could be the spy. This detecting was so much fun. Too bad the Pinkerton Agency didn't hire women. Maybe the United States would get into a war with Mexico and she could be a spy. Just a little war. Nothing that lasted longer than a few months. Longer than that would be redundant.

She laughed at herself. She wasn't spying. She was snooping. Spying was honorable. Snooping was a woman's skill.

Reggie entered the office and she smiled at him.

"Miss Delacroix." He touched his hat and smiled at her.

She tilted her head in a flirtation manner. "I told you to call me Esme."

He grinned at her. "Writing a letter to Luc?"

"I like sitting at his desk. It's the seat of power. And I do so adore power."

He sat on a corner of the desk. "You have power--the power to break my heart." He placed one hand on his chest.

"Lieutenant. Reggie. A bit of advice about women, never let them know they have power over you. You give them an unfair advantage."

He gave her a puppy dog glance as though he were a hungry man and she were a turkey leg. Young men were all alike. They saw her as a desirable woman even as they checked her bank account. Beautiful women were everywhere, but beautiful with money were a rarity, except maybe in Europe. "Reggie, have you ever considered a tour in Europe. You would be very popular there. With your connections, all you would have to do is lift a finger and every available woman would fall at your feet. European women adore men in uniforms."

Reggie shrugged. "My duty is here with Luc."

She put her chin on interlocked fingers. "Loyalty, is another quality women seek." Even though Luc and Reggie had been friends for years, she didn't know him except through Luc's letters. While on the surface Reggie had a cavalier stance, she sensed there depths to him that no one knew about. His comment about fidelity didn't sit right with her. She had the feeling that his expression of allegiance for Luc was nothing more than an attempt to impress her. Not that his admission was strange, she heard it all the time. Again, she sensed he was doing nothing more than plumbing the depths of her bank book.

She folded her list of names and tucked it into her reticule and stood up. Luc would be so pleased when he found out she'd done all the preliminary work for him.

"Leaving so soon."

"I'm having tea with Mrs. Adams and some of the ladies. I intend to find out every bit of gossip about everything."

"Luc said you were interested in opening a school for the darkies. I can help you."

She grinned at him. "Lieutenant, you are too busy defending the United States to worry about a school. Thank you for your offer, but Monty has already offered his services."

"I certainly can't do more than a General." He stood aside from the door to allow her to exit. "But if there is anything I can do, please don't hesitate to let me know. May I escort you to your tea?"

"Thank you, no. I'm sure you have more pressing business to take care of." She stood on the walkway and opened her parasol for her walk across the parade ground.

—◦◦◦—

Esme sat with a smile pasted on her face, listening to the boring chatter of Mrs. Adams and the other women of the post. During her several hours in their company, she'd discovered that the Major liked his whiskey. Lieutenant Magill kept an expensive mistress in Eagle's Pass, and Master Sergeant Lawrence had a gambling problem and his wife took in laundry for extra money. Lieutenant Rippy's wife was having an affair with a local rancher. And that every one of the officers' wives complained about a lack of money. All the women admired Reggie because he worked hard and sent home what money he didn't need for his mother and sisters.

Esme was disappointed. She had too many suspects and not enough information to narrow the field. Being around the Major's wife and her friends made Esme miss her own many women friends in Europe. She resolved to write each and every one of them a letter this very evening to catch them on her new life.

As the women chattered, Esme found herself drawing the women, one by one, showing their animated faces. European women were more sophisticated about their feelings. American women were more open, more willing to share. Esme liked that in them. As she completed each drawing, she presented it to the subject and was rewarded with appreciation and several requests to draw miniatures of their children.

When the tea finally ended, Esme returned to Luc's quarters to mull over the information that she had. She sat in the parlor, the front door open to let in the breeze, while she added the information she'd gleaned to her list.

A knocked sounded on the door and she glanced up to find General Hammond watching her. "How is your investigation going, my dear." He entered and seated himself across from her.

"How did you know?" She folded her list and put it away in a drawer.

"How could I not know? You've talked to everyone on this post and asked questions with the finesse of an inquisitor."

"I didn't realize I've been so transparent."

Monty grinned at her. "Back in Washington during the War, my job was to identify Confederate spies. You my dear, could bring about the downfall of an Empire."

"I'm going to take that as a compliment."

He grinned at her. "As it was intended. Would you care to share your information?"

"I know, you, me and Luc," and possibly Callie, but Esme didn't want to bring any undue attention to the young woman, "are not the spies. But who the spy might be, I don't really know. But I will find out as much as I can to pass on to Luc."

Monty smiled at her. "You're doing a good job, but be careful."

She smiled and nodded. "Always, Monty. Always."

=—⊙⊘⊙—=

Luc woke the next morning with Callie curled up next to him. She looked soft and vulnerable in the morning sunlight. He just wanted to look at her. He could stare at her for the rest of his life. He wanted to protect her.

He gently ran his fingers along the line of her cheek. She stirred, but didn't wake. He leaned back and closed his eyes. He had so much to think about. His father was dying and probably wouldn't live much longer, he had to stop the wedding between Jonas Ramsaye and Simone, and he had to decide what to do with Callie.

He'd never had so many life effecting choices to make in so

little time. And each one he had to make would ripple like a stone tossed into a still pond. He only hoped he had the fortitude to withstand the onslaught of waves crashing on the shore.

━━━━⌾⌾⌾━━━━

Luc sat in the bank President's office waiting for him to return. The window was open to the street and the bustle of the city. New Orleans had grown up in the years Luc had been gone. The city had changed from a domestic port to an international one, from a small city to a large one. Masted ships rode at anchor at the docks. People thronged the streets. Merchants hawked their wares from wheeled carts. The aroma of spicy Creole good scented the air.

Luc knew he could never live here again. He felt confined, closed in, after the openness of the west. He was anxious to return to Fort Duncan, except that he couldn't leave just yet, and a return to the fort meant that the relationship between him and Callie would change. In their hotel room, they inhabited a world of their own making, a man and a woman making love. Back at Fort Duncan, she would be Cal and he would Captain Delacroix again, at opposite ends of the social structure. He would be white again, and she would be black. He felt a deep dissatisfaction at the changes that would happen once they returned.

Grant Tigler returned to the office and settled behind his desk. He was in his middle sixties with slicked-back, silver hair framing a still-handsome face. "Captain Delacroix, I hoped your sister would be with you. Such a charming lady." Tigler was a native and his approving words told Luc that he knew exactly who Luc and Esme were, but was willing to overlook their heritage for the sake of having their money.

Luc smiled. "Esme is not in New Orleans. But she is deeply concerned, as I am, about this inappropriate arrangement between our half-sister, Simone, and Jonas Ramsaye." He felt a stab of indignation that the banker was so vital and alive while Luc's father, many years younger was dying.

Tigler frowned. "You realize I cannot reveal confidential information, but I can say that I attempted to speak to Madam Delacroix about this. I hinted to her that Mr. Ramsaye's financial situation is not what it seems, but ..." he paused as he considered his next words, "Mr. Ramsaye has an investment that appears sound on the surface."

"Meaning," Luc prompted wondering what the banker was hinting at. Luc needed more than hints, he needed direct information.

Grant Tigler hesitated and then nodded as though he had come to a decision. "Mr. Ramsaye borrowed heavily to invest in a shipping venture to China. The ship is now five months overdue and Mr. Ramsaye's loan will mature in less than month."

"Interesting. Thank you, Mr. Tigler." Luc stood. "I'll be in touch."

The bank president stood and for a moment seemed undecided about something, and then he put his hand out to shake Luc's. For a second, Luc was shaken by a white man knowingly offering to shake his hand. Their palms touched and Luc discovered the other man's grip to be firm and solid and again he found himself comparing this man to his father.

Luc walked down the stairs and out the double doors to the busy street. He gazed back and forth searching to see if Callie had followed him again. But he'd worn her out this morning. She'd been insatiable.

He refocused on Jonas Ramsaye and his five month overdue ship along with the loan which had to be repaid in less than a month. Jonas must be a very nervous man by now. Luc could use that. He had known that Jonas was in a financially precarious position, he just hadn't known how precarious. Why he wanted to take on another wife was beyond Luc's comprehension? Unless Jonas had some expectation of inheriting the French Quarter address once Luc's father died.

As he walked down the street, he ran all the information through his head trying to figure all the angles from Jonas' point of view. He had the feeling Jonas didn't know Esme had purchased the mortgage on the house. Jonas probably figured that Simone was a good catch. The Delacroix family had lived in New Orleans for over a hundred fifty years and was a fixture in Creole society even in their reduced circumstances. If Jonas married Simone he would have a prestigious address and an entree into the still closed and eminent Creole society. What more could a man want?

What about Natalie? What would she gain from the marriage. If Jonas' ship arrived, Simone would be an extremely wealthy young wife, and Natalie would be able to move about in society again. Simone could hardly put on a show of wealth while her mother lived in on the edge of poverty. Not that Natalie was poor any longer since Esme had been extremely generous with the trust fund. But Luc figured that Natalie found the strings of the trust fund too confining. She wanted more.

Oh God, he was thinking like Esme! He didn't know whether to be proud of himself or frightened that he had been able to decipher the twists and turns of such a scheme. Deciphering was Esme's realm. Luc just plowed straight ahead while Esme saw the mystery within the puzzle.

Before heading to Jonas' house, Luc took a side trip to the docks and talked to the sailors on several of the ships moored at the docks. No one had seen the Sea Maiden, out of Shanghai. No one knew if the ship was lost at sea, or simply slow getting back to New Orleans. While the sailors had heard nothing good, neither had they heard anything bad. And bad news always shot around the world long before the good. Luc came away with a plan.

———⟨ෞ෮ඉ⟩———

Jonas Ramsaye's house looked like a monstrosity. Built to impress, the Gothic style mansion didn't fit with the elegant plantation style of the other homes in the Garden District. A rumor stated that Jonas had come to New Orleans from New York in the 1840s under a cloud of rumor involving his first wife and her death. Since then he'd attempted to storm the southern social bastion by marrying into different families. Although his infusion of cash had been appreciate, Jonas had been barely tolerated. He'd never been able to catch a woman as prestigious as a Delacroix.

Luc opened the wrought iron gate and headed up the path to the front door. He knocked and found himself admitted to the house by a dour looking housekeeper.

"If you will wait in here, I'll inform Mr. Ramsaye you are here." The housekeeper showed him into the parlor, another ugly room with heavy, dark carved furniture and thick red drapes covering the windows.

The room needed light. Luc resisted the impulse to open the drapes and let the sunlight in. The house depressed him.

The housekeeper returned, a frown on her face. "Mr. Ramsaye says he has no interest in meeting with you."

Luc had expected this response. "Inform Mr. Ramsay that I have information about his overdue ship."

A few minutes later, Jonas Ramsaye entered. He was a man with heavy features and a body growing too round for its clothes. "What do you know about my ship, boy?" His voice was filled with scorn.

Luc smiled at the man. "Would you like to discuss your affairs here in the parlor for everyone to hear, or would you prefer privacy."

Jonas scowled. Then he gestured for Luc to follow him and led the way down the hall to an office with the same dark furnishings. Floor to ceiling bookshelves hugged the walls. Books, looking brand new, rested on the shelves. From the dust gathering on the spines, Luc doubted that Jonas read much.

Jonas settled himself behind an ornately carved desk and steepled his hands. "Well, I'm waiting."

Luc opened a cigar box and carefully chose one. Though the bands said the cigars were Cuban finest, once Luc lit one and inhaled, he realized Jonas had taken the identifying bands from the original cigars and placed around cheap imitations. Luc frowned and mashed the cigar into an ash tray. Then he sat down in a leather wing chair, crossed his legs and faced Jonas, to find the man's face contorted with fury.

"I understand that your ship hasn't come in yet."

"China is a long ways away."

Luc lifted his eyebrows. "You're very calm for a man whose ship is five months overdue, with the bank breathing down your neck and taking on the responsibility of a beautiful young bride and her family."

Jonas' scowl deepened. "Boy, if you think you can scare me, think again."

"I'm not here to scare you. I'm hear to deal with you."

A flicker of interest crossed Jonas' face. "What do you have that I might want?"

"Enough money to buy out your interest in the ship and to show a nice profit. Enough to pay off your debts and maybe start again."

"I don't do business with your kind."

"People with money?" Luc asked with an innocent smile.

"No, people with tainted blood."

"Even people with tainted blood have money. More money than you're ever going to see again."

"When my ship ..."

"The operative word here is if," Luc said. "There are so many hazards on the sea. Storms, mutinies, pirates, the list is endless. Sea ventures should never be undertaken by those who cannot afford to lose the money. Unlike me." He was so Esme at this moment, he couldn't believe it. He and his sister were truly twins. He took back that lie he'd told her when she was five that she'd been lost by a troll. They were blood kin, after all.

Jonas licked his lips. "What do you propose?"

Luc had won. "What you paid for the venture, plus a ten percent profit. And my sister's freedom."

"Forty percent."

Luc laughed. "Fifteen."

"Thirty-five."

Luc shook his head. "Twenty is my final offer and the name of decent cigar dealer." Luc glanced at the humidor knowing his superiority was showing.

Jonas didn't answer for several minutes. He stared hard at Luc, his mouth working as though he wanted to say something, but couldn't get the words out. Finally, he said in a strangled voice, "When would the cash be ready?"

"I have an appointment with Mr. Tigler at the bank set for tomorrow morning at 10 am. Be there." Luc stood and left.

As Luc walked toward the front door and opened it, he felt deeply proud of himself. He was sorry Esme couldn't be here to share the moment of triumph. Simone was safe, and as soon as the papers were signed and he could make arrangements, she would be on her way to Paris.

He turned back toward the hotel and Callie, his steps quickening at the thought of her creamy flesh and bright eyes filled with passion just for him.

CHAPTER SEVENTEEN

Callie sat in the courtyard trying to figure out a way to be comfortable despite the confines of her corset. No matter what Luc said, she'd never wear a dress again no matter what other people thought of her.

She'd never been anyplace so pretty as this small garden. A fountain dominated the center. A gold fish lazily swam through the clear water between strands of a water plant with a bright white flower as big as her hand. Overhead, a fragrant tree with huge creamy blossoms showered petals on her. A squirrel scolded her from the bottom branch.

Lauren Delacroix, Luc's youngest sister sat on the edge of the fountain staring down at the fish. She glanced up and gave Callie a innocent look. "You really get to shoot guns and ride horses and stuff like a boy. That must be so much fun."

Callie had never thought chasing outlaws was fun. "I was working."

"Doing what?" Lauren trailed her fingers through the water and then playfully splashed Callie.

Callie grinned. "I was a bounty hunter."

"What's a bounty hunter?"

"I chased bad guys who stole cattle, or robbed people."

"Didn't anyone care that you were a girl?"

Callie shook her head. How could she explain desert life to this delicate city-bred girl? "Everyone works in my village. We have to or we don't eat."

"Don't you have servants to cook for you? Mama says we used to have servants, but we can't afford it any more. But when Esme came, we had servants again. Do you know Esme? Esme is pretty. She looks like my brother Luc, but men aren't pretty. I don't know, I don't understand."

Callie smiled. Luc was more than pretty. The memory of his body pressed against her made her skin tingle. "You're right, men can't be pretty."

Lauren shrugged. "But I like Luc anyway. He's a good big brother."

Callie felt a wave of loneliness. "I have a brother."

"You do."

"His name is Rafe." How she missed him? Not knowing what had happened to him gnawed at her. "He used to be a soldier, but I don't know what happened to him."

"I'm sorry." Lauren slipped her soft hand around Callie's rough one. "Maybe you'll find him some day."

"I don't think so. He's been gone a long time. My mama thinks he's dead."

"My daddy's going to die." Tears formed in Lauren's eyes.

"My daddy died when I was a little girl about your age." Callie distantly remembered the pain of his death, but life was too hard to grieve forever. "Many people believe that when we die, we go on to a better place."

"To go see Jesus?"

"Maybe. And nobody hurts any more, or has to worry about putting food on the table, or cleaning the barn."

Lauren shifted closer to Callie. "I'm afraid to die."

Callie put her arm around the young girl. "You're young, you have plenty of time to grow up, get married, have lots of children."

"I don't want to marry a boy. Simone doesn't have to get married either. She's happy she doesn't have to marry that old man. She's excited about going to Paris. I'd like to go to Paris, but Esme promised me she'd send for me once she got to San Francisco. I think I'm going to like San Francisco. Mama doesn't want me to go, but I want to go. I want to be with Esme. Esme says she'll teach me how to paint and play poker. Do you play poker?"

Callie shook her head. "I don't play."

"You should get Esme to teach you. Esme knows how to do everything. She's going to teach me to fence."

"Fencing?" Lauren's artless chatter completely mystified Callie. "What's fencing?" Callie had an image of a long fence in her mind.

Lauren bounced to her feet and took up a position with one hand back and hooked up from the elbow, and her other arm pointed forward, fingers cupped as though holding a stick. "En garde." She bounced back and forth on the balls of her feet, her skirt swishing around her thin legs.

Callie was surprised as Lauren's pose. She had no idea what the child was doing. She glanced up at the window where she could see Luc standing. He watched her and that made her self-conscious.

176

Suddenly there was a scream from inside the house. Luc whirled from the window, and Callie jumped to her feet. Lauren ran toward the house, her skirts flying.

In the hallway on the second floor, Callie found Lauren and her two sisters standing in front of an open doorway, crying. She looked inside and saw Luc holding onto his father. Beside him stood Natalie Delacroix, her face stony and her eyes misted. She gripped the folds of her skirt in tight-fisted hands.

Callie found herself herding the girls away from the door and into a nearby bedroom. She could do nothing to help their grief, but she could comfort them. She held Lauren while Luc summoned the doctor who then pronounced Etienne Delacroix dead.

Natalie sat on the sofa, her head high and her eyes glittering. The black silk of her mourning dress made her look pretty with her white skin and her dark curls surrounding her face. "Well, I suppose you think you're the head of the family now. Just because you won this little triumph over Jonas doesn't give you rights over me and my daughters."

Simone shrank back against the chair she was sitting in. Like Callie she was trying to making herself invisible. Callie knew that Simone desperately wanted to go to Paris.

Luc's face tightened. "Natalie, things have never been good between us. You forced my father to send me and my sister to Paris, but my childhood resentment of you is long over. I care about my sisters and naturally that would extend to you as the mother of my sisters."

Natalie started to cry. The tears left blotches on her pale face. "Your father never loved me. He loved your mother. I was just a convenient way to sire a legitimate family."

"I appreciate how well you took care of my father," Luc responded. "I can never repay you."

"Yes, you can. Allow Simone to marry Jonas Ramsaye."

"Why are you so insistent on Jonas marrying Simone? He's poor. Everyone thinks he's a rich man, but I will tell you he's living on borrowed time."

"But he told me he was rich. Everyone says he's rich, and he promised he would take care of me." A plaintive note sounded in her voice.

In a moment of clarity, Luc understood that Natalie simply didn't want her children to be poor. She had endured poverty for so long, that she now feared it above all else. How sad that she understood so little.

Luc leaned forward. "You're being taken care of."

"Do you think I want to be beholden to my husband's black bastards." Natalie glared at Luc.

"Do you think I care," Luc said. "If you must rationalize the origins of my money, it originally came from my father's pre-war fortune. I just happen to have a sister who is financially astute."

"Jonas' money is honestly earned."

Luc started laughing. "Natalie, Jonas' money came from a munitions factory in Pennsylvania that supplied the northern army with weapons and ammunition."

Natalie looked crushed. "I don't believe you."

Luc's voice softened. "You must believe me. You forget I fought for the North. And I know that Jonas' money isn't as pure as you would like to believe." And that one decision caused such a rift between him and his father that only death had healed it. "I will care for you and your children for as long you need me. All I ask is that you mourn my father properly. Once the mourning is over, if you wish, I will help you find a new husband. You are still young and pretty."

Natalie smiled at the compliment. Then she glanced at her daughters. Even Luc could see the thought in her mind that three daughters was a liability to husband-hunting. "And what type of husband can you find for my daughters? I will not allow them to have poor husbands who cannot safely support them."

"Esme has already arranged for them to have their own trust funds. They won't need husbands if they don't want them. They will all be free to make their own choices."

"But they are just girls. How can girls make a choice?"

"Contrary to popular belief, women are able to handle their own lives when given a chance." Luc's mother had handled her own life and so did Esme. Callie handed her own life, too. Why should Natalie think her daughters should rely on some man to make the decisions about their futures. Luc understood that Natalie came from a society where women were treated as affable pets, but the war had changed things and more women were taking charge of their futures. "I know you have intelligent daughters."

"What about me?"

"With letters of introduction, I can present you to the nobility of Europe."

"That's not what I mean. If you can make my daughters independent, then you can make me independent, too. I'm not sure I want to marry again."

"Then I will make it so that you have a choice as well. I have homes in

London, Paris and Monte Carlo. You can live in any of them."

Callie sat in a corner huddled with Simone, Josette, and Lauren. She held Lauren's hand and Simone leaned against her. In the last few days, Callie had proved to be a rock of strength. Death was a very different experience for her, and she had accepted Etienne's death with a stoic equanimity that had made her the one person in the house the others could depend on.

"But what about you. What happens if you chose to marry and bring your bride to one of those homes. I will be homeless again."

"You will never be homeless." Luc found himself smiling at Callie. Callie looked up and returned his smile. Her face was transformed. "I'm not ready for marriage, yet."

"I think maybe you are." Natalie followed the direction of his glance. "She's very pretty, if you like that type of woman."

Luc glanced at Natalie. "What's wrong with Callie?"

"She's very Indian looking and dark. What do you see in her?"

What did he see in Callie? "She's a woman who understands my world. She has spirit and is independent." Just like Esme. A light seemed to go off in his head. "She doesn't need me. She simply wants me."

"Those are great qualities in a woman," Natalie said in a scornful tone. "She's can't sew, or do needlework, or cook. I don't understand what her mama was doing, not to teach her these things."

Luc smiled. "She can track an outlaw, shoot a gun, and ride the wildest horse." The other skills she'd learned in the last few days were not the type a man talked about. He was impressed with how much she embraced the new direction of their relationship. She was insatiable and she had none of the coy qualities that seemed to permeate European women in their intimate relationships. Luc's mistress in Paris had constantly needed to be maintained as the price for her favors. Callie asked for nothing. She wanted him, not the objects he could give her.

In an off-hand tone, Natalie said, "I wonder how your superior officers would feel about your relationship with her?" She fanned herself with a languid gesture, smiling at him as though she had the better poker hand.

Luc's heart went still. How nice of Natalie to hit at the crux of the matter. How smart of her to leave unsaid, the most important part. She knew more about him than was comfortable, though he knew she had already given him power over her. "Consider your threat carefully, your fortunes rise and fall with me."

Natalie blanched. Point taken.

"Tomorrow," Luc said, "your daughter leaves for Paris. I think you need to help her finish packing. Callie and I have some business to attend to."

The superior look on Natalie's face told him that she thought she knew exactly what type of business was at hand. Nothing could be further from the truth. Luc intended to take Callie to see his mother's house.

Callie watched as a dock hand wrestled Simone's trunk up the gangplank to the ship waiting to take her to Paris. Lauren held tightly onto Callie's hand. She seemed a bundle of repressed excitement.

Luc directed the dock hand. He looked so handsome in his suit with a broad-brimmed white hand shading his face. She marveled at his ability to be so at ease in so many different situations.

"Luc," Simone said, "is Paris really the most beautiful city in the world."

"Yes, but compared to you, it's a factory town. You're going to set the place on its ear." Luc hugged her. "Be good, the Countess is a dear friend and her husband is a prominent government official. She'll adore you. She was Esme's patroness. I would trust my sister with no one else." He kissed her hand and Simone giggled nervously.

After a second's hesitation, she threw her arms around him. "I love you so much. Thank you for what you've done for me and for my sisters."

A loud whistle pierced the air. A ship, pulled by a tugboat, had come into view and Callie strained on tip toes to see. Why did she have to wear a gown today when she could have climbed up a pole to see what had caused so much excitement.

"The Sea Maiden," came a shout.

Luc turned toward the commotion and at the shout, his face lit up. "The Sea Maiden." He grabbed a passing dock worker. "Did someone say The Sea Maiden?"

"Yes, sir. The Sea Maiden. She made it back. Late, but that is one seaworthy old girl. Made it all the way back from China. I knew she wouldn't disappoint us." The dock worker leaped into the air and started running toward an empty dock space.

Callie grinned at Luc. She touched his sleeve. "My mama's cat looks like you when she's caught herself a big juicy bird."

"Calisto, I believe my ship has come in."

"Do you own that ship?"

Luc nodded. "As of five days ago, I own fifty-five percent of her cargo."

"Is that a lot?"

He grinned at her. "That's a lot." He turned toward Simone's ship.

180

"You'd best be getting on board."

Simone hugged him again. "Thank you, Luc." She turned and hugged Lauren.

Callie hugged her, too. "I'm sorry your mama and sister Josette couldn't come." Josette wasn't feeling well and Natalie had stayed behind to care for her.

"I'm afraid, Callie," Simone said.

"You'll be fine. All those big people in France will love you." Callie kissed Simone on the cheek.

In the few days since she'd been introduced to the Delacroix household, Callie had come to like Luc's sisters very much and Luc had told how pleased he was she had made such an impact on them. She'd told them stories about her life in the desert, even as she tactfully avoided telling them she was a scout for the Army and really worked for their brother.

After Simone was installed in her cabin with the woman who would be chaperoning her to Paris, Luc insisted they check out the Sea Maiden. He was filled with suppressed excitement and Callie didn't understand why. The ship was just a ship, a little larger than the others, but still something that floated on water, even if he did own a part of the cargo.

Luc asked Callie to take Lauren home and wait for him there.

Luc stood on the docks waiting for the ship to be tied to its berth. He thought of all that cargo he owned. He had no idea of its eventual worth, but he could see Esme rubbing her hands together over it. Money equaled power and forced acceptance. Some people didn't care where he and Esme had come from, but many people did, and having money made their background more tolerable.

"I hate you," Jonas Ramsaye said in a dead voice. "You've ruined me."

"You ruined yourself," Luc replied.

"You knew the Sea Maiden was going to arrive. You swindled me."

"I didn't know anything." Although he could smell the stench of greed coming off of Jonas. Luc clasped his hands in front of him. "If you want to threaten me with a lawsuit, go right ahead. I can see the headlines now. Black man outsmarts white one. You and your children will be humiliated for the rest of their lives. No one likes to be a laughingstock. You're old. I can tie you up in court until all the great-great-grandchildren, you don't even know about yet, are old enough to marry."

Jonas' face was as red a mulberry. "Not if I kill you first. You may look white, but I know who and what you are. I can tell the world."

Luc stepped up to Jonas until they were almost face to face. "You can tell the world whatever you want, but the end result will be the same. I did not swindle you. You took my money of your own volition. I have witnesses who would rather have my money in their bank then yours. The courts will believe them because they have more credibility than you do. So if you want to challenge me in a court of law, you do so at the risk of your own reputation. So if you please, stand out of my way."

Jonas stepped aside and Luc walked closer to the dock just as the gangway was being dropped into position. Once it was open, he walked up onto the ship and asked to see the captain.

━๑๑๑━

Callie was curled on her side, her eyes half open, her hand cupped under her cheek. She felt satiated and drowsy with his love-making. The knock on the door startled them both because of its lateness.

Luc pulled on his robe to answer the door. He walked through the bedroom and into the parlor. Distantly, Callie heard the sound of voices. Luc laughed and Callie wondered what had so caught his attention.

She closed her eyes, thinking of nothing but having him back at her side. Every moment she spent with him was to be savored and tucked into her heart for the future. Once they were back at Fort Duncan they would revert to their former situation. She couldn't think of a time when he would no longer be hers and she hated the thought that she would be alone again.

Luc entered the bedroom and she watched him through half-closed eyes. A red cloud descended on her, feeling good on her bare skin. The cloud smelled beautiful. She didn't know the scents, but she inhaled them deeply. She opened her eyes and sat up. Luc sat on the edge of the mattress grinning at her.

"This is so soft."

"The finest silk from the Orient, meant only to grace the skin of the most beautiful women."

Callie smiled at him. She hugged the cloud of fabric to her breasts. She snaked her hand around his arm and pulled him toward her. "Make love to me on this silk." She wanted to feel him and the silk against her skin at the same time.

He undid the belt at his waist and tossed his robe on a chair and reached for her.

CHAPTER EIGHTEEN

Rafe watched as the war party raced around the outside of the village hooting and screaming. As they calmed and came into the village, Rafe confronted the leader of the party, Red Claw, who boasted of his kills. The Mexican bandit, Juan Valenzuela, smirked at Rafe as he dismounted from his horse.

"What is the matter with you?" Rafe demanded of Red Claw. Anger consumed him. "Our war is with the army. You risk our future by attacking men doing nothing but trying to feed their own families."

Red Claw snarled. "Who cares. They were Mexicans carrying gold."

Rafe couldn't believe that Red Claw had taken a great risk that could bring the Mexican government down on their heads. "You stole Mexican gold?"

"Gold is gold. Gold buys weapons." Valenzuela said.

Rafe stared at the two men. "Do you understand what you have done?" Allowing the Mexican bandit into camp had been a mistake. He had come with grand ideas on how the Comanche could help him with his own war, and in return he would help them with theirs.

Red Claw glared at Rafe. "I did what any warrior would do. I met my enemy and killed them all."

Fool Rafe thought. Mexico was not their enemy. "Your raid will do nothing but make our job harder."

"You have the soul of a rabbit," Red Claw beat on his chest. "The army doesn't care about Mexico."

"But Mexico cares about Mexico. And the U.S. Army isn't going to stand in their way if they are hunting us too." Rafe reached for his knife, but his wife stopped him. "You have added to the list of our enemies. We're barely one step ahead of the Blue Coats. And now you have given the Mexicans a reason to join the fight against us. I will kill you."

Valenzuela jumped out of the way, a startled expression on his face. "I am Mexico, and I have helped you in your battle with the army. You have much to thank me for, including your friend at the fort. If not for me, you would not have the information he has provided for you. If not for me, you would not have a way to even contact him."

Willow touched his arm. "Husband, they are not worth your time. Do not insult your knife with their blood." She pulled her own knife from the scabbard. "Let me kill Red Claw. He is nothing more than a coward at heart."

Red Claw glared at Rafe. "You will allow a woman to fight your battles?"

Willow growled deep in her throat. She looked so fierce and protective, Rafe wanted to allow her the kill. But he couldn't. The tribe needed all their warriors including a coward like Red Claw who killed innocent men to prove himself brave.

Rafe shook Willow's hand off his arm and laughed. Red Claw's face contorted with fury. "You took young, inexperienced warriors against an enemy of unknown strength. That is not bravery, but an attempt to look like a man in the eyes of boys. You're not strong, just lucky."

"I will kill you." Red Claw stepped back.

"You will try," Rafe replied. "If you think you can challenge me then do so now." Rafe crossed his arms over his chest. "Otherwise, I have no time for you."

Red Claw glanced around at the crowd which had surrounded them. Many of the men looked stern and disapproving, and the women watched Red Claw with menace deep in their eyes. They all understood what was at stake and Red Claw had done.

Night Feather pushed through the crowd and stood in front of Red Claw. "You have disgraced your name. You've chosen to disobey my orders."

Red Claw bared his teeth. "I did what a warrior should do, fight his enemy."

Night Feather glanced at Willow's knife. "As far as I am concerned, you are still a child. And until you have learned to be a warrior, I will have nothing to do with you." Night Feather turned his back to Red Claw. Slowly the other members of the tribe did the same, turning away from him.

Rafe watched a mixture of emotions cross Red Claw's face. He felt sorry for the man who had started out with such noble thoughts and was now being shunned. Valenzuela was escorted from the camp by two warriors and put astride his horse and sent on his way despite his loud protests.

Willow glared at Red Claw and tapped Rafe on the shoulder. She turned to face away from Red Claw and Rafe found himself following suit. When the tribe had drifted away, Rafe headed toward his horse.

"Where are you going?" Willow asked him as he jumped astride his horse.

"We cannot keep this gold. I must find a way to return it." He angled his horse toward the desert. He had to get away or he'd kill Red Claw.

Buzzards circled the sky. Callie shaded her eyes with her hand. "Something's dead." They'd been following fresh wagon ruts for two days. She pointed them out to Luc.

"The army isn't due for another supply train for a month."

"Maybe this isn't army." Callie spurred her horse forward and they trotted over a rise to confront a field littered with dead animals and overturned wagons. Five graves with twigs formed in the sign of a cross had been lined up beneath the leaves of a large cottonwood.

A man with a slouch hat and worn clothes, using a branch for a crutch, limped out onto the road and took a deep sigh. He waved at them.

Luc reined his horse to a halt. "Sir, what happened here?"

Callie could see this little wagon train had seen a heap of trouble.

The short Mexican man took off his straw hat. "A troop of seven Comanche with a Mexican came out of nowhere. They attacked us and took our supplies and our gold."

Luc glanced around at the devastation. "What is your name?"

"My name is Hector Portillo," the man said with a thick Mexican accent in his voice.

Luc and Callie dismounted their horses. "Where were you headed," Luc asked.

"My orders were to take the gold to Austin."

Luc handed the reins of his horse to Callie. "You should have requested an escort."

The man spat at the ground. "Our escort never showed up. Waited two days at the border, but no one came. So we crossed the river and hoped for the best." He dug into his pocket and handed Luc a letter. Luc read it, his eyes moving over the paper swiftly. When he folded the letter and put it in his pocket, his jaw was tight with a deep tension.

Luc frowned at the man. "Why didn't you just head for the nearest fort?"

The man spat at the ground near Callie's boots. "The army gringos didn't come when they said they would. I wasn't going to trust them again."

"Did you wait for the army?"

"For three days." He glared at Luc.

Callie wished she knew of a way to help him, but knew he couldn't settle Mexican-American relations in a day. They needed to get out of here in case the Comanches decided to come back and check their handy work.

Luc took the reins of her horse from her and handed them to the other man. "Mr. Portillo, I can see you're wounded and in need of medical care. We're less than a day from medical help, food and a clean bed at Fort Duncan. I'm not leaving you out here alone and vulnerable." He got on his horse and extended his hand. "Climb up here behind me."

His first order to her as her commanding officer since they left New Orleans. They were back to their original roles and Callie mourned the easy camaraderie they'd developed. She had hoped for a few more days of his companionship.

She climbed up behind Luc. She closed her eyes. New Orleans was a distant dream, a fantasy gone like smoke on the wind. She thought of the clothes Luc had arranged to ship back to her village. Her fingers craved to caress the silks and satins, to bring back the evenings spent in fancy restaurants. He'd even taken her to the opera even though she hadn't had no idea of what was being said. The music has been so beautiful, she'd cried. She had to refocus her mind on her goals.

She kept the dream of land in her mind for the next two days. They were torture, being close to Luc and being unable to touch him with the man they had picked up on the trail.

While Luc was in a meeting with General Hammond and the senior officers of the fort to discuss the situation with the Mexican gold, Callie sat with Esme on the front porch of Luc's quarters.

Esme looked very pretty in a green silk gown that almost matched her eyes. "How was your journey to New Orleans?" She sat in a slatted chair on the veranda in front of Luc's quarters her sketch pad across her lap and her fingers smudged with charcoal. A floppy hat shaded her face.

Callie sat on the step and looked across the parade ground toward Luc's office. He'd been there all morning catching up on all the activities that had happened during the weeks they'd been gone.

"Why are you always so nice to me?" Callie inquired of Esme.

Esme gave her a languid smile. "You have adventures I can never have."

"I don't understand."

Esme smiled, a faraway look in her eyes. "You don't wear a dress. You hunt, shoot, ride a horse like a man and you never have to fight to be respected. People respect you automatically because they think you're a man. That kind of respect must be intoxicating. For me, respect is a game and I have to beat the men before they will give me the littlest crumb. Men think that admiration is enough to keep a woman happy. But we really want respect, equality and dignity. You have these. The soldiers here respect you and your abilities. They trust you with their lives. No man on this post, but Luc, would do that for me simply because I wear a dress."

Callie didn't know what to say. "But I live a lie." So did Luc.

"Only to fulfill your dream." Esme sighed. "How much of our past did Luc share with you?"

"I know everything." Knowing Luc's background had changed so much between them.

"Then you understand the reasons behind our deception."

Callie did, but she could help feeling that lie made Luc feel different. "The lie is eating at him."

"I know. I want him to resign his commission. But he always has one more task he must accomplish, one more mission to complete. I'd hoped that now he'd made peace with our father, he would be free to find a new life."

"But he doesn't know anything else."

"He can go back to Paris, or come with me to San Francisco. He owns land in Canada. He doesn't have to stay here. He can be what he wants to be."

"But why would he want to leave?" Despite Luc's lie, Callie knew he loved army life. The army was bigger than himself. More important that the little details. For Luc, the army was his tribe, his family, his reason for being. Callie understood that. She had the same feelings toward her tribe, her family. Though for her the army was a means to an end, if she could make this kind of money doing anything else, she'd go.

"Because I think he must. The army is like reliving his boyhood every day. He gets to ride, shoot and rattle his saber at the enemy. This is so typical of being a man, they are afraid if they grow up they get old." Esme laughed. "Cal, I believe you and I are too intelligent for our own good."

Callie didn't think she was intelligent, but if Esme thought so, it might be so. "But I don't know how to read." Rafe had known how to read and write. He'd promised to teach her, but he'd left instead.

"My classes are going well, you can join in. You will be reading in no time. Trust me. You just need to know your letters and I can start right now." She flipped a page on her pad and started writing.

Callie didn't know. She'd had little time for book education in her village. Only the chief and his wife knew how to read. Why should she? Yet she thirsted after knowledge. She wanted to do more than make a mark on a piece of paper in place of her name. She wanted to be worthy of Luc. He could read and write and was a wealthy man. What would he want with a woman who couldn't read?

She glanced at Esme whose fingers flew over her sketch pad. For all her lady-like manners, she was a strong woman. Despite the way she looked, Callie didn't one moment doubt that men respected her. In a different way, maybe, but still they respected her. Callie envied Esme and thought it strange that Esme would envy Callie. Callie had nothing. Esme had everything. The world was a very odd place.

✦✦✦

Luc sat across from General Hammond. General Hammond sat at Luc's desk, frowning as he brought Luc up to date on what had been happening and Esme's part in it. Luc wasn't certain he wanted his sister involved any more than she already was.

The meeting was over. Major Adams was setting up a patrol to head back to the ambushed gold train and see what could be determined from the mess. He'd also sent a messenger to Austin to inform them of what had happened, and sent another messenger along with the survivor back to Mexico.

The General sat back and the chair tipped slightly. "Our spy appears to have struck again."

Luc gazed out the window. A herd of new horses had been delivered and off-duty soldiers hung on the corral fence watching as each animal was separated and then led to the blacksmith for shoeing. "That appears to be the case, sir."

"Who would have handled the request for the military escort?"

"I would have." He pulled the letter Hector Portillo had given him and handed it to the General. The letter, sent to Hector's supervisor and promising a military escort, had been signed by Luc himself, or rather someone impersonating Luc. The signature was a good one, but not Luc's.

General Hammond quickly read the letter, his face turning thoughtful. He tugged at his mustache. "The signature is a good forgery. Can you tell who signed your name?"

"I can't, I don't have that skill, but I know someone who does."

The general leaned forward. "Who?"

"Esme does." Luc found himself smiling, remembering when Esme as a student had studied the European masters and then leaned to flawlessly copy them, right down to the artist's signature. "If not for her career as a portrait artist, I believe she would have made an excellent forger."

The General scanned the letter again. "The letter is dated after you left for New Orleans. Sloppy mistake on the spy's part." He twisted in the chair. "Who took over your duties?"

"Everything was parceled out to all the junior lieutenants." Luc had a sick feeling in his gut. One of his people was a traitor. Someone he'd worked with and trusted. Who could have betrayed him? Betrayed their oath to the United States government.

A horse slammed into the fence and several soldiers shouted. Hammond glanced out the window. "Which means, one of the junior officers on this post could be the traitor. I don't know if I want to believe that. Anyone could have written this letter, an enlisted man, or even one of your precious Black Seminole scouts."

"Maybe," Luc replied, "but most of them don't have access to this office or my mail, or have any reason to be in here. As for the scouts, the government has never understood about the Black Seminoles. They have great pride in who and what they are, and simply want the government to fulfill its promises. Once their loyalty is given, it never wavers. Loyalty cannot be bought, but must be earned. The United States tries to buy loyalty."

Hammond's lips thinned as he digested Luc's information. "How do you know so much about how the Black Seminole thinks?"

"My scout, Cal Payne."

"That fourteen year old boy. They don't grow them big in Mexico, do they?"

Luc laughed. Callie grew up just fine in Mexico. She was just the right size. For everything. "He gave me a quick lesson in Indian history. Cal was willing to share what he knew with me. Smart kid. Given half a chance, he'll go far."

"Okay, so the scouts are loyal. Just to be sure, what about your black troops. Many of them are ex-slaves and have ambitions to get ahead."

Luc shook his head. "Most of the black troops fought in the war and they're also loyal. I don't think we even need to look at the newer recruits. They wouldn't know how things were done yet. From what I can see, the information being passed would only be known by an officer."

"You have four junior lieutenants and one senior lieutenant. That would be Rippy. Major Adams is already checked out and is beyond reproach. I already trust you implicitly. Which one do you think is the spy?"

Luc had to think about that. "What would a spy gain from his betrayal?"

"I don't know. What can the Comanche pay him?"

"The Comanche doesn't want anything from the white man except guns. But they can sell guns for money. So someone has money to pay the spy."

"Who wants money?" The first name that popped into Luc's was Reggie whose family was in such desperate need, but would Reggie lower himself. Would Reggie's greed be more than his pride. Reggie's family heritage was a source of pride and betrayal didn't fit with his Boston superiority for the under-classes.

Lieutenant Cox knocked at the door. Luc motioned him to enter. He entered carrying a dispatch bag. He saluted. "General, our daily dispatch is here. The messenger wants to know if you have anything to send back to headquarters."

"Not today," Hammond declared. He thanked the Lieutenant as Cox hefted the bag on the desk. Cox smartly saluted the General and was given leave to depart.

Luc's mind wandered down the list of officers. Lieutenant Rippy had a wife and two children to support, yet they seemed quite comfortable on what they had. The children weren't going barefoot and Rippy's wife was good with a needle and did sewing for the other wives. Though Esme commented that gossip suggested Rippy's wife was having an affair with a rancher in the area, Luc didn't know when the hard-working woman would have time for an affair. She seemed quite happy with her husband and family.

Lieutenant Magill was new on the post. He'd only been transferred four months ago. He had a mistress in Eagle Pass. Luc had seen the woman. She was looker with a fondness for pretty clothes, expensive jewelry, and big floppy hats. He'd been at headquarters before being posted to Fort Duncan. He could already have been working as a traitor before his transfer here.

Lieutenant Cox was the youngest and most junior officer. A graduate of West Point, he seemed to enjoy what he did and didn't appear to mind much that he made so little money. Despite the Major's daughter aggressively tossing her hat at him, he seemed content to remain single, in no hurry to take on the responsibility of a wife and family.

And of course, there was always Reggie. As much as Luc's mind shied away from considering Reggie, he had to be objective despite his long friendship. Reggie needed money to support his mother and sisters who had an upper class life-style and were not too accepting of their newly acquired poverty. But Reggie was Luc's friend, and they'd been through a lot together during the war. Luc just didn't think Reggie would sell his loyalty so easily.

They had to flush the traitor out and he tried to think what he could do. "What would happen," Luc said, "if we planted false information? Something that would be of interest to the Indians and that the traitor would want them to have."

"What kind of false information?"

"A change in the supply routes again. Or an unscheduled shipment of guns or gold bullion." Luc studied the dispatch bag. "You receive dispatches daily. So you would be informed immediately of supply trains. We could use that to set something up and see who takes the bait."

Hammond nodded. "I like the gun idea. Either that or we have a witch hunt. Glad I thought of that."

Luc hid a grin. The General was the General. If Luc could supply him with the spy, he'd retire in glory and show his gratitude.

"Pull this off, Delacroix," the General said, "and there is nothing the army won't do for you. You do know you're being groomed for bigger and better things. You have friends in high places."

For a second Luc was pleased the army had such faith in his leadership abilities. But he wondered if he wanted those bigger and better things. He wondered if the army would feel the same way if they knew about his heritage.

Since Callie had come into his life, he didn't know what he wanted anymore. If he stayed in the army, he wouldn't be able to keep Callie. And having her in his life had become of utmost importance. To be with Callie, he needed to be honest. The idea of resigning popped into his mind, but he immediately recoiled from it. He couldn't give up the life he'd worked so hard to create. He had to find another way.

Evening shadows lengthened across the ground. With evening mess completed, most of the soldier had retired to their barracks, though a few sat on the long veranda. Luc sat on a log beneath the silver cottonwoods shading the main corral. As the post slowly calmed down for the night, he puffed his cigar. The General had decided on a two-fold plan and was currently implementing with the help of Esme. Luc turned the plan over and over in his mind rooting for defects. There were always flaws and his job was to spot them and call them to the General's attention. Plans could always awry, no matter how careful the planning.

A rustle sounded at the edge of the stand of trees. Luc saw Callie watching him, poised as though ready to flee should he not want her. He nodded and she approached to sit next to him, perching lightly on the log. He inhaled the sweet fragrance of her hair pushed up beneath the brim of her wide hat. In her over-sized man's clothes she looked like a child playing grown-up.

Each time he saw her, he marveled that she hid her identity to easily. No hint of the sweet young woman he'd discovered in New Orleans could be detected. She had turned back into a soldier like a chameleon changed its color depending on its location.

"There's a spy at Fort Duncan," Luc said to her. "Someone who's selling confidential information to the Comanche."

Her eyes went wide. "Who would do such a thing?"

Luc shrugged. "I've been assigned the task of finding out."

A thoughtful look came over her face. She seemed to be thinking about something. "The night the General and Esme arrived, I saw a soldier sneaking away from the Fort. I was curious and followed him. He took off for the stream." She pointed.

Luc felt a stirring of excitement. "Who was it?"

Callie shook her head. "I don't know. Never got a good look at his face."

"It was a man."

"Yes, sir," Callie replied calmly as though she didn't know she'd just handed him a bomb.

"Could you tell if he was an officer, or an enlisted man." A shiver of excitement slipped through him.

"I couldn't tell if he was black or white."

"You didn't think to say anything."

She frowned at Luc. "You're out here by yourself. I just thought someone needed to be alone for awhile. There was a lot of big things happening that day. I know I need to get away sometimes."

"If you thought he just needed to get away, why follow?"

"I don't know. Something didn't feel right, but afterward I forgot about it."

Luc stood. "Can you show me where this person went?"

Callie jumped up and led the way along the path of the stream. Overhead birds chirped as they settled in for the night and a rabbit, flushed by their passage, hopped into a thicket of mesquite. At a small clearing shaded by spreading live oaks with thick vegetation and underbrush beneath the spreading arms, Callie showed him a rotted log laying half in and half out of the stream. "Put his hand in here, but I couldn't tell what he was looking for." She suddenly thumped the log. "Just checking for snakes." When she was satisfied nothing reptilian hid within, Callie moved toward the end of the log and watched him.

Luc knelt down and stared into the shadowed interior of the rotting log. He shoved his hand inside and felt around, but couldn't feel anything that didn't belong there. When he looked up, he found Callie with her hand out-stretched. "What is this?"

"I found this." In the palm of her hand rested a shiny gold button that caught the dying light of the sun.

He didn't scold her for not giving it to him sooner. She hadn't known the importance of her find, and earlier it wouldn't have meant anything even to him. Luc took the button, studying it. The button could have come from any uniform. Not much evidence, but it did prove the spy was at Fort Duncan. He pocketed the button. Once the traitor was exposed, maybe Luc should think more deeply about his future. He could angle for a transfer back to Washington D.C. and set Callie up in a little apartment in Arlington.

Or they could just leave. Maybe he could talk her into running away to Paris! They could live openly in there. Luc a little apartment in the city. "Come away with me to Paris." Luc touched her arm.

She stared at him in surprise. "Are you loco? What would someone like me do in Paris. Paris is for ladies. I'm not a lady."

She was adorable in her indignation. "You could be a lady."

Callie snorted and said, "How would I become a lady? I don't have any schooling and I can barely be bothered to wear a dress."

"I could teach you." The idea appealed to him. "A lady isn't always something a woman is born to. It's something a woman usually learns."

She shook her head. "I don't want to be a lady. I'd have to wear a dress all the time and learn to use the right fork."

Luc stood and brushed dirt from his knees. "I thought you admired Esme."

"Esme isn't really a lady. She only pretends to be one to get what she wants."

If Esme knew how well Callie understood her, she'd change all her tactics and Luc would have to relearn how to deal with his adorable sister whom he loved so dearly.

"Besides," Callie continued, "I have my family, my tribe to take care of." Her voice softened and drifted away.

"I have enough money for everyone." He could buy her tribe all the land they needed to make a new start. Not in France, surely, but someplace else, where they would feel they belonged.

Callie shook her head. "My people wouldn't fit in Paris."

Luc laughed. "That wasn't what I meant. I can buy their land and you wouldn't have to work so hard to satisfy so many other people's dreams. You could have a life of your own. You deserve to have one.

"My tribe is my life."

Of course, it was. She wouldn't be Callie if she didn't believe in herself.

"I love you." The words sipped out and Luc couldn't believe what he'd just said. He was so surprised he dropped his cigar and then bent to pick it up again.

"No," Callie said, "you just think you love me because I'm different. Away from here, I'd simply be another woman."

Luc protested. "You would never be 'another woman' anywhere." She was a refreshing breath of air in his life.

"How can you be honest with me when you can't be honest with yourself?" She turned and walked away.

Luc watched her go. He had no answer. Her words shook him to the core.

$$\rightwave$$

Esme dimpled flirtatiously at Lieutenant Cox as he passed her. He smiled at her with the foolish smile men seemed to develop when a pretty woman showed interest in them. Not that she was interested in this man, but in what he might know.

Her heart pounded with excitement. She had a mission. General Hammond had told her he had total faith in her. Esme would not fail.

Cox hesitated at the sight of her. She crooked her finger and he stumbled over his feet in his eager haste to get to her.

"Miss Esme, what can I do for you?"

The puppy look of adoration on his face told her he would do anything. She patted the empty space on the double swing hanging from the porch roof in front of the mess hall. From inside came the sounds of the cooks getting ready for dinner.

"I've been feeling so lonely," Esme pouted, "Won't you sit with me for a moment. Please." She batted her eyelashes at him. "I won't keep you from your duties for too long."

Lieutenant Cox sat down next to her. Despite his age, he blushed like a school boy. All in all, he was attractive. A little rough around the edges, but nothing an attentive wife wouldn't smooth out of him. She remembered that his family harvested maple syrup in Vermont and that he was anxious to prove himself as capable as any battled-scarred soldier. He'd missed the war by a year, being too young.

Esme placed a hand on his arm. "I appreciate all those very nice things you've done for me. Taking me to Eagle's Pass and helping me get supplies for my school. It's going very well and I was hoping to show my appreciation."

"How?" he asked bluntly. Then he blushed again and glanced away in embarrassment.

Esme laughed. "You farm boys are so eager. As much as I might enjoy your company, a woman demands to be wooed."

"How would I go about that?"

Esme sighed. "Pretty words. Women adore pretty words, especially when they are written on paper and we can keep them next to our hearts forever." She clasped her hands over her breasts and fluttered her eyelashes at him. Men were so simple.

He shook his head. "I'm not a poet, Miss Esme. I can barely find the words to write reports."

Esme patted the back of his hand. "You don't need to be a poet. Your words just need to be passionate and true. I can tell you are a passionate man." She handed him a pad of paper and a pencil. "Let me help you. Just a few short words. In Japan, a form of poetry has just a few words. I believe it is called haiku."

He leaned over the paper and wet the tip of the pencil with his tongue. "Like I said before, I don't know any pretty words. Not the words that would do justice to a beautiful woman like you."

Esme could tell he wanted deeply to impress her. "You'll do fine. Make it up." She leaned toward him and pursed her lips.

He blushed again, the red creeping toward his ears.

When he finished the poem, she kissed him lightly on the cheek and sent him on his way. She folded the paper and slipped it into her drawing box and sighed. Men were so predictable.

Lieutenant Magill was busy. He sat at his desk reading something and making notes on a slip of paper.

But Esme persisted. "Come for a walk with me." She pushed out her bottom lip and pouted. She tapped him on the wrist with her fan. "Please. It's a pretty day and I'm lonely."

The young officer stared at her as though she were icing on a cake. "But I have work to do." He glanced at the stack of paper of his desk, even though his blue eyes betrayed his eagerness. "Your brother will be upset with me if I don't complete these requisitions. You should know the army runs on paperwork. I sometimes feel like I'm drowning in it."

"I shall speak to Luc about working you so hard." One of the things about American men Esme adored. They weren't game players like Frenchmen. If they desired a woman, they made their desire plainly known, taking a lot of the guess work out of seduction.

He glanced at the paperwork on his desk. "I don't think I should."

"Then I will extract from you a promise, in writing, that you will walk with me this evening, under the cottonwoods." She pushed a piece of paper at him. "I will dictate it."

This was much too easy. Luc would be pleased with the results, but she was already bored with all her manipulations. Maybe Lieutenant Rippy would provide her with more of a challenge. After all, he was married.

Lt. Rippy stood on the porch of the post store. He wiped his face with a white handkerchief which he folded neatly and returned to his pocket. "How can I help you, Miss Esme." He wasn't falling for her charm. He was polite because she was his superior's sister, but he wasn't interested in her flirting. In fact, he looked slightly alarmed, as though he expected his wife to come darting around the corner and catch him in an indiscretion.

"I know London, Paris, Rome, but I don't know the United States." Esme fluttered her eyelashes at him, but he was immune to her manipulative flattery. "If you could write down all the state capitols for me, I and my students will be eternally grateful."

He looked almost relieved that he wasn't being tempted into something he didn't want to do. He was a man loyal to his wife and family. She wondered if he knew how unfaithful his wife was. Though she had no particular proof that the woman was straying.

Life on a military reservation was a microcosm of society. They had their own pecking order, their own gossip mill. Nothing went unseen, or was unknown. The mostly carefully guarded secrets had a way of being discovered.

Esme was most curious about a peculiar custom called ranking out. When a new officer and his family arrived, they took their position in the line of quarters according to their position in the official hierarchy of the post, which mean anyone occupying those quarters had to move down to the next set of quarters and anyone living in those quarters had to move until the whole line of officers and their families moved down. Mrs. Rippy had once complained that they had to move into a sod hut when she had first been married and her husband was the lowest man in the ranks. She had told Esme of the mushrooms that grew up through the floor planks and the small black and yellow striped snake that had lived in the wall and curled up on her parlor chair as though coming for a friendly visit.

Lieutenant Rippy took the pad of paper and the pencil. He leaned against a post as he quickly wrote down the states and their capitols.

Esme practically danced with excitement. She had Reggie Cooper left to do. She tracked him down to his office. He sat at his desk, feet up on the surface of the desk, smoking a cigar. Smoke swirled around his head and he appeared to savor the fragrant tobacco.

"Luc tells me," Esme said with a girlish giggle, "that your penmanship is absolutely exquisite. I would like a sample to show to my students. They must understand how beautiful cursive writing can be. Unfortunately, Luc and I are sadly lacking in that talent." She let her shoulders droop and dazzled Reggie with a smile that sent his feet off the desk and the cigar on the ground.

"My pleasure," Reggie Cooper said with an expansive gesture. "But as payment for my help, you must go riding with me."

"That's not a payment," Esme giggled, "but a pleasure."

"Alone," he teased her.

She dimpled at him and stroked his cheek. "I cannot think of a better payment."

A silly grin spread across his face, and Esme saw his whole body stiffen. If she could arouse him with a touch to his cheek and a practice giggle, what would he be like in bed? Would he go the distance? She doubted he'd last long enough to get her out of her corset.

He accepted the pad of paper and the pencil and sat down at his desk. "Do you want me to write anything."

"Anything that my students can read."

"How about a love poem. I know one that almost makes me cry every time a read it."

"And that would be?" Esme coaxed.

"Let me compare you to a summer's day."

Esme sighed. "The English Bard. I so adore Shakspere?"

"His poetry is exquisite." His bent over the paper, and cast longing looks at Esme as he wrote.

Esme leaned over his shoulder and sighed with delight as each word was formed on the page. A pity, he did have beautiful handwriting. She wished she could admire him as much as her brother did.

CHAPTER NINETEEN

Rafe pulled his horse to a stop and raised his hand. Something felt wrong. An odd feeling seeped over him as he glanced around the prairie. A peculiar smokey smell filled the air.

"I smell death," Night Feather said, pulling his horse to a stop. The warriors behind him followed suit.

Rafe pushed his horse forward, the other warriors following him. Rafe and Night Feather had left two days ago to hunt and visit several neighboring bands of Comanche. They had spread the story of Red Claw's betrayal of his people.

Rafe hadn't figured out how to return the gold, but he'd visited the log near the fort and left a note asking how he could do this. He didn't want the wrath of Mexico to fall on the heads of his adopted people. They had enough to worry about without making an enemy of Mexico.

Rafe heard the wailing long before he topped the rise and saw their small camp in chaos. The tee pees had been pulled down across cooking fires and lay smoldering. Children cried and old women stood in the center of the camp cradling them. Bodies lay sprawled across the ground and Rafe's heart seemed to stop.

Willow, Rafe thought. He kicked his horse hard and raced toward the camp, Night Feather and the others racing after him.

"What happened?" He asked one of the old women as he slid to a stop and dismounted from his horse.

The old woman stared at him, not seeming to recognize him for a moment. "Everyone is dead," the old woman wailed, cradling a baby in her arms. "Your woman made me take the children and hide in the underbrush."

"Where's Willow?" Rafe demanded.

The old woman wept huge tears. "Red Claw and that Mexican bandit returned last night with others. They wanted the gold. We fought them, but they took it anyway, and killed everyone. Including your woman."

Rafe stared at the devastation, his mind numb. "My son," he asked, his throat dry. He tried to think, but no thoughts formed.

"Safe with the other children." The old woman pointed at the edge of the camp where another old woman parted the bushes and led several children toward him.

Rafe shook his head. He glanced around trying to spot his wife, but saw only blood and dead bodies. He didn't believe his Willow was dead. "Where is she?"

The old woman pointed at the center of the camp. A body sprawled on the ground surrounded by other bodies. The long black hair and the familiar curving of breast and hip told him it was Willow.

He stood over her staring down at her lifeless face. Strands of black hair covered her eyes. He knelt, pulling Willow into his arms and holding her, wiping her hair out of her face. She still held her knife clenched in one hand. Dried blood stained the blade and her fingers. Her leather tunic was drenched with blood, a gaping hole in the side of her head showing the gunshot wound that had killed her.

Two men lay near her. Both dead. One of them was Red Claw, a look of total surprise on his face as he stared unseeing at the blue sky. Willow had killed him. She had told Rafe she would not allow Red Claw's blood to insult his knife, and she had kept her promise.

Grief replaced the numbness in his heart. Not his Willow, he thought. She couldn't die. She was the fiercest of warriors—invincible and strong. He held her tight against his chest. Tears blurred his vision and he knew his life would never be the same again. He would never again have her to warm his bed, to mother their son, to be his friend. Her laughter, her passion was gone.

He held her for a long time, then gently placed her back on the ground, arranging her arms and legs in a more modest position.

One of the old women thrust his son at him. Rafe took the boy and held him tight. His son clung to him. Rafe studied his son's face seeing the shape of Willow's stubborn chin and the sloping of her cheeks in his features. He remembered when Willow had presented him with his son, the pride in her eyes, the love she had for them both. That moment had filled his heart with love. Her death was now draining his heart of everything he had once held close.

He hugged his son tightly. "Your mother was a warrior among warriors. She died bravely." Rafe handed his little son back to the old woman. "What about the Mexican?"

She grimaced and spat at the ground. "Once he was done with his killing of women and old men, he took the gold and left."

Rafe scanned the horizon. "Which direction did the Mexican go?" Hardness formed at the core of Rafe's soul. He could not bare to look at Willow, laying on the ground. He knew he would grief deeply later, but the time for action was now.

The old woman pointed east. Rafe caught the reins of his horse and after a long good-bye to his wife, he led the horse toward the edge of the camp.

"Where do you go, brother?" Night Feather asked, his voice breaking with his own grief. Though his wife had been gone many years ago, lost in childbirth, the daughter born of the wife's sacrifice was one of the dead.

Rafe swung up onto his horse. "To avenge our families."

"Then you do not go alone."

Rafe shook his head. "What I do I must do alone. It is because of me that our wives are lost. I brought the Mexican into our fight because he promised us guns. I let him use us for his own purposes, and this is what happened." He gazed at the camp, at the children with no mothers, the warriors with no wives, into the dark eyes of his dear son.

He had thought their cause noble and just. But the end was lost. They had nothing left to fight for.

Rafe reached toward Night Feather and clasped his hand. "Thank you, brother, for your offer, but I cannot accept it. When you have cared for the dead seek out Quanah Parker. He will welcome you. His fight is now our fight. Send the old women and the children to my village in Mexico. I know my people are not your friends, but my mother has a kind heart and will help them to settle some place safe. My mother will care for my son." He reached to the back of his neck and undid the leather thong threaded with the alligator tooth his mother had given him as a child. "Give this to her. She will know it's from me."

Night Feather accepted the tooth. "What about you?"

"I'm going after Valenzuela. Soon he will be dead and so will I." His soul was dead already.

Reggie. Luc couldn't believe Reggie was the spy, but Esme had offered him incontrovertible proof. She had shown Luc Reggie's writing and compared that sample with the signature. No matter how hard a person tried, some basic elements of his handwriting he could not hide. In the end, his perfect, Boston-bred penmanship had tied the noose around his neck.

Luc hid in the brush watching the log. Across the clearing he could see the spot where Callie was hiding, but he couldn't see her. Several soldiers, hand-picked by him, hid in different areas, all of them prepared to uncover the traitor.

Luc waited. All the while he kept asking why. Why had Reggie chosen this path? Reggie could have done other things to make money, but he'd chosen betrayal. The army was a big, hulking beast easily scammed and Reggie had found a way to work the system for himself. Luc wondered how long Reggie had been using the army as his bank.

A rustle sounded in the underbrush. Luc made himself small and as invisible as he could.

Juan Valenzuela stepped into the clearing and Luc tensed. Then Reggie rode up and dismounted from his horse.

Reggie approached the log and glared at Valenzuela. "I got your note, but I want you to know I'm not your lackey. And contacting me was dangerous."

Valenzuela laughed. "You're a fool, gringo. I own you. Your own greed has made you my lackey."

Reggie's face went red. "What do you want?"

"My pet Indian has betrayed us."

"Is he dead?" Reggie asked.

Luc leaned forward to hear them better.

"Not yet, but he will be here soon enough. We will wait for him." Valenzuela sat on the log. "If nothing else, you can capture him since he is a deserter from your fort."

"You mean he's a darky?"

Valenzuela shrugged. "Los Negros and the Indians have formed many alliances in the past. It's a good thing you don't think my gold is beneath you."

Reggie turned a stiff face toward the bandit while his hand crept toward his pistol.

Valenzuela laughed. "You can hate me, if you wish. I don't pay you to love me. One day we'll no longer need each other and perhaps I'll kill you. But now we wait."

"I can't be away from the post for too long. My absence would be noted. Besides, I have information you need." Reggie reached into his shirt pocket.

"What information?" Valenzuela eyed Reggie greedily.

Reggie held up a piece of paper. "A dispatch for the General. A new shipment of guns. Guns you have an interest in. But then again, maybe you don't." Valenzuela reached for the paper, but Reggie backed away, refolded the paper and put it in his pocket. "I want my payment first." He held out an empty hand.

Valenzuela grinned at him. "I have gold. Lots of gold. More gold than you can ever imagine."

"I can imagine a lot." Reggie grinned. "Get it. Then you can have the information you seek."

Luc's heart sank. He had his proof. Reggie was indeed the traitor. He had disgraced his family and betrayed his country. If Luc had known his family was in such dire need, he would have attempted to do something for them. But Reggie had always shaken off any offer of help from Luc. Luc had thought Reggie's pride kept him so independent, but now he knew that Reggie had simply developed an independent source of income for himself.

Luc stood up and Reggie whirled to face him. The hidden soldiers, except for Callie, all stepped forward, crashing through the underbrush. Luc wondered where Callie had gotten. He'd wanted to leave her behind, to keep her safe, but couldn't. She was soldier, no longer a woman. He was having a hard time keeping the woman he loved separate from the soldier he needed.

"Reginald Cooper," Luc announced as he stepped toward Reggie, "you're under arrest for treason." The word 'treason' seemed to reverberate through the clearing.

Reggie whirled, a look of astonishment on his face. Valenzuela stepped back and grabbed Reggie's arms, pushing him toward Luc. Reggie staggered to his knees and Luc stepped around him, his pistol aimed at Valenzuela. "Halt."

Valenzuela grabbed at his weapon and aimed his pistol at Luc. Suddenly, Callie popped up seemingly out of nowhere and shoved Valenzuela as hard has she could. The man stumbled backward, his pistol flying out of his hand. He turned toward Callie, raising an arm to strike her, but she jumped up and clung to him with such force, they went down in a tangle, half rolling into the stream.

Valenzuela struggled to get an arm loose and Luc saw a knife in his hand. Luc leaped toward them. Reggie struggled to his feet and started to race toward his horse, but two soldiers tackled him, struggling with him.

Luc reached Valenzuela. Callie hung on the man, her arms and legs wrapped around him so tight he couldn't move, much less escape. They continued struggling until Luc grabbed the bandit by the shoulder and hauled him to his feet. Valenzuela punched Luc and pain radiated from the impact. Luc staggered, but landed his own punch on Valenzuela. Valenzuela slipped and fell backward, sprawling in the mud.

Two more soldiers stepped forward to restrain Valenzuela. Luc knelt down next to Callie and gathered her into his arms. She felt so frail, so fragile.

Blood seeped from her chest. She gazed up at him, her eyes unfocused. "I'm bleeding. Am I going to die?" She closed her eyes and went limp.

———⟨◦/◦/◦⟩———

"Cal Payne is a woman!" General Hammond exclaimed. He stood in the doorway of Luc's office. Major Adams sat at Luc's desk while Luc prowled the room unable to stand still. Esme sat in a chair waving her flushed face with a fan. She was deeply proud of her role in uncovering Reggie. Too proud, Luc thought. He was caught between annoyance at his sister's interference, and pride in her abilities.

So much had happened in the last two days, but his worry was mostly for Callie. He had worried that she would die. The doctor had declared her stab wound to be serious, but for the most part, it had missed any vital organs and the possibility was she would recover if she didn't develop an infection. Luc knew how fatal an infection could be. He'd seen men die in the war because the doctors had nothing to treat them with. He didn't want Callie to die. He loved her in a way he'd never loved another woman. If she died, a part of him would die with her.

Outside on the parade ground, the troops stood at ease after the morning's inspection. Since the revelation of Reggie's betrayal, the post was on edge, filled with tension and worry over what the Comanches would do once their source of information was at an end.

"According to the doctor," Major Adams said, "she's about twenty years old, or so. Too bad, she was a damn good scout. I'm going to be sorry to see her go, but the army is no place for a young, single woman, no matter how efficient she is." He scratched his chin. "Now that I know she's a woman, I can't understand why I didn't see it. Not even my wife saw through her disguise. I always thought women instinctively knew things like that."

Luc wanted to say that Esme had seen through Callie's disguise, but a glance at Esme told him to just keep quiet. Esme was unusual, why point out how unusual she was.

Hammond turned on Luc. "Do you have anything you care to speak to me about? You were with Miss Payne for almost six weeks ... alone."

Luc opened his mouth to speak, to confess his culpability in her masquerade, but the words wouldn't come out. He feared if he told the General what he had done to enable her disguise, he would confess how he felt about her, how deeply he cared for her.

Hammond raised his hand and shook his head. "I don't think I really want to know."

"Sir," Luc said, "I wanted to send her home, but she was so determined to get land for her family, I couldn't. She's a very stubborn woman. I realize I've risked my own career in keeping her secrets, but I thought she'd pull it off." He couldn't reveal her secrets, because she knew his.

The General frowned. "What land are you talking about?"

Luc tried to remember how the promise was worded, but couldn't remember. "I was told that if the Black-Seminoles served as our scouts, they would be paid in land. Forty acres per scout. Callie feels that if her family owns their own land, the government won't be able to force them to move, or take it away from them."

"I haven't heard of that promise." Hammond stroked his chin, a thoughtful look in his eyes.

Luc stared at him. A part of his brain told him he shouldn't be shocked. The government had a long history of breaking promises with the Indians. The Seminole in particular. "They were promised this land. Why do you think the Negro-Seminoles are here? They have no love for the United States." The government had treated them as shabbily as they had all the other tribes over the last hundred years. Luc never once thought he was being lied to. He has accepted the promise on faith because he thought it had been honorably offered.

"I can look into it," Hammond said. "Your scouts have served you well, but I can almost guarantee that nothing about this land was put in writing."

No, Luc thought, the government was too careful of its own needs to really consider what was happening to those people being hurt by the policies.

Esme struck the closed spines of her fan against the arm of her chair. "Does that mean that the United States Army is going to cheat these people after they have put their lives on the line for this country? Mon Dieu, France would never do such a thing. The United States doesn't deserve such loyalty. The Black-Seminoles don't deserve to be treated so poorly for their service."

Luc wasn't certain he agreed with his sister's assessment of France. Their adopted home was as guilty of similar abuses as the United States. But then again, despite all her worldliness, Esme had an idealistic streak that always popped up at unusual moments.

"I'm sorry, Esme," the general said with regret in his tone, and a bit of guilt in his eyes. "The Army may not be the most ideal place, but I do know promises of that caliber cannot be made without Congressional approval, and I have not heard of any proposal offering land to the scouts for their services even being discussed. I don't know where Luc received his information, but I suspect it was an error ...."

Luc interrupted, "From the Recruitment Department." A small worm of anger ate its way through him. The United States Government couldn't be allowed to get away with such underhanded manipulations. But Luc had no idea what he could do.

Hammond took a deep breath, "I'm sorry, Luc, but I have a feeling someone may have over-stepped their authority. But I will do whatever I can in my power to see that some provision is made for your scouts. Except for Callie. She enlisted under false pretenses and this negates all promises made to her"

"But General," Esme said, "She was a scout, regardless of her sex. And she did a good job. You cannot blame her for wanting more than what she has."

The General clasped his hands behind his back. "I understand why she did what she did, but my hands are tied here by the law. But, I can say, a $10,000 bounty exists on Juan Valenzuela. A bounty a United States soldier could never collect, but one that private citizen Callisto Payne can." A brief smile passed over his lips. "I will personally see that she receives that bounty."

Esme clapped her hand. "Tres bon, mon General." She rose and kissed him on the cheek. The General blushed. "My friend in Baltimore will be pleased with you. She is a honorable woman and you have shown yourself to be an honorable man. I demand the second dance at your wedding."

A knock sounded at the door. Luc opened it to find one of his soldiers at the door with a black man wearing a tattered uniform. "Sir." The soldier stood at attention. "This person insists he is a deserter and demands to see Major Adams. He wants to surrender."

Luc stood aside and the black man entered. He had a look to him that seemed familiar, but Luc had no idea why.

The black man offered a snappy salute and wry grin. "My name is Corporal Rafael Payne. I deserted four years ago, sirs, and I wish to turn myself in."

"Rafe, the Captain said you were here, but I didn't believe him."

Callie said. Seeing her brother in the flesh brought back so much of the worry which had consumed her over the years. He wasn't dead and she didn't know if she felt relief, or anger that he had deceived her and their mother. She winced at the pain in her chest as she raised her arms to her brother. "Mama thinks you're dead." She lay in Luc's wide bed with Esme to care for her. Luc had temporarily moved into Reggie's empty quarters. She felt odd laying on Luc's fine sheets while his sister fussed over her.

She shifted, trying to ease the ache in her chest from her wound and the bulky bandages that cris-crossed her breasts beneath the fine lawn of Esme's nightgown. She felt odd wearing Esme's beautiful nightgown with its delicate embroidery about the collar and cuffs. But Esme had insisted.

Rafe bent over and kissed Callie's cheek. "I'm sorry, little sister." He was neatly dressed in his uniform, but without rank insignias. He looked tired and sad and seemed somehow distant, as though the years separating them were a huge burden he couldn't share. "I acted thoughtlessly. I should have let you both know, but somehow I couldn't." He opened his mouth as though to say more, but then didn't.

Callie struggled to sit up wondering what secrets he was keeping from. The secrets stood between them as a barrier Callie didn't think she could break down. She had to be happy just having him with her again. She couldn't press him for all the things that happened in the years he'd been gone. The look on his face told her that subject of the missing years was closed. At least their mother would be at peace, knowing he was still alive. Though probably on his way to jail.

Esme, hovering at the door with concern on her face, scolded. "Don't you tire her out." She shook a finger at Rafe, then softened the gesture was a smile. "She doesn't have much strength."

"I'll be mindful of her, ma'am." Rafe eased himself down on the edge of the mattress and took Callie's hand.

Two guards stood just inside the doorway warily watching Rafe. But Esme gently drew them outside into the hallway where they leaned against the far wall, their eyes never leaving Rafe.

"I'm glad you're here now." Callie clasped his hand and held on tightly despite the pain that wracked her body. She had never been wounded before, never felt such agonizing physical pain. She had been so surprised when Valenzuela had stabbed her, she had almost let him go. But she hadn't been able to release her grip on him. He was Luc's enemy, therefore her enemy. And she would have died keeping him restrained.

Rafe sat on the edge of the bed. "Not for long. I'm going to be court-martialed and probably end up in jail for awhile."

"No. No," Callie protested, fear clutching at her heart. "I have money. I can take care of this for you." The money still awed her. Never in her life had she thought she would have so much. She could hardly wait to go home and tell her mother, but the doctor had told her she wouldn't be going anywhere for a week or so.

Rafe laughed at her. "Where did you get money, little sister?"

Finally, Callie could do something for the brother she adored. "The bounty on Juan Valenzuela. I captured him." She felt a spurt of pride. She whispered, confidentially. "Ten thousand dollars. I can buy anything." Ten thousand dollars bought a lot of dreams. She had even tried to pay Luc back for the money he'd spent on her in New Orleans, but he'd refused to take a penny from her.

He smiled at her. "You don't need to worry about me, just take care of mama."

"I am. And the whole tribe. We can go anyplace we want. Even Florida." She could buy land now. And no one, not even the United States Government would be able to take it away from her. She would have a home, a future, a place to grow. Her mama would have a garden as big as she wanted. Despite her excitement, a lonely future stretched in front of her. She would no longer have Luc. He had his life in the army, and she had hers with her people.

Rafe ran his fingers lightly over her cheeks, as though memorizing through touch the planes and angles of her face. "How did you get hurt?"

"I joined the army, just like you."

"And they let you join." The incredulous look on his face told her he didn't believe her.

Callie grinned at him. "I was a scout for the army. But not any more. They found out I'm a woman. And I've been 'separated" as Captain Delacroix says. Women can't be scouts in the army. Someone high up thinks women can't manage the hard work, or the life. But I proved them all wrong. Captain Delacroix says I was as good, if not better, as any solider. He's a good man. He can help you." She felt a warmth flood her face. The hardest part of returning home would be leaving Luc behind. But she had no part in his life. He wanted something different than she did. She didn't want a part in his life, as long as he lived as a white man, betraying his own heritage. Yet she loved him and the love ached in her.

"Now why," Rafe scoffed, "would a white officer want to help me?"

"Just talk to him. He'll help. I promise." She couldn't betray Luc's secrets. Only Luc could make things right for himself. If she had to continue without him, she would. Though her heart would break. As much as she loved him, she wouldn't live with his lie.

CHAPTER TWENTY

Callie saddled her mule. Old Silas sat on a stool. He shook his head, mumbling, "Little man, little man. Guess I can't call you that anymore, can I Callie?"

Callie cinched the saddle tight. Her mule grunted. "I'm gonna miss you, Silas. You've been a good friend." Her chest still ached, but the wound had healed. The scar across her chest, she would wear forever.

"What are you gonna do know?" Silas said. "You got money. You gonna live high in the big city?"

"No." Callie turned to Silas. "I'm gonna buy myself the biggest piece of land I can afford, build a house and just sit awhile."

Silas shook his head. "Not a bad plan. But what are you gonna do about Mr. Luc?"

"What do you mean?"

"A pretty girl like you and a big, strong handsome rich man like him. You can't tell me nothing happened on the trail alone. No way. No how. I see you looking at him. You got eyes for that man. At first, I thought it was just hero worship, but now I know better."

"Shut up, old man. You don't know anything." She tugged the reins. "I have to go." She gave him a big hug and dragged her mule out of the corral. At the gate, she found Esme, waiting.

"You were trying to sneak away and not say good-bye. I'm hurt." Esme crossed her arms over her chest.

Callie didn't reply. She couldn't deny her desire for a quiet leave-taking.

Esme touched her shoulder. "You could come to San Francisco with me."

"What is it with you and your brother? Always wanting to take me to the big city. No. I don't belong there."

"Luc and I could be your people."

"I don't think so. I have to be where I can be who I am."

"This is not just about the big city, is it, cherie? It's about the color of our skin."

"Maybe."

Esme put a finger beneath Callie's chin. "Luc is who he is because of the color of his skin. I wish the world was different, but it isn't. You must be who you are in the world, not change the world to suit who you are."

"I know. I will have to live with my lie every day. But in the end, my people will prosper. I was willing to pay the price. Who profits from Luc's lies?"

Esme gave Callie a sad smile. "To be allowed to be who he is, Luc lived the lie."

"That's a shame, isn't it?"

Esme leaned forward and shook her finger. "Then you, better than anyone else, should understand."

"I do. But we can never be together because he cannot accept what he is."

"He loves you."

"I love him with all my heart. I will always love him. But I will not lie for him. I've done enough lying in my life."

Esme sighed. "These moral dilemmas, they give me a headache. You will continue with your reading and writing, won't you?"

"I will. I promise." Callie swung up on the mule. "The first thing I'm doing after I find some land, is hiring a teacher to teach all of us how to read and write. I understand the power of words now."

"I just purchased the Hotel DeVille in San Francisco. If you change your mind, there's always a place for you." Esme reached up and took Callie's hand, pressing a sack into it.

Callie tried to gave the sack of coin back. "I have my own money now."

"I know, but this is just for you and no one else. So you can come to me if you need to. You are my sister." Tears sparkled in Esme's eyes. "I hate good-byes. Au revoir. The French way is better. Until we meet again." She walked away never looking back.

Callie nudged the mule away from the corral, heading toward the road. She found that saying good-bye had drained her. She didn't look back.

Callie was a mile from the post when she heard hoofbeats. She turned in the saddle and saw Luc riding after her. She drew her mule to a halt.

"Don't leave me, Callie," he pleaded when his horse came to a halt. A cloud of dust rose from the animal's hooves.

"I can't stay, Captain. Luc."

Luc studied at her set face, the way her chin jutted at him and her eyes sparkled with unshed tears. He felt barren, empty. She was leaving and taking a part of him with her.

"Is there anything I can say that will make you stay. I can rent a room in Eagle's Pass."

Callie's head went up. "I'm not your fancy woman. In New Orleans I felt as though I was playing dress-up in my mama's clothes. I can't be that woman forever. I have responsibilities."

"Callie, I love you."

"I know you do, and I love you, too. But there are too many things standing in our way. You have an important job to do here and you've done a lot of good. You take care of the Black soldiers like men. You treat them with respect."

Luc thought his heart would break in half. "Do you think that's enough to keep me warm at night?"

"No, but I have a job to do, too." A tear dripped down her cheek.

He nodded. He knew that she was leaving not because of her people, but because of his choices. She would not give him an ultimatum forcing him to choose. He loved her more than she would ever know, but he had so much more to accomplish. Texas wasn't safe yet and the Comanche problem would not be settled for years. He could think of all the tasks he had to do, but none of them were what he wanted to do. He wanted to be with Callie, to make babies with her and grow old, yet so much stood in their way.

"Let me go, Luc. It's for the best. I can't ask you to give up everything you hold dear. That would be wrong." She turned her mule and headed down the road.

Luc watched her go. His throat opened and closed and he felt utterly impotent.

Luc sat at his desk unable to concentrate. Two days ago, he had put his sister on a stage bound for the nearest railroad station from where she would head to San Francisco. The General was leaving in the morning. He'd completed his most pressing tasks. Rafe was taken care of. Reggie was off to Federal prison. And he had one last task to perform. He read his letter of resignation one last time.

"Can't I talk you out of this?" General Hammond asked as he clipped his cigar and then lit it.

"I've known you for over ten years, Sir. You've been more than my commanding officer, you've been my friend. I've lied to you, sir."

"About what?"

"I'm not what you think I am."

"You mean you're not the son of a New Orleans plantation owner and his mulatto mistress."

Luc sat up straight. "You knew."

The General took a deep drag on his cigar. "As much as I loved my sister, it just bothered the hell out of me that she married herself a Johnny Reb out of New Orleans. The Delacroix name is a pretty big name there. And there's one thing my sister knows is gossip. You say one name to her and you chapter and verse all the way back to the birth of Christ."

Luc didn't know what to say. He held the letter in his hand and picked up his pen. "Then you know. Why didn't you do anything?"

The General smiled at him. "You can forgive a man who saves your life pretty much anything, especially a minuscule little fib." He held his fingers up. "I've known two great soldiers in my life, you and Robert E. Lee. I lost Robert, and I wasn't losing you. Didn't matter to me. Twenty years ago, maybe, but not anymore. I watched this nation rip apart at the seams because the notion that color mattered. I know my opinion is not popular, but I don't ever want to see such a devastating event happen again.

Luc took a deep breath. "You would have married my sister in a minute had she given you any indication that she cared for you in more than just a fatherly way."

General laughed. "A beautiful woman with a lot of money is a beautiful woman with a lot of money." He winked.

Luc held out his hand. "It's been a pleasure to serve under you." He signed the letter.

"You're going to go after that little Seminole girl, aren't you. I don't blame you. Again, she is beautiful and she does have some money. Not that her money is a problem for you." He puffed contentedly on his cigar. "Where to you intend to go?"

"I have property in Canada. And I've always had an inclination to raise horses and babies."

"Good luck to you, Luc. I want you to keep a bed made for me, I hear there's good hunting in Canada." The General stood and took Luc's resignation letter. "I'll be seeing you."

Luc felt hot and dusty as he rested his horse for a moment before going on. In the distance, he could see Callie's village, a green oasis in the heat of the desert.

He pushed his hat back and felt the stiffness of the brim. He still had trouble believing he wasn't in the army any longer, that he'd given up a goal that had been so important to him. But with Callie gone, somehow the situation didn't seem so critical anymore.

He had weighed all his options very carefully, and each one had come up short, except for being with Callie. He discovered that he couldn't continue without her love, without her respect. The army could take of the Comanche situation without him, but there was only one Callie.

He spurred his horse toward the village and discovered a hive of activity. Wagons had been drawn up in front of adobe houses and women loaded the backs of the wagons with boxes. Children played in the dirt, stopping to stare at him as he passed. Some of the children wore Comanche clothes and he wondered where they had come from.

Callie walked out into the sun, shading her eyes with the palm of one hand. She balanced a small boy on her hip. A boy who resembled her brother.

Luc reined his horse to a halt and stepped down. "Callie," he said, holding out his hand.

"Captain, what are you doing here?" Callie put the little boy away and he ran back into the house yelling something that sounded like grandma.

"I'm not a Captain anymore."

Her eyebrows rose. "You mean you left the army?"

"Black men can't be officers. I could live the lie, or I could live with you."

She nodded at him. "That must have been hard, giving up your dreams."

"I didn't give up my dream, I just rearranged it." He took her hands in his. "I love you."

She went into his arms, her hands cradling his cheeks. "I love you, too, Luc. But are you sure?"

"Never in my life have I been so sure about anything."

"Where do we go from here?" She molded herself against him, her face upraised.

"Canada, where we can be legally wed."

She smiled at him. "My tribe is going back home to Florida. But I understand it's as hot there as it is here. I think I'd like to try something colder for a change."

He kissed her, his mouth covering hers, their tongues meeting. He moaned with his love for her.

She drew back, breaking contact. "What are we going to do in Canada?"

"How do you feel about raising horses and babies?"

She nodded at him. "I like that." She tilted her face up to him and laughed. "I like that a lot. I can do anything with you by my side."

"Me, too." He kissed her again, long and hard and filled with promise.